THE EX

BOOKS BY S.E. LYNES

Mother

The Pact

Valentina

The Proposal

The Women

The Lies We Hide

Can You See Her?

The Housewarming

Her Sister's Secret

The Baby Shower

THE EX
S. E. LYNES

bookouture

Published by Bookouture in 2022

An imprint of Storyfire Ltd.
Carmelite House
50 Victoria Embankment
London EC4Y 0DZ

www.bookouture.com

ISBN: 978-1-80314-511-2
eBook ISBN: 978-1-80314-510-5

For our Rob, with love.

Love is a familiar. Love is a devil. There is no evil angel but love.

William Shakespeare, *Love's Labour's Lost*

CHAPTER 1

December 2021

It's over three months now since Sam Moore was pictured on the *Lyme Times website* for reasons no one would ever have wanted. The headline read: *Child Abduction: Local Man Held; Wife Still Missing.*

That was the morning after, before the press had fully caught up. Since then, of course, the news has moved on and we are back to new variants and vaccinations, the threat of yet another lockdown and what that means for our much-loved seaside town.

I should probably introduce myself. My name is Miranda Clarke, and Sam Moore was my closest friend. My reasons for trying to tell this story are partly to make sense of it, partly to set the record straight and partly to ask myself what I could or should have done differently.

Where to begin? Just over eight months ago, I think. The world is blinking in the light of post-lockdown. We have spent over a year shielding our loved ones, trying to protect people we don't even know, and our nerves are still jangling. Some of us have suffered unimaginable grief and anguish. Most of us have experienced stress and anxiety. Some of us are poorer. Some of us richer. Some have become more determinedly sociable than before, some lonelier, more isolated. No one has come out unscathed. We are changed in ways we don't yet know. And maybe that's what this story is about too: change.

As for me, I'm one of the lucky ones. On the professional front, as a garden designer, I've been able to work either from home or outdoors during these crazy and difficult times. Sam was my chief landscaper, the guy whose talented hands gave life to my technical drawings, who transformed paving into patios, scrubland into lawn, rubble into rockery. In short, I showed the clients the dream; he was the one who fulfilled that dream.

For the purposes of this account, I'll do my best to keep myself out of it, though I suspect there will be times when I'll jump in. There will be things I'll want to make sure I get across. It's all been so complicated. It's all been such a mess.

So please – bear with me.

Sam's story starts as it always would: on a hike, muddy boots, no phone. That was Sam – a hard man to reach.

It is a sunny spring day towards the end of April 2021. Here is Sam, leaving the lush jungle of Ware Cliff at his back. He is heading down through the holiday chalets towards Monmouth Beach when he sees her. Another step down, another, his eyes fixed now on the slowly coalescing form of a woman half obscured by the bowling green wall, a woman walking from town towards the car park. Because that's all she is as yet: the shape of a woman, a half-figure in the distance.

But still in his stomach a knot of dread tightens.

The woman emerges from behind the wall and he sees she is pushing a stroller, the seat tipped back, what he presumes is a baby tucked underneath a blue blanket. Not her then, he thinks. It never is. She used to appear to him constantly, like a host in other women's bodies: today a young mother, out for an afternoon walk.

The knot of dread loosens. It is not her. Thank God.

Beyond the stony beach, vanilla sunlight bounces off a graphite sea. It is warm enough that his hike has left him sweaty, the sleeves of his jumper tied around his waist, cagoule rolled up and nestling in his rucksack in the space left by his sandwiches. His gran, Joyce, made these sandwiches for him early this morning. He ate them on the bench at the viewing point just before dropping down: wide skies over Charmouth, the rise and fall of the land's edge tracing a lazy line over to Weymouth – to Portland on a clear day. Walking has kept him sane this last long, solitary year. The elements have brought him the peace he has craved.

Down on the green to his left, an older woman trots behind a bowling ball like a dog handler at Crufts. The ball rolls promisingly towards the jack, but at the last moment curves away and settles behind a cluster of nearer bowls. The woman throws up her hands in exasperation.

The young mother is nearer now. She is passing in front of the cars, the zigzag of beach huts to the rear. Her outline clarifies a little. And then she stops, hand rising to rub the back of her thin neck. The knot of dread returns as swiftly as a hammer blow. This gesture is... it is hers.

Hot familiarity races over his skin. And now he sees that the pale pink puffer jacket she is wearing is the one he bought her, the black beanie hat the one she always wore.

This time it is not a woman who could have been her but who actually is not. This time it is her, yes, yes, it is, as he knew it would be one day. Oh God. Lockdown reinforced their separation. Sometimes he thinks it was the only thing that gave him the strength not to return to her. But now, instantly, white-hot chaos fills him, and just like that he is back there: on Cannington Viaduct, one leg either side of the concrete barrier, rain falling in rods, his mud-caked boot lifted in the black air.

He shuts his eyes, shakes the image away before opening them again: to her.

Her wide jeans are cropped at the ankle. On her feet, her thick-soled lace-up shoes are so familiar he almost laughs. The telltale diagonal stripe of a shoulder bag. She always made everything she wore look cool: shirt cuffs she would fold back over the thin sweaters she liked, collars she would button to the top like a geek – the effect the exact opposite. Old satchels she would hold up at Bridport vintage market and ask him what did he think – this one, that one, which did he prefer or should she get both? He would shrug, no idea, but then later he would see her wearing the same unpromising battered purse, the strap across her chest, and he would think: yeah, that looks good.

He hasn't seen her since a little over a year ago, when he left the keys to the flat they shared on the kitchen table with a note apologising for his own diminishment at her hands, a shrinking of himself he only realised had happened after-wards, when Joyce gently pointed it out to him. And again he sees himself, scrambling up the slope to the viaduct, snipping through the barbed wire, bolt cutters shaking in his hands, half mad with confusion, scaling the metal fence and stumbling in the rain across the forbidden arches, throwing one leg over the concrete barrier, willing himself to do the courageous thing for once in his life and just...

His hands tighten into fists. It's possible she hasn't seen him.

He is about to turn back and creep up the steep steps between the chalets, but she looks up, as if she has heard his thoughts or perhaps sensed him there, watching her. He falters, feels in that moment like he's been caught stealing. She leans forward; he can tell by the angle of her body, by the visor of her hand flat against her forehead, that she is figuring out whether or not it is him. Behind her sunglasses – pink to match her jacket – he can't see her eyes. But she is peering at him, he knows.

She straightens then, one hand rising in a tentative hello. He cannot see her features clearly but has the impression she is smiling. Mirroring her, he too smiles, raises his hand, finds her name on his lips.

'Naomi.'

She is waiting for him. There is no avoiding her. He cannot turn on his heel and escape to the refuge of the undercliff.

Stay calm. She does not know about the viaduct. She does not need to know. No one does. No one except Joyce.

Blood thrumming in his temples, he descends towards her. Better to get this over with. Keep it civilised. If she shouts or swears, he can walk away. He is not trapped, not here. What can she do to him really? There are bowlers on the green, dog walkers, out-of-season tourists out for a stroll. She won't make a scene.

With each step down, her even features solidify – her generous mouth, her fine nose, the delicate point of her chin – until there she is, as harmless and as dangerous as he remembers.

She takes off her sunglasses. Her eyes are no less deep, no less brown. And today they are soft, as they could be when she wanted. His breath catches.

'Hey.' Her smile is tender. From her hat, a lick of black curl.

Her lack of fury is disconcerting. He pushes his hands deep into the pockets of his combat trousers.

'Naomi,' he manages. 'Hey.'

In the stroller, a baby sleeps – eyelids red-threaded like chard leaves, mouth a tiny pink cyclamen. The blanket is blue. A boy then.

'He's... he's my friend's,' Naomi says, as if in a rush and despite the fact that he hasn't asked. Her white cheeks flush pink beneath her freckles. 'His name's Tommy. Thomas. He's... he's my friend's baby. My friend Cheryl's.' She fusses a moment with the blanket, though it is perfectly tucked in, the baby undisturbed.

'Are you... were you going for a walk?' Asking the question, he has the impression he is trying to help her out of her embarrassment. It occurs to him that she might feel as awkward as he does, seeing him like this after so long, the last time a hazy memory of insults shouted down a flight of stairs, himself cringing, hurrying out to the van, his meagre belongings in his arms.

But she is not shouting at him. There has been no scratch of sarcasm, no disdainful narrowing of eyes. Instead, she looks behind her, towards the thick, sloping girth of the Cobb, the boat masts thick reeds in the harbour. And back, meeting his eye, but only briefly. She always looked away and back at him when she was about to lie.

But, 'I was just in Chideock,' is all she says.

'Is that... is that where you're living now?'

She shakes her head. 'Still in Brid.'

'You still in the flat?' Their flat. Hers now: his parting gift, his apology.

'You still living with Joyce?' she counters.

He rolls his eyes, an attempt at humorous self-deprecation. 'Saddo. Still living with my gran.' He tries to laugh. Fails. 'I'll start looking for somewhere now things are opening up again. Hopefully we're through the worst.' His feet feel heavy; the soles of his boots are clogged with clay. He wonders if she is about to make some caustic remark about his choice to live with Joyce during lockdown, the choice that finished them in the end.

But again, 'You still landscaping?' is all she asks.

'Yeah. It's not been too bad. Outdoors, you know. We've been busy actually. You still at the doc's?'

She presses her mouth tight. Her eyebrows rise – well, here we are then, is the expression. 'I was thinking,' she says, 'I might go and sit on the beach for a bit.' She shivers – the kind of shiver Joyce would call someone walking over her grave, though to be fair, it has grown chilly. She appears to be suggesting they go together, that she'd like to go and sit with him amidst the ghosts of day-long picnics here on this beach, their giggling games of dare – *dare you to run into the cold sea without stopping; dare you to kiss me, properly, in front of everyone; dare you to slide your finger inside my swimming costume right here, right now.*

He shakes the images away, ignores the heat climbing up his neck.

He clears his throat. 'Might be a bit cold for sitting about.' He glances down at his hiking boots, the brown splashes of mud on the bottom of his khaki combats. When he returns his gaze to her, she looks away. He has rejected her, he thinks. A small rejection to open the wound of the much, much larger one. She will not like that one bit.

'We could grab a coffee?' he asks, to make amends, the beginnings of old panic low in his gut. It is not what he wants to do at all. God knows, he can barely look at her, let alone sit opposite her in some warm café with no easy means of escape.

Thankfully, she thumbs over her shoulder to the rows of cars at her back. 'I'd better get him back. To his mum, you know?' A rejection for a rejection. Touché.

'Of course.' He is nodding too vigorously but can't stop himself. 'I'll... I'll walk you to your car.'

'If you like.'

They cross the car park, to the back of the beach huts. He can hear the crash of sea on stones, the yelp of a dog. Sulphurous air: black wigs of seaweed stranded by the tide.

At her car, she stops, opens the back door and lifts the top of the buggy out of its frame with easy expertise. The baby stirs, blinks awake. His eyes are blue, like Sam's own. His romper suit has a hood with cute fluffy animal ears on it, his head hidden, his eyebrows no more than a white downy fuzz. A fair, blue-eyed child. He groans, a half-hearted protest, both arms coming up, fists tight as Venus flytraps. His eyes find Sam's, stare at him, into him, almost. Something in him shifts.

Her friend's kid, she said. She definitely said that.

'I'd better get him back,' she says.

'Yes.' He nods, confusion growing by the second, a faint familiar churning in his gut. 'Back to his mum, you said.'

She casts her gaze behind her, towards the Ladies' by the bowling green, back to him. 'Bye, Sam.'

A year ago, he had to break free of her just to carry on breathing. Now, at the thought of her going, he is filled with the urge to grab the sleeve of her coat, to say, *Stop. Wait. Just...*

'Look after yourself,' is what makes it out of his mouth. The words sound flat and lame.

'You too.' She doesn't look at him. Instead, she clips the baby into the seat belt, touching her nose against his, grinning and cooing at him before she rounds the front of the car – her trusty red Golf, repository of more memories, more games of dare: himself at the steering wheel, in broad daylight, open traffic; her lowering her head to his lap...

He feels himself blush, wonders if she will notice, for one crazy moment, whether she will read his mind.

But she starts the engine, causing him to step back, and reverses out while he stands there, inert, caught between leaving and staying. Briefly she lifts a hand before pulling away – if she looks at him at all, it is only a cursory glance in the rear-view mirror. He watches, still rooted to the tarmac. The car disappears around the shop that sells buckets, spades and the paraphernalia of holidays by the sea.

His hand is still raised in a wave. He lowers it.

CHAPTER 2

Sam arrives home, an attack of the nausea he hasn't had for months now passing through him. He opens the front door to the porch, then the inner door.

'Sam?' His gran's voice reaches him. It seems to be coming from the sitting room. 'Samuel, love, is that you?'

'No, it's Sir Paul McCartney.'

A pause. He knows she is smiling, shaking her head at this game they play, and this settles him a little.

'Tea?' she calls, and he hears her footsteps moving through the back of the house.

'Please.' He drops his bag and takes off his boots, places them neatly in the porch before peeling off his damp hiking socks. Barefoot, he hobbles on his heels over the cold chequerboard tiles of the hallway to the utility room, which smells of damp plaster, even in the summer. Here, he throws his socks directly into the washing machine with the clothes he loaded this morning. A mixed colours cycle set to run, he slides his feet into his old Birkenstocks and goes to find Joyce in the kitchen, already stirring sugar into his tea. A homely bell of welcome, the teaspoon clanks against the china; steam curls against the black kettle on the red range cooker. He kisses her on the cheek and takes the mug from the countertop.

'Cheers,' he says.

'There's chocolate digestives in the barrel.'

He takes three and eats the first in two bites, sits down and groans at the stiffness in his thighs.

'How've you gone on?'

'Good, yeah. Very boggy still in the undercliff, but I took some nice shots. Might sketch them later, get my watercolours out. I caught the bus to Seaton and walked back. Popped down to Monmouth before coming back up.'

'Good for you. I'm jealous. Good workout that. I've been three times round the garden and done my yoga with Adriene. Well, not the headstand, but I managed some of it.'

He lifts his tea, but it is too hot to drink, so he puts it back down on the battered kitchen table.

'I saw Naomi,' he says,

Behind her reading specs, his gran's pale eyes widen. She lowers herself onto a high-backed chair. Tuts. 'Suppose it had to happen sooner or later.'

'That's what I thought. Still a shock though.' He blows on his tea, observes the mini wake.

'How did she look?'

'Well. She looked well.'

When he looks up, Joyce is staring at him, blinking as if she's just put in eye drops, not missing a trick. Those lenses really do magnify everything. 'Actually, she had a baby with her,' he adds.

'Did she?' Emphasis on the *did*. 'Did she indeed?'

He eats another half-biscuit. The milk chocolate melts on his tongue. He wonders what he wants to say. Or doesn't. He knows exactly what he wants to say. What he's wondering is whether or not to say it, whether it is simply too explosive to voice aloud.

'Boy or girl?' Joyce asks.

'Boy.'

She lifts her own mug to her lips and slurps the top layer of tea with the asbestos-tongued prowess of octogenarians everywhere. 'How old?'

'Decent size. Not a newborn. A few months, I'd say, but not walking yet, I don't think. It... he was in one of those car seat things. Maybe six, seven months? Big. Biggish.' He sips his tea, sweet and hot. From the bird clock on the wall, the spotted woodpecker rat-a-tat-tats. Four o'clock then. 'It was her friend's, she said.'

'She said that, did she?'

'Her friend's, yeah. Cheryl, I think. Or Sharon. Must be a new friend, because I never heard her mention a Cheryl or a Sharon. She was taking him for a walk anyway. His name's Tommy. Quite an old name for a baby, don't you think? Not that I'd know.'

'Tommy.' His gran runs her bottom row of teeth across her top lip. 'Kind of her to take him out. For her friend, I mean. Very kind.'

'Yeah.' He knows what she means. She means Naomi isn't known for her kindness.

There is something else too, but this they leave between them like the last chocolate in a tray. Neither wants to touch it for fear of upsetting the other. Naomi liked to give gifts, organise surprises or nights out, but he can't imagine her spending hours doing something she would find boring, not unless she had to. And she would find hanging out with a baby very boring indeed. So why was she taking her friend's kid for a walk on her own on a chilly afternoon in April? Either she has turned over a new leaf, or...

Or what?

He knows what. The knowledge is the last chocolate. The temptation of it nudges at him. He is waiting for Joyce to pluck it from the box and hold it up so that he can say, *Yes, that's what I thought too.*

'She seemed different,' he offers, finishes his second biscuit, breaks the third in half, quarters.

'Different how?' There is a firmness to his gran's voice.

'Older, I think. It's been a year, I suppose. She looked more... mellow. She was friendly, but reserved, in a way, which is understandable. I feel better for seeing her. For getting it over with. But yeah, she was... nice. I asked if she wanted to go for a coffee.'

'Oh, Sam.' Joyce sucks air through her teeth.

He holds up a hand. 'Not like that. Just, you know. We were together a long time.'

'Yes, and by the time you got out of it, you were scared of your own shadow, love.'

'I know that. I know.'

Joyce is fixing him, in the way she does. 'But do you? I know she's pretty, more than pretty. And I know sex is a powerful force—'

Again his hand comes up: stop. He wishes she wouldn't say stuff like that.

But Joyce is having none of it. 'Well, it is. Brings down governments, does sex. And young people have needs. I should know, I was one once. And I know this last year has been lonely for you, living with an old woman—'

'It's been fine! It's all fine. I love living here. Let's drop it, OK?'

This time it's his gran's turn to hold up a hand. 'I'm not saying I'm not excellent company, not to mention a passable alto to your baritone, but you're barely thirty, and hanging out with your granny listening to Miles Davis and playing chess of an evening is no life for a young man, even a kind, lovely man like you. I'm not trying to do her down, love. Just watch it, that's all. In my experience, leopards don't change their spots. And just because they retract their claws doesn't mean they're not still there in those big fluffy paws.' She presses her mouth tight shut, seemingly finished, but then opens it again. 'And you're sure it's her friend's, this baby?'

There. The last chocolate. She has plucked it out of the box.

CHAPTER 3

Joyce studies her grandson closely and decides he looks about as comfortable as a bug under a magnifying glass on a particularly hot day. She's thinking: oh no, here we go. Not Naomi. Please God, not Naomi.

'My legs are aching a bit,' he tells her, shifting in his seat – an abrupt and in no way subtle change of subject that of course, being no fool, Joyce spots straight away. 'OK if I run a bath?'

'Should be plenty of hot water,' Joyce replies impassively. No point pushing it. She does not add that she could see Naomi bloody Harper in him the moment he came into the kitchen – in the high set of his shoulders, the tightness of his jaw; that she can still see her now in the slow lift of his body from the chair, the barely perceptible deepening of the lines on his brow.

Once he's gone to run his bath, she refreshes the pot and pours herself a second mug of tea. She takes it back into the living room, and after a quick inspection of her handiwork stares out at the receding tide, the rhythmic spray white over the Cobb. There'll be new findings on the pebbled shore. Treasure or junk, depending on your point of view. Overhead, water rumbles through old pipes. She can hear Sam whistling, the sound coming and going as he flits between his room and the bathroom.

A baby, she thinks, and tries not to think. Despite her attempts to stop it, Naomi's far-too-pretty face comes into her mind, her wheedling tone of voice, the jokes that weren't jokes, the coy incline of her head as she browbeat Sam into taking her out to that celebrity chef place in Langmoor Gardens with money he didn't have. My God, she had some moves all right. Like feminism never happened. Women like Naomi let the side down. They need a poke in the eye.

A six-month-old or thereabouts, Sam said. The baby.

They both knew what the other was thinking.

And now what?

Now what?

The iPad Sam helped her order last March is on the kitchen table. She opens Facebook – Sam helped her with this too, so she could keep in touch with her old Clapham friends, plus Susy, Mike, Helen and Daryll and the rest of the Sea Shanty Chanteurs. He helped her with Zoom too but she had no patience for it, preferring FaceTime by far. It took some getting used to, but a one-to-one video is far and away better than those awful *Celebrity Squares* boxes where by the time you've figured out who's speaking, someone else is, and every time you want to chip in, which in Joyce's opinion is how conversation works, the whole thing seems to freeze.

She sifts through the countless Facebook Naomis, but there is no Naomi Harper. Either she's gone private or she's no longer there. Or, of course, being no fan of Joyce, she has unfriended her or even blocked her. But having not looked at the profile since Sam showed it to her almost a year ago, there is no way of telling when or if Naomi has deleted herself. Or why.

'Odd,' she mutters to no one but herself.

Sitting back in her chair, she sips her by now lukewarm tea. Why the dickens would Naomi delete her profile at a time when most people are living through their computers? What is she, *shy* all of a sudden? Perhaps not so keen to broadcast her life once her fella left her, eager as she always was to show the world that she was living the dream, that she was the bee's knees. Or is there another reason, something or *someone* she wanted to keep secret?

Not for the first time, Joyce wonders about how Naomi was after Sam left. She must have been *seething* that he had finally found the courage to walk away, especially if she then found out she had a bun in the oven. But she ran him ragged. The sight of him on her front step in the rain that night is one Joyce will never forget. Ashen, he was, his eyes black, looking like he had at ten years old when she'd returned from the hospital to break the news about his mother, her own beloved Frida, always so full of life it had been beyond torture to watch it empty out of her like milk from a carton. A bad memory wrapped up in another bad memory. The night Sam left Naomi, Joyce hadn't seen him in over two months – two months! – but there he stood in the dark, soaking wet, shaking from head to toe.

'Can I come in?' That was what he said. As if this wasn't his home, as if it wouldn't always be his home.

Later that night, once she'd dried him out and fed him and poured him a large glass of her best brandy, he told her that when he'd floated the idea of the two of them moving in with Joyce for the duration of the lockdown, he and Naomi had had a terrible fight. It had been building for months. He hadn't had time to call ahead, had simply thrown his belongings into his van in blind panic and driven over.

It wasn't until the next morning that he told her he'd trespassed onto Cannington Viaduct and spent a long time looking over the edge. He didn't name what he'd almost done. Didn't need to.

'The main thing is,' she said, holding one of his hands in both of hers, 'you're here now, love, and that's what matters.'

The following evening, having been awake all the night before chewing it over, she said, 'Sam, listen to me. I'm going to pay what you owe on the mortgage. Let her keep the flat.'

He looked at her, horrified. 'I can't. I can't let you do that.'

'You can. You'll get everything I own anyway one day. May as well have this bit now you need it. Make a clean break. She has no claim on you then.'

Joyce closes Facebook and returns her gaze to the sea. A clean break. No claim on him.

But despite her best efforts, could that dreadful woman have a claim on him after all?

CHAPTER 4

What follows is an extract of a letter from Naomi Harper to Sam Moore, which was found by police in the glove compartment of Joyce's MG after Sam was arrested.

Dear Sam,

When I saw you today, I so wanted to tell you the truth, but I couldn't – I just couldn't.

I'm back home now and Tommy's asleep, so I thought I'd try and get everything down while it's clear in my mind. Funny, my horoscope this morning said: Something startling will happen today. And I know you'd laugh even though you're a classic Virgo, but you see, something startling did happen, didn't it? Nearly startled the life out of me. I thought I was over you, but I don't think I am. I'm literally shaking.

It was hard seeing you today, really hard. You look so well. The colour is back in your cheeks, and your hair looks nice a bit longer like that. You're still so handsome, so built, so tall. It was quite gutting actually. Not sure about the beard though. Only joking! And by the way, there's nothing wrong with living with your gran, especially now she's getting older. That house was too much for her even before – the cleaning took her ten hours a time, and OMG, the repairs! Do the windows still need replacing? They must be mostly filler by now. I remember how the wind used to make the bedroom windows bang sometimes – it used to whistle under the doors too. It was freezing, wasn't it? We used to have to wear woolly hats and jumpers in bed, didn't we? Great sea view of course, but brrrr.

Seeing you today brought back so many memories. I suppose you're the only person I want to talk to about them, the only one who'd remember what I remember. Like when we came back from Ibiza that time and the courgettes you'd planted had turned into marrows and Joyce made that bolognese sauce and she put it in the marrows for dinner. Do you remember that? She put star anise in it. I'd never tasted it before. I didn't eat the marrow – it was all watery – but I ate the sauce, didn't I? It was delicious. See? See how much I remember? We had some good times, didn't we? I know that's easy to forget sometimes, but we did.

Thing is, I probably shouldn't have lied to you today, but now I'm home, I don't know if I'll ever tell you the truth. Even now that things are finally easing up, I'm not sure I'll see you, especially if we're avoiding each other, which I suppose we will be. Maybe you'll come over this way. Maybe I'll bump into you at the market one Saturday... but it's not like you'd bother with the market without me, is it? The way I see it, there's no real need to tell you. Because the thing is, Sam, we live separate lives now. And that's on you.

I don't have to tell you anything. Not anymore.

CHAPTER 5

I think anyone who knew Sam would've said he wasn't what you'd call an alpha male. He wasn't fey or effeminate or anything, just a bit quiet. I always thought he was like the jazz he loved so much: you had to listen to the pauses. His love of music came from his gran, I think, as well as the gardening; it's just a shame he never inherited her business smarts. She'd had a successful chain of launderettes in London back in the day, but she was a local girl originally – local girl makes good, returns to her roots a rich woman. When she came back, she bought the big Georgian house up by Ware Cliff. This is going back twenty years; I was just a kid. By the time I met her, she was as much part of the landscape as the famous Jurassic geology.

Sam needed someone with more of a grasp on the mate-rial, administrative aspects of life, and I guess that's where Naomi came in. He told me she always handled the money side of things, and there was no surprise there, I can tell you. Money flew out of his hands, and working out budgets with him was a nightmare; I could laugh just thinking about the constipated look he'd get on his face, the panic-induced glazing of the eyes. In the end, I'd do the calculations for a prospective job and tell him how much he should charge me for the work. It takes a lot of trust to operate like that, but obviously, in the cold light of what happened, I think it might've been better to have insisted he become a bit savvier. I let him down in that regard as well as so many others.

Working as well as we did together, I guess I always hoped that one day Sam and I would become business partners, and OK, I'll admit, maybe more. I didn't think he saw me that way; he wasn't one to pick up on signals even if you stood there in your underwear pointing to the bedroom – not that I ever did that. Christ, no. But as the year went on and he and Naomi got closer, we hung out less and less. And maybe here too I let him down. If I'm guilty of something, it's of not saying enough – to him or to others. If I had, maybe the disaster could have been averted.

I didn't tell him, for example, that Darren had once told me that the Harpers had a bit of a rep over in Bridport. Naomi's dad had done time for burglary, and Darren had heard her mother was a tricky one. But I wasn't about to start slinging mud at another woman's family so I could get the guy. As for expressing my concern to the lads, as the weeks went on, the bottom line was he was obviously hiding his relationship from them. It wasn't for me to divulge information he wasn't ready to share. I didn't want to break his trust or cause him to feel ashamed and end up isolated.

Or by that do I actually mean I didn't want him to distance himself from *me*? With hindsight, can I honestly say I wasn't secretly flattered to be his confidante, that I didn't hope that our closeness might spill over into something else? God knows. I know now I should have taken the risk of him turning away from me. Maybe if I had, I could have stopped him. Maybe I should have told Darren. Maybe Darren would've taken him for a pint and had a word. Maybe Darren would've said, *Mate. Slow down.*

The fact is, I didn't do any of those things. But back to Sam: there he is, under the bathwater, eyes closed, the pulse of blood throbbing in his temples.

Naomi.

Naomi, Naomi, Naomi.

The coldness in her narrow red eyes. 'You're asking me to live with you and your *gran*? Are you fucking serious?'

Himself, tongue-tied, no longer sure his request was even reasonable. Shrugging, shaking his head.

'I don't see why we have to do that when we could just do her shopping, couldn't we? She's got loads of friends. Sam? Sam? Say something!'

Himself, walking away from her, closing the bedroom door, pulling the holdall out from under the bed. The door opening. Her, a shadow.

'What? So that's it, is it? You're going to her? No discussion? Just... leaving? That's what you're doing?'

Himself: the impossibility of finding words, any words at all, against the torrent of hers. He can't remember the rest, only that it went on for the time it took him to pack his things, continued unrelenting through every return trip from the van for more of his stuff; that somewhere inside he knew he was not leaving for this alone, only that this, finally, had become the reason.

'If you walk out,' she shouted after him, 'you can never come back, you know that, don't you? Sam? Sam!'

The click of the catch. His own quickening feet. Her primal wail of rage – all that was left now her words had run dry. The pale linoleum of the shared stairwell blurring beneath him, the rapid tap-tap-tap of the metal stair runners against the soles of his boots. The banister cold against his grip. The dizzying descent. And out into the chill kiss of the March air. The metallic thunk of the van doors shutting on the pathetic sight of all he had taken with him: two bags, one filled with clothes, one with books. His gardening tools, his toolbox. A box of vinyl records already loaded up, the vintage Pye record player she had bought for him from Bridport antiques market, a box of shoes, a coffee maker, his mother's Le Creuset casserole dish.

That's it, he thought, the enormity of what he was doing growing from some dark corner of himself. This is the material sum of my life. I have failed. I am a failure.

Panic took him towards Uplyme, his mind blank. At the sight of the hundred-foot arches of the viaduct, he swerved the van into the hedge and jumped out, raided his tools and headed up the muddy rise.

Somehow, *somehow*, he did not throw himself off. Who knows how? Perhaps the extreme height gave him some perspective, the glass rain diving into the black abyss. Whatever, minute by minute, his breathing steadied. He stepped back, climbed down, returned soaking wet through the muddy grass and then on, down to Lyme, to his gran's, his home since he was ten years old. Joyce had brought him there from Clapham after the death of his mother: a fresh start, a chance, after he'd gone off the rails at school.

'This is where I grew up,' she'd told him – still so careful in the way she spoke to him back then, none of the easy teasing that developed between them over the years. 'I was thinking of moving back anyway once I'd sold the business, so may as well be now. We'll be happy here – you'll see.'

She was right. Eventually. In his final year at primary school, his teacher, Mrs Colston, asked him to help her with the school garden. She did this, he realised only recently, to help him get over his crushing shyness, his mortification at being the new kid with the weird London accent. He stayed after school, and together with a few of the other kids, they dug the earth and planted seeds and made an arched dome out of willow, and he felt that churning feeling inside him shrink away.

That summer, he worked with Joyce on her garden, all thoughts of London – the fighting, the spray-painting of obscenities on the school toilet walls, the throwing of eggs at buses – almost gone. Later, together, he and Joyce dug trenches in her back garden. She showed him how to mix concrete, which they poured into the hollowed-out ground. Once it had set, they laid railway sleepers on top and filled the raised rectangles with fresh soil and compost, then stood back and drank their tea from white mugs, and Joyce said, *Look at that, would you look at that? We've only gone and built a vegetable garden.*

When Sam was fifteen, Joe, a local landscaper, let him help on small jobs during the school holidays. He earned pocket money mowing lawns at weekends, learnt how to pave, how to lay bricks. Later, he built sheds, planted beds, levelled ground. He had a good eye, Joe said, a practical brain and the knack for handling plants. That was Sam: in his element in the earth.

Joyce was right about him being happy in Lyme. And when she first met Naomi, she was right about her too, telling him to mind how he went. But as he and Naomi became serious, Joyce said less and less. When he told her they were moving in together, she said only, *Wonderful, love. As long as you're happy,* and gave him five thousand pounds towards the deposit.

Just now, in the kitchen, Joyce's expression had hardened the moment Naomi's name was mentioned.

And you're sure it's her friend's, this baby?

Could she be right again – in what she'd almost said?

This afternoon, Naomi looked behind her towards the Cobb before she spoke. Was it before or after that that she said she was looking after her friend's child? He can't remember. Was still trying to get his sea legs against the rushing wave of her. But he does remember her manner when she said it: nervous, embarrassed, as if caught off guard.

Caught in a lie? Or just embarrassed to see him after their messy break-up?

He rubs in the shampoo, fingertips hard against his skull, trying to disperse the tension. During lockdown, he had to stop himself from texting her to check she was OK, knowing that one text would be the first knot in the noose, the end of the rope wound tight around her delicate white hands.

But that was before today, before he saw her with the baby, whose colouring matches his own, whose age ties in perfectly with a pregnancy that would date from before he left. Did she know about it then, when she shouted after him, accusing him of choosing his grandmother over her, as if he was not allowed to have both in his life?

This afternoon it was as if he'd caught her doing something she shouldn't. She hadn't expected to see him there, that much was obvious. He'd burst out from behind the chalets; there was no way she could have seen him approaching. It would've been too late for her to make a dash for the car. But then it isn't comfortable bumping into an ex at the best of times, he imagines – can only imagine since he hasn't had any direct experience before today. And he was awkward too, embarrassed, tongue-tied.

The pendulum swings back and forth: it was merely the

discomfort of lovers no longer together/it was something more. The way that baby stared at him/all babies stare. His blue eyes, his blonde brow/lots of babies are fair with blue eyes.

Oh, but if... and he hardly dares think it, but *if* the child is his, Naomi will have known he might suspect, even hope. When they were happy – and they were, at first – all he wanted was to have a child together. Two. Three even. But she refused.

'Children cripple women.' Her words, not his.

It was their first argument, an argument they would have over and over again.

'I can go part-time,' he said. 'You can have a career if that's what you want.'

'We won't have enough money!'

'We don't need much. Kids go to school soon enough.'

'No,' she said. 'No way.'

She would know, know without any doubt whatsoever, that even if they were no longer together, he would want to be a big part of their child's life.

So why didn't she tell him?

His breath comes quick and shallow. How typical of her, to keep the one thing he always wanted from him, as a kind of revenge. As awful as it is to think it, she is capable of such a thing.

He pushes his feet against the side of the bath, making the water swish up and down the length until the soapy residue clears. Remembers himself, the night he left, reaching Joyce's house, the brass lion's-head knocker in his hand, banging on the great red door. There he stood in the fat rain: hair sticking slicker and slicker to his head, drops running off his oilskin, jeans dark, saturated. When the door opened, he saw immediately that she had aged. He had not seen her as recently as he should've done. And this, too, was Naomi's doing. *You're not going there again, are you? Didn't you see her last week? We're supposed to be booking a holiday/looking for furniture/going to the supermarket.* It was never a good time.

Joyce peered into the dark as if trying to recognise him. 'Love? Sam, love, whatever's the matter?'

In the warm kitchen, the savoury smell of meat and vegetables, the soft click and woof of the boiler. Joyce made him sit on the old chesterfield sofa while she fetched the Remy Martin she only usually got out at Christmas.

'It's over,' he said. 'I suggested we move in with you for the lockdown and she said no. She was so... I just couldn't believe she could be so... so hard. Mean. Five years of my life... all gone.'

'Oh no, love. Not gone – spent! You'll have learnt a thing or two, honestly you will. No one gains wisdom by never getting into a pickle. It's the getting out of it that makes you stronger, and get out of it you will. You just need a bit of time and some peace and quiet, that's all, and I think peace and quiet is what we're getting for the foreseeable if this bloody virus does what they say it's going to do. And when it's gone, you can come out fighting, OK? Plenty more fish in the sea. Any clichés I've missed? Here's another: you're not old yet.'

No, he is not old. He is thirty-two. And if he's right about the baby, as he is beginning to dare to hope, a family is not impossible after all.

The bitterness clears. Himself, a father to a son. A little guy to take walking, to teach stuff to, to take to the pub one day. Today Naomi's smile echoed all her smiles from before, when they were happy. Her smile is a mark he has not been able to scrub away after all. She seemed changed.

No one changes, Joyce would say. Leopards, spots.

But what if something dramatic happened? Like serious illness. An accident. A death. People change then, don't they?

A global pandemic.

A pregnancy.

A birth.

He sits up quickly, sending water sploshing over the edge of the bath.

'Motherhood,' he whispers. Motherhood changes a woman. He's pretty sure Joyce said that too, once.

He will call Naomi. There is no choice now. He has to know, if only to stop this... this obsession. It's possible that seeing him, she regretted a choice made in anger, stuck to out of stubbornness. Why not? When she found herself pregnant, she would have been apoplectic, would have vowed to keep his child from him, to punish him. Her sister, Jo, would have egged her on, that's for sure. Jo could pick a fight in a yoga retreat. But then the baby arrived. Motherhood humbled her, softened her. And today, confronted with the *reality* of her ex rather than the *idea* of him warped by the spiralling fury of absence, she was not as sure of her hate as she had been.

Or was she simply looking after her friend's child?

'Argh.' He dries himself and returns to his room. Picks up his phone and opens WhatsApp.

CHAPTER 6

Her last message makes him flinch.

You said you'd be home by six? You'd better bring a take-away with you cos I'll be fucked if I'm cooking after the day I've had.

Ignoring this, he writes: *Can we meet?*

No. Too obvious. She'll know what he's after. If the baby is his, it's clear she doesn't want him to know. He has to play this carefully. He has to look right into her eyes when he asks her, study her every micro-movement. Years spent living with her, he's pretty sure he can read her up close.

But he needs a pretext.

His room is untidy. He scans it, not sure what he's looking for, before his eyes settle on the stack of records in the corner. Still wrapped in his towel, he drops to his knees and lifts the albums one after another. Finds the Frank Ocean: orange vinyl, limited edition. It his hers; he took it by mistake. Here is the pretext. He will make no mention of the baby. He deletes the message and tries again.

Hi. Good to see you today. Forgot to say, I still have your

Frank Ocean album. I could bring it over to Bridport this Saturday – we could have that coffee? Sam

The two grey ticks turn blue: she has read the message. But a moment later, she is offline. She has not replied.

Unsure what this means, his belly heats with anticipation, but he forces himself to get dressed, go downstairs and focus on cooking dinner.

Joyce crosses him on the stairs. She's going to jump in the bath, she tells him. She's aching all over from holding a funny position at the top of the stepladder.

In the kitchen, on the draining board, her tools are drying: the round-ended trowel, the float, the scraper. On the countertop, a large bag of powdered plasterboard adhesive and her water spray gun. Yesterday, he found her glossing the kitchen window, one hand in her wrist brace. Last summer, he had to stop her from climbing the extendable ladder to refresh the paint on the upstairs windows, telling her he would do it; in that moment, he reminds himself he must do before she tries again now the weather is finer.

So discombobulated was he by Naomi and the child, he has forgotten to pick up groceries on the way home. A quick examination of the various tins and jars suggests a simple store-cupboard puttanesca, one of Joyce's favourites. He skins a tooth of garlic, crushes it against the flat of his knife. Don't think about Naomi. Put her out of your mind. The garlic simmers in olive oil, is followed by the grey slither of anchovies. Naomi. Gently pushing her nose to the baby's. He tips the bright, heavy falling sludge of tomatoes from the can. Naomi. Tenderly clipping the baby into the back seat of the car. He chops the black olives in half, throws them into the sauce. Naomi. Softly talking to the baby, her voice lilting. It was all so instinctive, so natural. These were not the exaggerated gestures of a woman unused to children, but the much smaller intimacies of someone close to the child, very close. It reminded him of the way Miranda is with little Betsy. He rinses the capers, empties them from the sieve into the red, bubbling shallows.

It is the small things that give us away, he thinks. It is not what we say but what we do.

Above him, Joyce's bath gurgles away. He lights the gas under the pasta water and is lowering the spaghetti into the pan when she appears, pink-faced, her white hair sticking up in short wet spikes. She is wearing her black silk pyjamas, her tan leather clogs and the calf-length grey cashmere cardigan she often dons in the evening after a day engaged in her ongoing battle with the house. She doesn't like to wear slippers or a dressing gown; they make her feel depressed, she says. As for the house, it will win one day. It is a wonder it hasn't already. Even the mighty Joyce is no match for this great Georgian pile.

'Red?' She passes behind him to the wine rack. She has started to waddle a little; the pain in her hip must be getting worse.

'Sure.'

Minutes later, he has brought the serving bowl to the table. His gran sits and takes a sip of the cheap Pinot Noir they buy in bulk from the big Morrisons outside Bridport.

'Thank you for this beautiful meal,' she says with feeling.

'Bon appétit.' He sits opposite her and begins to serve.

'I've been thinking,' Joyce begins, twizzling an oily ball of orange strands onto her fork.

'Me too.'

Over the round gold rims of her half-steamed-up glasses, her pale blue eyes meet his. 'And?'

'I think the baby might be mine.'

Her eyebrows rise, though not in surprise.

'He has my colouring,' he goes on. 'And just... the way she was with him, you know? And I've never heard of a Cheryl, so that would have to be a new friend, which is weird. I mean, who made new friends in lockdown? And if he's six or seven months old, that would mean she was around three months pregnant when I left. I know I said today she seemed... I don't know, nicer. Softer. But at the same time... it's just the sort of thing she would do. Keep him from me, I mean.'

His gran nods, her mouth a grim line. 'What are you going to do?'

'I've texted her. I've got an old record of hers I said I could give back.'

Another pause. Joyce's fork hovers. 'Have you thought about what you want?'

He takes a mouthful, the sauce salty and juicy on his tongue.

'Not really,' he says, swallowing. 'I mean, I'd like to know. I have a right to know.'

Joyce says nothing. They eat, drink, talk in gentle flurries about Sam's walk, the beach hut for sale on Monmouth.

'Three hundred grand.' She snorts. 'Three hundred grand and no lav!'

While she rolls her after-dinner cigarette – medicinal, for her various muscular pains – they discuss what they might watch later on Netflix. She has always known how to leave him the space to get to where he needs. Their conversation is twenty-two years long: plenty of room for going round the houses until you arrive back where you began.

'So,' she says, with an air of finality, 'this kiddie.' She

lights the joint and leans back in her chair, takes a drag and blows out a plume of sweet smoke.

'If he's mine,' he says into the space, 'and I'm not saying he is, but *if* he is, I think... I think I have a right to see him. As in, be part of his life. I want... I want to be, y'know, his dad. I mean, if I am, that's what I am, isn't it? His dad? It's not like I knew. It's not like I left *him*, and maybe if I'd known, I wouldn't have left. It's just, I didn't have a... I mean, I only had Mum till I was ten, so... Not that you weren't... I mean, you were... you are... we're—'

She waves her hand in dismissal. 'I know what you mean, don't worry. We're grand. But let's not get ahead of ourselves. We don't know anything, do we? Let's not go waltzing off into what might be.'

'I'm not. I promise I'm not. But at the same time, I feel like I know, do you know what I mean? I kind of felt it.'

She smiles kindly, furrows carved deep at the edges of her eyes. 'All right, but as I say, let's not rush in. Only fools do that, don't they? And you're no fool.'

CHAPTER 7

Dear Sam,

In case you were wondering, Pete left Jo about a month after you walked out. That's how come we bubbled up together. You won't know that, I don't suppose, no reason why you would. Not like anyone's seen anyone, is it? It seems like a big coincidence seeing you this morning, but it was on the cards, I'm sure you'd agree. And a lot of relationships failed during lockdown. I saw it on This Morning. Divorces went up. Domestic violence was off the scale too apparently. I really feel for those women.

But violence isn't always physical, is it, Sam?

You wouldn't recognise Jo now, by the way; she's had a serious makeover. I think that's common when you split with someone – new hair, new me sort of thing. Britney Spears did it, didn't she? Shaved her hair off.

I'm batch-cooking some chicken right now, just FYI. Chicken with rice and veg for little Toms. I call him Toms, sometimes Tom-Tom, sometimes Tom-Toms. Picture it: wholesome grub simmering away on the stove, me on my laptop at the kitchen table, multitasking like some sort of domestic goddess. Honestly, you'd barely recognise me these days. I'm wondering now if you cook for Joyce like you used to cook for me. Do you do all the odd jobs around the house? I bet you two were self-sufficient during lockdown – bet you had more vegetables than you could eat!

Just had to change Toms's nappy. Where was I? Can't remember. Have I told you about Dawn yet? My therapist. She helped me after you left. I had PTSD apparently. Dawn said just because it's not, like, war or anything, it's still trauma, what I went through. I didn't realise that. I told her about how we met and how I recognised you from school. I told her we had a deep connection, literally straight away, and how you just threw it away when things got a bit difficult. She said maybe I chose the silent type because my dad spent time away from the family home. But she also suggested you might be afraid of connection because of your mum. Like, deep down you feared that if you allowed yourself to love me like you loved her, something would take me away? Might be something in that, I think. What do you reckon? If you were here, I wonder if you'd tell me or just clam up. You never did like talking about that stuff, which is a shame, because it would have brought us closer.

I think all I'm trying to say is: people evolve. That's what I learnt from Dawn. I've evolved. It's hard, I can tell you that much, and there's been quite a few changes to my circumstances. It's so sad, when you think about it. We could have evolved together. We could have had so much.

I don't know what I'm saying really. I'm not saying I wasn't difficult sometimes, but I was unhappy, that's all. Unhappy people aren't easy, and I know I said mean things, expected you to read my mind and stuff, but you're not so easy yourself, you know? Any little issue we had, it was like trying to talk to a stone, and then I felt like I was hysterical or mad or something. Like when you left: I was getting more and more upset, and you just carried on packing like you couldn't wait to get out of there. You didn't stop or try and comfort me at all. That's gaslighting, did you know that? Dawn explained that to me as well. Denying my feelings. I think a good counsellor could have helped us, but you didn't want to even try. You just put your head in the sand as usual and went to live with your gran.

I can feel myself getting angry again, and that's not what I want to be, Sam. Anger won't help. I'm learning to deal with my feelings in a more useful way. I follow loads of therapists on Insta, and they post great stuff, really insightful, about boundaries and stuff.

I'm sorry I didn't tell you the truth today. I almost did, but the moment passed and then it was too late somehow. Now I'm thinking if you didn't delete my number, you might even ring me. If you do, I might tell you. See how I feel. As I said, I don't owe you anything anymore. I really noticed Tommy's little blue eyes today, his blonde eyelashes, how similar he is to you in his colouring. Are you thinking about that now you're back at Joyce's? Or are you thinking about that time I dared you to make love to me at Chimney Rock? You were so worried it would collapse under us or that some hikers would appear on the path and see us, but that's what made it so intense. I bet you remember that, don't you?

I think about you, Sam. Maybe that's all I want to say. I know I felt something today. I was trembling when I got into the car. Literally. I could barely clip Tommy into his seat belt. I thought about you all the way back to Bridport. I'm thinking about you now. I wonder actually if I went to Lyme just so I'd bump into you – you know, like a subconscious thing. But even so, what are the chances? I suppose it had to happen sooner or later.

Joyce will tell you not to contact me, I'm sure, but I wonder if you will. I hope you do. It would be good to see you again. See you properly, I mean, and to feel like you want to see me.

OMG. You just messaged me!

Talk of the devil.

CHAPTER 8

He has just climbed into the van the following morning when Naomi finally replies.

I can meet you this Saturday. The Bull. 1pm?

Great, he replies immediately. *See you then. Xx*

He exhales. Has the sense of rope running through his hands, his own foot tied to the end. But no, he has tight hold. He has no idea how he will broach the subject, only that he must. He wonders how or if she will explain it away. Perhaps she genuinely believes he didn't spot the likeness or work out the dates, or that she can pass it off as a coincidence. She always believed herself to be more intelligent than him, than everyone for that matter.

'What're you reading now?' she would ask in the evenings, when he was trying to relax with a book.

'*Moby Dick,*' he remembers answering once, already dreading her response.

'*Moby Dick?* Oh my God.' Sure enough, she laughed, then asked if it was pornography.

'It's about a whale.'

She rolled her eyes and shook her head. 'A book about a whale. How exciting.'

She used to complain that they never spent any time together, by which he understood he was at fault for not wanting to watch the programmes she chose. But he found her documentary-style soap operas about the wives of billionaires as boring as she found his books – boring and a bit upsetting. Naomi, however, used to point at the television and laugh out loud. At first, when he was high on the drug of her, he found this cute: the way she could giggle at people treating each other so badly and apparently enjoying it. There was an innocence to it, he'd thought back then. Until it began to grate on his nerves.

He folds Joyce's shopping list into his jeans pocket before starting the van. It's early. Half past seven. He's got a new project on Higher Mill this morning and has texted Miranda that he's on his way.

When he gets to her cottage, she is already waiting outside with Betsy, who waves madly as he pulls up to the kerb. Now, at the sight of Miranda with her little girl, and preoccupied by what might be his own situation, he sees the parallel: another woman abandoned to raise a child. A parallel too with his own mother, even his grandmother. Is that what he has done, walked out on a family? Except Miranda's ex was having an affair and she asked him to leave; Sam's mother was never really with his father, and his gran kicked his grandad out for being a lazy arse – Joyce's words, not his. And not one of these women hid the fact that she was pregnant. No, he is not like those men. His story, if it is his story, is different.

'Hey.' Miranda is climbing into the cab and pulling Betsy up after her.

'Hi, Sam-Sam,' Betsy says, smiling with all her baby

teeth before her features close in determination as she clam-
bers over her mother's lap. She wiggles to the back of the
seat between him and her mum, her pink trainers sticking
out in front of her.

'Hey, Bets,' Sam says. 'Could you start the engine
please?'

She bends forward and pushes the phone charging
point with her thumb, then claps her hands, her fingers
spread and rod-straight.

Silence. She looks up at him, eyes wide and green.

He frowns. 'No luck. Another try?'

Again she pushes, her little thumb whitening around
the tiny pearl of her nail.

Sam turns the key in the ignition. The rattle of diesel
engine fills the van. 'That got it. Thanks, Bets.'

Ten minutes later, Betsy safely dropped at nursery, he and
Miranda are alone, and talk turns inevitably to the project: a
former holiday let opposite the river. Miranda won't come
every day; she is the designer, and as such has a supervisory
role on site as well as liaising with the client. For Sam, who
is in charge of the physical work, Darren, Lee, Scott, Josh
and Callum, the young apprentice, the work over the next
few days, possibly couple of weeks, will be grubby and
strenuous, as it always is at the beginning. This job could
take a few months, weather depending.

Sam believes he's been chatting perfectly normally, but
as he turns into the driveway of the bungalow, Miranda asks
him what's wrong.

'Nothing,' he says, parking up next to the property.
'Why?'

'You seem a bit distracted, that's all.'

He can feel that she's turned to look at him but keeps his gaze forward. Beyond the windscreen, a greened and dilapidated shed slumps behind a ramshackle dwarf wall. The shed is too large for the space, the felt roof peeling. The rotten wooden side flakes like slow-cooked meat.

'I'm fine,' he says. 'Bumped into Naomi yesterday, that's all.'

'Your ex? Wow.'

The fabric of Miranda's combat trousers swishes as she shifts position. In the corner of his eye, her hiking boot dandles. When he sneaks a glance past her red weather-proof jacket, he sees that her cheeks have pinked and are puffed out like a trumpet player's. Nodding slowly, she blows a long jet of air, then flushes deeper; he's not sure why – it isn't particularly hot in the van.

'Are you OK?' he asks.

'Yeah!' She frowns. 'I'm thinking you might not be though.'

'It was fine.' He returns his gaze to the windscreen. 'Bit awkward, that's all.'

'Horrendous, isn't it? I remember the first time I handed Bets over to my ex. Used to be sick after he'd left. But it'll be easier next time, I promise, then easier again, until you get used to it.' The click of the passenger-side door opening, but Miranda is only halfway out of the van.

'I'm not sure I will.'

'Oh, you will. Honestly. Time heals and all that.'

'See her again, I mean. I mean, we don't have to share custody of... anyone.' He does not tell Miranda his suspicions, nor that he's seeing Naomi on Saturday, though he can think of no reason to keep this from her.

'True. At least you'll be prepared if there is a next time.'

'Not sure you can be prepared for Naomi.' He shakes

his head, half laughs. 'She's like an unexpected punch to the jaw, you know?'

Miranda grins. 'I suppose a punch to the jaw is always unexpected.'

'Ha!' He is about to come clean about Saturday, but she has jumped out of the van. He follows, slams the door shut.

The others aren't here yet, so he and Miranda have a good look around the site. The job is challenging but will be satisfying too. At the moment, it is a mess of contradicting levels, weeds, brambles, a broken fence and some dodgy paving. The V-shape of Lyme Regis means that almost every street is on a steep rise, the gardens sloping violently uphill, rockeries, root systems and stone walls securing the soil.

'I reckon we'll rip this out first.' Miranda pats the seventies-style concrete balustrade, pushes it to test its stability. 'Then we'll build decking as far as here.' She draws an invisible line with her hand over the narrow canal-like trench that runs across a short section of the garden, empty save for some dark damp earth and one rather magnificent *Gunnera manicata*.

'What's that trench for?' Sam asks.

'I *think* it's the old mill race.' Miranda holds up her sketch and the two of them study it, mentally matching the reality with her vision of what the space will eventually look like. 'They split the river further up the hill, and this channel runs down from there and across the back of all these properties. It once powered the mill over there.' She points towards the flats to the right. 'When it used to be a mill, I mean.'

'Higher Mill flats.'

'Exactly. Like the mill race down to the brewery as you go into town. Except that one's still in use obviously.'

'Gotcha. So... does it run all the way under the garages?'

'I've not inspected it, to be honest. Only the exposed bit is on the surveyor's report.'

She jumps down into the shallow trench, bends to shine her iPhone torch where the channel passes under the concrete base of the ancient shed. She crouches, peers into the gloom, then kneels before lowering herself onto her elbows, her head disappearing momentarily beneath the concrete.

'It's closed off up ahead, but...' She backs up, her head reappearing. He holds out his hand, pulls her up. 'It looks like there's another channel off to the right. Hard to tell.' She pockets the phone, chafes her hands together.

'To the right as in towards the river?'

'Yeah. Not sure. It's pretty dark in there.'

'There might be an opening though. At the river.'

Sam wanders out of the garden, jogs down the driveway and across the lane. At the railings, he leans over. It's overgrown; he can't see much, so he vaults over and scrambles down the bank. The water races past, down towards the salmon steps, the brightly painted houses of Jericho. Against the flow of the river he strides, cold water leaking into his socks now. And there, almost opposite the property and hidden in the bank, is a rough man-made arch of sandstone bricks, the mouth of what looks like a tunnel.

'Mi,' he calls out. 'Miranda! Over here!'

The opening is tall enough that if he bends forward, he can walk right inside. It is dry, the rush of the river at his back. He takes out his phone and shines the torch ahead. It is a kind of secret grotto, like a mine shaft. He keeps going, bending lower and lower as the tunnel closes in, sensing he has passed beneath the road, that he must be somewhere under the driveway. It is cocoon-like. Silent.

'Sam?' Miranda's voice echoes in the chamber. The passage darkens. He glances over his shoulder, sees her outline at the entrance. 'Be careful,' she calls to him. 'If it collapses on you, I'll never... Look, I'm not insured, OK?'

'Nice.' He laughs, dropping now to his knees. There is a wall ahead, as if he is coming to a dead end. It looks far enough away to be under the garden, under the shed maybe. He is down on his elbows now. From the left, light penetrates. He crawls towards it, sees that the right-hand side is completely blocked, as Miranda said, but that the left emerges exactly where she was standing a few minutes ago. Wriggling on his belly, he manages to squeeze himself out and stand up.

'Mi!' he shouts. 'Hey, Miranda! Look where I am!'

A moment later, she appears at the gate, her eyes round. 'What the hell?'

'It's a secret passage! It's like something out of the Famous Five, like a smugglers' den or something!'

She laughs, her expression of infantile joy mirroring his own. 'That's insane.'

'I know!'

'It must have been the old floodgate. Must be. What else could it be? That's what the other mill race does further down, right? You see it when the rain's heavy; the water comes battering through that little door thing in the wall. Well, the floodgate.'

He drops to his knees. 'I'm going back in.'

'Oh my God, you're braver than me. Meet you at the river!'

Heart beating with childish excitement, he crawls back, using his phone to take photos all the way along, the camera flashing white. 'Bloody hell,' he mutters. 'This is epic.' And, 'I can't believe it.'

On the riverbank, Miranda is grinning down at him as he straightens up out of his stoop. Her delight so obviously matches his own that for a moment he thinks he might hug her. Instead, he passes her the phone, their heads almost touching as she scrolls through the photos.

'This is so cool,' she says. 'I can't believe it wasn't on the survey. I wonder who else knows about it?'

'No idea!'

'I tell you what though.' She hands the phone back to him. 'It's a great place to hide a body.'

Look, I wish I'd never said that about the body, OK? I didn't mean anything by it; it's just the sort of thing you say if you come across a dark, spooky hidey-hole. A joke, less than a joke. I wasn't to know what Sam would end up doing. And I know there were those who judged him harshly for what he did, but what I say to anyone who stuck the knife in afterwards is: can you honestly say you'd have been in your right mind? Can you actually stand there and *judge*?

CHAPTER 9

Dear Sam,

So you've finally contacted me to meet up. Typical you. You never could make your mind up, could you? But opposites attract, even I know that. I never told you this at the time, but you know the night I met you? Well, that morning I'd read in Cosmo that Pisces vibes well with Virgo, because they're opposites! How spooky is that? That's why I smiled when I asked when your birthday was and you told me 28 August. I was like, this is a sign!

You were my family, Sam. That's how I thought of you. Maybe because I met you so soon after Mum died – met you properly, I mean. That's why you leaving like you did was such a betrayal. Being sensitive, I took it personally. But asking me not to be sensitive is like asking me to change my eye colour, and anyway it's pretty hard not to take total rejection personally.

But I've grown up a lot since then. I know people are complicated. We're all so complicated, aren't we?

Don't get me wrong, I'm not saying I was perfect, but

I was perfect for you. Honestly, you were always such a neek at school. But that's what I loved about you – not at school, but later, when we met as grown-ups. You're still the cleverest person I know, although that's not saying much – I know some right lemons. But you knew how to do stuff, and I didn't appreciate that as much as I should have. I was young. I just wanted to have fun. I'm older now and I can see the value of all your old-school skills. Looking after Tommy has changed my priorities, you see.

My therapist was always going on at me to write you a letter. I never did, but now I can see why she suggested it. Tell you what's weird though. I just thought this: if you ever read this letter, you'll never be able to picture me now, while I write it. Isn't that weird? Like, I know everything about myself in this moment, but you won't even know where I was or when I closed my laptop and opened it again.

So weird.

But if you do ever read this, I do a few paragraphs here and there between seeing to Tommy's needs. I've just given him his banana porridge. Weird. I've gone all funny just thinking that when you read this, in your reality, Tommy won't just have had his banana porridge, will he? Because time will have moved on. He might even be talking or something by the time you read about the porridge!

Is it normal to think about this stuff when you write a letter? I don't know, I've only ever written texts or Whats-Apps and they land pretty much in the same time zone. Actually, I'm going to stop thinking about it because it's actually freaking me out.

Tommy loves his banana porridge, by the way. You always took a banana with you to work, didn't you? He's in bed now, dead to the world, bless him. I'm putting my feet up with a magazine and reading my horoscope. You'll never believe what today said! It said: A chance to come clean. Can you believe that? Well, maybe I will. Maybe I'll tell you the direction my life took after you left, just to see the shock on your face.

I knew you'd text instead of calling because that's classic you. I could plot you like one of those graphs on the government press conferences. I'm enjoying talking to you like this, Sam. Maybe this isn't a letter. Maybe it's more like a conversation. You were often so silent in conversations, so in that sense it's the same. Except that when you don't reply, I feel like I can cope.

CHAPTER 10

The last time Sam was in the Bull was with Naomi and Jo, and Jo's boyfriend Pete, the Christmas before lockdown, he thinks. Jo got very drunk very quickly on espresso martinis and was sick on the pavement outside. Pete had to walk her all the way to her dad's because the cab wouldn't take her. Sam has never been sure why Jo drinks cocktails – or alcohol, for that matter; it never did agree with her. Naomi's sister is a nightmare all round. A bit scary even.

He and Naomi met just round the corner from here, he thinks. At the Electric Palace. He'd gone with Darren and some mates to see a comedy gig. Naomi was at the bar. Sam was surprised when she remembered him from school; she was the It girl even then. She and her sister never troubled the yard or the sports field, instead taking up residence in the girls' loos, shrouded by clouds of illicit smoke, not that he ever saw them with his own eyes obviously; it was common knowledge, part of the Harper girls' myth. The pair of them had the glamour that comes with being a little bit beautiful, a little bit hard, a little bit dangerous.

'I'm here with Jo,' Naomi told him that night, staring so

directly into his eyes it was like she was daring him to do something he was afraid to do. 'You remember my sister, don't you? She's gone for a puff. We're cheering ourselves up. We lost Mum last month.'

'I'm so sorry,' he said, a little confused by her familiarity. At school they had exchanged not one word. Her mother, he seemed to recall, had a reputation for marching into school, jabbing poor quivering teachers in the chest and telling them to lay off her girls or she'd do something about it.

Naomi shrugged. The challenge in her eyes subsided. 'Not your fault. These things happen.'

'Well, I'm sorry for your loss. If you need to talk... I just... I know how it feels, that's all.'

She cocked her head, her smile slow. 'Aren't you sweet?'

Out of nowhere, she reached forward and squeezed his upper arm, then laughed. 'Sorry! I just had to see if that was real. You a gym bunny?'

It was his turn to laugh. 'Landscaper. A lot of heavy lifting. But no gym, no. Just walking and... er, working, I suppose.'

'And you used to be such a skinny little thing too.'

'I'm amazed you even remember me. Even *I* barely remember me.'

She laughed so much at that, he thought she must have heard someone else tell a joke, somewhere nearby. He even looked round to see this person. But no, she was laughing at him.

Did he walk her home that night? Or was that after their first date, a long daytime walk over the cliffs, stopping for a drink at the Anchor Inn. Maybe that was a few dates in actually – he can remember them laughing a lot, making then losing eye contact, falling in love. The memory is hazy and golden. It confuses him, as early memories of Naomi tend to do.

He orders a latte; they said coffee, so it seems like the right move. The girl tells him to go and sit in the garden, as they're not serving indoors yet. He can take off his mask when he sits down. The garden is actually a courtyard, which a year ago was a lot plainer. Now, there's a large brazier, which is smoking a little. They should have lit twigs first, used more firelighters. You need to get these things raging hot.

There's no one else here, only a discarded newspaper on a seat. He grabs it just as the girl from the bar brings his coffee, telling him she's sorry it took so long. When she speaks, her face flushes red. He thanks her, unsure why she looks so embarrassed, heat flushing through him as it occurs to him his fly might be open or something. A quick check. No, thank God. And anyway, the blushing girl has returned into the pub.

A glance at the paper's headline – further easing-up measures due next month. It is harder than he thought it would be, being back in Bridport, not just because of the disaster-movie-style eeriness of the deserted streets, the near-empty pub, but because everywhere is full of memories of himself and Naomi. On the way here, he passed an Indian restaurant, scene of one of their many arguments. A female client had been there, dining with a group of girlfriends. When Sam walked in, she recognised him and called him over. She was pink-cheeked, a little tipsy, as she introduced him to her friends: *Girls, this is Sam, the gardener.* She raised her eyebrows at them, some hidden meaning in her expression, their mouths and eyes rounding in apparent understanding.

'Oh,' they said. 'So *this* is Sam.'

More giggles. A round of nice-to-meet-yous, large half-empty glasses of rosé wine held up in manicured fingers.

He left as quickly as he could. At their table, Naomi was scowling at him from behind the tealight. In his belly, a familiar pit of anxiety hardened.

'Nice,' she said. 'Take your girlfriend out for dinner, then leave her sitting on her own for half an hour.'

'It was only a minute or two,' he whispered, not wanting the client to overhear. 'Would've been rude not to say hi.'

'Well, it felt like longer. You made me look like a right lemon. So humiliating.'

'Sorry. I had to. She's a good client.'

'Client.' Naomi rolled her eyes, picked up the menu, sighed heavily. 'Not sure I'm even hungry anymore.' She could do that, make something small grow so huge that whatever they were doing got lost in its shadow, the whole evening spent trying to claw his way back to where they had started.

'Sam.'

Startled, he looks up. Naomi is standing in front of him, her smile tender. His breath catches; he has the urge to stand up and kiss the pale skin of her cheek, to plunge his face into her neck. Her hair is cut shorter than a year ago, making the black waves look even thicker. Her beauty is as overwhelming as it was the other day, as it always was. The feeling of confusion returns.

'Naomi.'

Beside her, there is no child, no stroller, no one.

'You're having coffee,' she says. 'I thought we were eating.'

'Oh. Sorry, I...' He said coffee, he's pretty sure, but he can't exactly check the text thread while she's standing there. And now he has drunk a large latte, which has killed his appetite. At least, something has. 'You order,' he offers. 'I will too, I mean. You know me – I can always eat.' He smiles, but Naomi's face has closed a little.

'No, it's fine.' Her mouth purses. 'I can eat later.'

He has ruined things before they have begun.

'Seriously,' he tries, keen to rescue the situation. 'I'll have a bowl of chips or something. Please. Let me order you something, come on.'

Her shoulders lower a fraction. She sits down, unloops her long yellow scarf once, twice, unhooks a battered turquoise shoulder bag over her head. 'I'll have some cheesy chips then. And a vodka and Diet Coke if you're having a drink.'

He isn't. He's driving. But he orders the vodka and Diet Coke for her, lime and soda for himself, and the chips. Pays for them up front so it won't become embarrassing later. He is, he realises, afraid of how she'll react to what he must ask her. He is afraid of her.

'Sorry,' he says, returning with the drinks. 'About the coffee. I've ordered two bowls of cheesy chips. It's cold, isn't it? For April? Still, they've got the fire. At least it's not raining. Chilly though.'

'It is.' She takes a swig, places her drink on the table.

'I brought your album.' He passes her the Frank Ocean. 'Didn't realise I'd taken it. Sorry about that.'

She takes the record, gives it a desultory glance before placing it on the chair beside her.

'You wanted to see me.' She is looking at him incredibly directly. 'Or was it really just to give me my record back?'

'Right.' The wooden slats of the chair creak beneath him. 'I did, yeah. I thought it might be nice to... y'know, catch up. Actually, I thought you might be with the baby. The baby you were with the other day. Tommy, was it?'

Her eyes narrow. 'Why would you think that?'

'I don't know.' Oh God, this is harder than he thought it would be. Already he can feel his armpits prickling.

'He's at home,' she says.

He nods, slowly, as if she has explained something to him. 'Right. Right.' His mouth has gone dry. He takes a sip of soda, another. 'Everything's so weird,' he says. 'All a bit post-apocalyptic, isn't it?'

'Post-apocalyptic.' She shakes her head. 'Only you, Sam.'

She asks after Joyce, he after her sister; she tells him Jo has split up with Pete and shaved all her hair off.

'Crikey,' he says.

'Crikey,' she repeats, as if what he has said is stupid, and again shakes her head.

The chips arrive, ketchup, mayo; cutlery wrapped in serviettes.

Naomi dips a long chip into the mayonnaise and bites off the end. 'Yum.' She dips it again, this time into the ketchup, and slides the rest into her mouth.

'I thought...' Sam begins, consciously avoiding looking at the shine the chip has made on her bottom lip.

'You thought what?' Another chip makes it whole into her mouth. 'Sam? What did you think?' Her voice is not unkind.

'Nothing.' Suddenly short of breath, he sips then gulps his soda. Feels it running down, cold inside him.

'Sam? What's this about? Why are we here? I thought the record was an excuse to, you know... see me.' Her chin juts, her eyelids half lower in what looks like a challenge.

'I thought...' he says again, inwardly cursing himself. Naomi used to call him a coward. She was right. He slides the salt across the table like a chess piece, makes himself let go of it, look up, meet her eye. 'I just... I mean, what is he, about six, seven months old? Tommy. The baby you were... looking after.'

'He's seven months. His mum had to have him in hospital in the middle of the pandemic, poor thing. Can you imagine that?'

'Who's Cheryl?'

She frowns, her eyes downcast. Shrugs. 'She's... she's a friend. Just a girl from work.'

'I'd never heard of her before, that's all.'

'Why would you have? She was kind to me at a difficult time, not that you'd know anything about that either.'

It's all going wrong. His breath is coming fast now, shallow. Naomi dips another chip, eats it. Another. She sips her drink, puts the glass back down on the table and stares at him. Another moment of painful stillness passes.

'I'm sorry. I thought when I saw you with him that he might be... I mean, he's fair, with blue eyes, like... I mean, I thought...'

'Oh my God,' she almost whispers, as if to herself, before looking at him again with that intense burning directness. 'You thought he was yours, didn't you?'

His neck is hot, his face. 'I... no, I...'

'You did, didn't you? You actually thought...'

He can't look at her. Instead, he lets his eyes fall to his lap. There is a blob of ketchup on his jeans, which he wipes with his thumb, smudging it into a dark smear. 'I didn't think anything, I—'

'Well he's not, OK?'

'I'm sorry,' he says. 'I didn't mean anything by it.'

'Wait.' She frowns. 'Is *that* why you arranged to meet me? Not to see me at all, but... Did you *actually* think I'm capable of doing something like that?'

'Of course not! It wasn't as thought out as that. I... It was good to see you.' His scalp prickles, all sense of what he planned to say gone. 'It was just... it was difficult, seeing you out of the blue like that, that's all. A shock, I suppose. And you seemed quite nervous. I mean, I guess it could've been me that was nervous, not you, but maybe you were too. You seemed like you didn't want me to have seen you and the baby. And the baby... Tommy... he's blonde, with blue eyes, and the dates and everything... and afterwards I... Look, I didn't just think it, OK? I *hoped* it. I hoped it.'

Naomi shakes her head. When she speaks, it is with her mouth full; she covers it with her fist. 'Well, that's why you're a fool for leaving. Precious little chance of having a kid now, isn't there?'

'But you didn't want a family. You said—'

'I said I wasn't *ready*. Not the same thing, Sam. Not the same thing at all.'

Momentarily, his confusion clears. She did not say this. She said she never wanted children, not ever, even said once that she hated them. So why would she say now that she does, or did? Why would she be looking after her friend's child when she doesn't like kids and isn't really the sort of person who would go out of her way to help others?

'Sorry,' he says. 'Forget I said anything. I didn't mean to—'

'You never mean to.' Her tone is drenched in bitterness. 'And yet you do. All the time. You always did. Classic Sam, the whole lack of emotional intelligence disguised as oh-don't-mind-me.' She imitates his voice, moving her head from side to side like a puppet, her hands spread, her eyes wide. 'It's only gentle giant Sam; he doesn't mean anything bad.'

He shakes his head but can think of nothing to say.

'Oh, and here comes the silent treatment,' she says. 'I'm getting all your greatest hits.'

'I'm sorry, I—'

'Please tell me Tommy wasn't the only reason you wanted to meet me.'

He makes himself look up, expects to see her features twisted in spite, but her eyes are brimming, and when she speaks again, her voice trembles.

'Please, Sam. Tell me you wanted to see me. Give me that at least.'

'Oh God,' he says. 'I didn't mean to upset you, Nomes. Of course it's not just about the... It really was good to see you the other day. I mean, I did miss you. During lockdown.'

'But you never contacted me. Not once. Not even a text to see how I was. Nothing.'

'But... but that would've been confusing, wouldn't it? I was trying to be clear. To behave clearly, that's all. So you could, y'know, move on. The last thing I wanted to do was hurt you. You must know that.'

She sniffs, sighs, shakes her head. 'I'm still a bit raw. It's been a lot. You have no idea what I've been through.'

His breath shudders from him. 'I really am sorry. I guess I got carried away with the idea, that's all. The baby, I mean. I shouldn't have got my hopes up. I wouldn't have got my hopes up if I hadn't wanted to see you again, would I?'

She stands abruptly. 'Actually, I'm just... I need the toilet.'

'Sure.'

Head bowed low, wiping at her face, she walks into the pub. Immediately he plunges his face into his hands, swearing over and over under his breath. She has had to get away from him to compose herself. He is a pillock. A twit. A moron.

Outside, a bus whistles past, back towards Lyme. He should go. There is nothing here for him, not now that he has added insult to injury. Classic Sam, she said. And she was right. Well done, mate.

Minutes pass. He takes a chip. It is barely warm, almost cold. He pushes the bowl away. Thinks about putting a log on the fire but doesn't. Wonders about knocking on the loo door, calling to her to ask if she's OK. But doesn't. Instead, he waits, hands clasped between his thighs for warmth.

'Sam.' Naomi is back. She is sitting down. Her face is red, her eye make-up all but washed off. She is chewing the inside of her mouth. Her eyes flick towards his, down to the table. She drains her glass. Appears to take a deep breath, blows it out like exasperation itself.

'Are you OK?' he asks. 'I really am so sorry.'

'I didn't bring Toms today.' She opens her watery eyes, meets his gaze for a second, closes them again. 'I left him at home.'

'What do you mean, left him? Isn't he with his mother?'

'No,' she whispers, shakes her head. Her eyes are open now, but she is looking past him towards the brazier. The courtyard has filled a little since they got here. From inside the pub drifts the smell of roasting meat.

'But you said—'

'I said he was at home. But he's not with his mum, he's with my sister.' She is still staring into the grate, her eyes flickering. She turns to meet his gaze. 'Look, I didn't bring him because I wanted to see what you... I suppose I hoped you'd want to see me, you know, for *me*. For *us*. I hoped...' She shakes her head. 'Doesn't matter. I've been a... I feel like a complete lemon.' Her bottom lip trembles; her eyes fill. She looks away and quite suddenly slaps herself on the forehead once, twice.

Panicking, he reaches for her hand, but she withdraws it.

'Please,' he says. 'I'm so sorry. I didn't mean to offend you. Of course I don't think you'd do something like that. I was just blinded by... Look, I'm sorry. Forget I said it.'

'No.' She shakes her head, causing a tear to escape down each cheek. The urge to dry them with the paper napkin is almost overpowering, but he makes himself stay still. He has the sense that nothing she has said so far is true, that as ever, it has all been a test, which he has failed. She seems to be talking in circles.

'I did want to see you,' he says quietly. 'We were together a long time. I never stopped caring about you, I just... we just... we drove each other nuts – you know we did.'

'Stop. Don't say anything else. It's not your fault. Not all of it anyway. I got my hopes up, just like you did, only my hopes were... I mean, I'm the idiot, because it's not to be. But for once, you actually got it right.'

The hairs on his forearm lift. 'What are you saying?' He knows what she's saying, somewhere, the meaning pushing through his veins, pushing, pushing, towards his heart.

She reaches for the napkin and presses it to her eyes. When she lowers it, finally, she fixes him with her dark stare, and when she speaks, her words land slowly, as a dream clarifies in the moments after waking.

'You got it right,' she says. 'He's yours. Tommy's yours.'

CHAPTER 11

Naomi's chin is tilted, her head cocked slightly. She is blinking fast, her eyes glossy with tears. She has told him he was right. It is possibly the first time this has ever happened, yet there is no pleasure in it, none whatsoever.

'I wasn't going to tell you. But yeah, you're a dad.'

He closes his eyes. His head spins. He opens his eyes, afraid he might pass out.

'I should've told you,' she says quietly. 'I know that was wrong. I do know that. But you left me. *You* left *me*, Sam, and things were just... they've been totally shit.' She laughs, though without mirth. 'Funny, you said I was mean, you know, at the end, but turns out I was hormonal.' Another laugh, brief and bitter. She looks miserable. Miserable and a bit lost.

'Did you know?' he asks softly. 'When I left, did you know?'

She shrugs, wiping her eyes again with the napkin. 'I'd missed a period. But things between us were pretty strained, so I thought it was just that. You closed down, you know? I was so stressed. I'd lost weight. Your silence was...

It felt cruel. I tried to talk to you, but there was just this wall. I was so lonely. I never thought you could share your life with someone and be that lonely. So yeah, I couldn't eat. And sometimes my cycle goes a bit haywire if my weight drops too much.'

He nods, remembering her constant dieting, all the things she wasn't allowed, or didn't allow herself, how irritable hunger made her, how no matter how many times he told her she was beautiful, she didn't believe him. She wanted to look like the women in the magazines, she said. She seemed to think he would prefer that, or that he even took any notice.

'So you *didn't* know about the baby?'

She shakes her head as if to free a bug from her hair. 'Not in any concrete way. Even if I had, I wouldn't have wanted you to stay out of *duty*. Or pity. Maybe I'd've told you if you'd bothered to get in touch.' The last word she almost spits, distaste remaining in the set of her mouth for a few seconds after she's stopped speaking.

A silence falls between them. It is not awkward. It is not painful. It is shock, he thinks, for both of them. He has no idea what to say next, has not thought this far ahead. *Have you thought about what you want?* Joyce asked him. Yes, he told her. I want to be his dad.

And now he is. He is Tommy's father. How strange it is, to get what you want.

'Look,' he says, straightening in his seat. 'I'm sorry I upset you, but it wasn't fair of you to keep him from me. I have a right to see him.'

He is expecting her to shout, to release a torrent of criticism, for her hands to curl into fists and hammer on his chest. But instead she begins gathering her things, as if in desperation.

'Naomi? Nomes?'

She winds her scarf round her neck, her face blazing. Hooks her bag over her head and stands up.

'You can't go,' he says. 'We need to decide what to do.'

'We?' She sniffs, wipes the back of her hand across her nose. When she speaks, her voice is low and shaking. 'There's no *we*, Sam! *We* ended when you walked out on me. You left and I never heard from you again, and now you want to be in my life all of a sudden? Can you even imagine what it's been like for me? Can you imagine going through something like that on your own? Every morning throwing up with no one to hold your head, no one to bring you a glass of water and ask if you were OK, if you needed a cup of tea. Every check, every scan. The birth. Giving birth on your own, all on your own, Sam. Every sleepless night, every heated bottle, every bout of colic. Alone.

'If you'd even called once. If you'd even bothered. But you didn't. You dumped me like an old pair of shoes. So you'll excuse me if I didn't tell you. Why should I have? You wanted nothing to do with me. And now you want to play happy families? You want me to hand him over every weekend so I can stare at the wall and cry myself to sleep? No way. No way in hell.'

'You could go out.'

'Oh my God,' she hisses. 'I don't care about going out! You don't get to abandon me then come back now there's something you want – don't you get it? He's *mine*. Tommy is *mine* and there's no way I'm going to let you take him away from me because you've decided you want a family. Go back to your gran, Sam. She always did need you more than me.' Hands closing into fists, she closes her eyes, opens them again. 'Look, I'm gonna go before I say something I regret. I hate what you turn me into with your... your big trampling feet. Just... just don't contact me again, OK? Leave me alone.'

With a sob, she leaves, one hand cupping her forehead as if trying to stop the contents from spilling out. He stares after her, hot with shame and dismay. She disappears around the corner at a furious clip.

At the other tables, people turn to look at him, the source of a woman's distress, before turning away. His cheeks burn. The fire spits. He pushes his face into his hands again. What has he done? What the hell has he done? He was so convinced that Naomi's motives were mean and spiteful, he has not stopped to consider this: that she is horribly, terribly hurt. He has not imagined, not once, that he might have completely broken her heart.

CHAPTER 12

I could see it from both sides, of course, when he told me, much as I would've liked to see her as wrong. Being a woman in these situations is always worse. No amount of feminism can alter the fact that it's us who have to carry the baby, at least until it's out. And of course we're the ones with the milk on tap, so to speak, and then the hormones kick in and you're off your face on them, loved up to the eyeballs in ways you never knew were possible, tripping on sleep deprivation like a hippy at Woodstock. So yes, tempting as it was to judge Naomi, it was lockdown and she was abandoned, hurt, alone, with a baby to look after. And there was Sam in his big house, having his laundry done and his dinner cooked, going out for his hikes, painting his watercolours, spending cosy evenings by the fire without a worry in the world. But just as I could sympathise with Naomi, I could equally picture Sam walking in a daze back to his van, climbing into the cab, sitting with his head in his hands, frozen with shock and shame and regret.

There he sits, as yet unable even to start the engine. Everything has been turned upside down. What Naomi has done is not right, he knows this. No amount of hurt on her part can excuse it, but still... but still. He gets it, he does, and his heart swells with feeling for her. He should have called. Texted at least. He thought it was kinder to make a clean break, but he can see now that it was not. Not after they had lived together, loved one another. The money for the flat was dealt with entirely through Paul Thompson, his gran's solicitor. That was cruel. Even without the added complication of a pregnancy, it was heartless.

And something else, something else that has come from seeing her again, something he always knew would blind-side him.

Because a misguided attempt at kindness was not the only reason he didn't call her. This was: this beating of his heart, this tingle on his skin, this *confusion*. He didn't contact her because he had to get her out of his head. But seeing her on the beach and today, even before he knew what he knows now, was exactly as he feared. He never did get her out of his head. It was stupid to think he could have.

With a sigh, he starts the engine and pulls out of the car park. Oh God. Just now in the courtyard, Naomi was shaking, actually shaking, with the effort of containing her hurt. Hurt and rage caused by him. That it came so instantly, he thinks, is because it was already there.

I hate what you turn me into with your... your big trampling feet.

His big trampling feet. It is not the first time she has used this phrase. She used to get hysterical – before, when he let her down or insulted her without meaning to. Used to whip herself into a frenzy, accusations and disappointments and tears pouring out of her. It could come from nowhere. Once, one evening, she looked up from her magazine and asked him, 'Hey, Sam. Which Hollywood actress do I most remind you of?'

An innocuous enough question. But he couldn't answer, couldn't think of a single actress, couldn't understand, really, the point of the question.

'Not sure.'

'Come on! There must be one!'

'Actually, I'm just reading,' he made the mistake of saying. 'You look like yourself,' he added, when her face fell. Then, 'Why would you want to look like someone else?' Sensing rising tension, he tried to lighten the mood. 'If you looked like someone else, how would I recognise you?'

She didn't find it funny. He was patronising her, putting her down. She was only trying to make conversation; not every conversation had to be serious. And now she felt stupid, just stupid. Why did he have to always make her feel stupid?

'It might be enough for you to sit in silence all evening,' she went on. 'But it's not for me. Why don't you start a conversation for a change? Why don't you organise something for us to do, then we can talk about that instead of this... this quiet all the time? Just because I don't read books about whales and white men and their problems every night doesn't mean I'm not interesting.'

On it went. She ended up in tears, told him it was like trying to argue with a rock. He took it, hunched in his chair, as a soldier waits for bullets to fly overhead. At the time, he was unable to see where she was coming from. Now in the cold shell of the van, he can see that he was dismissive, and that he was dismissive a *lot*. And that, for someone who had been dismissed all her life, his behaviour must have pierced the heart of her. Each time, he reminded her of his privilege. His class perhaps. His big, trampling, annihilating feet.

But if she ranted and raved, it was not from a lack of love. He sees that now too. That is not how you react to someone to whom you feel indifference. She loved him. If she hadn't, she would have let him leave without a fight. They could have shaken hands and agreed to be friends. It is indifference that kills relationships, not rage. She raged at him because she loved him. She raged at him just now in the pub.

Does she still love him then?

The A35 takes him home; the van knows the way. It was true what Naomi said about his silence. He *did* retreat into himself those last months with her. Maybe he'd done it from the start. All these certainties he has held on to for over a year are crumbling. It is exactly as she said: he didn't, wouldn't talk, wouldn't engage in the kinds of conversations she wanted to have.

But only because in those conversations he was always, always wrong.

His thoughts shake; his grasp on them loosens. She wasn't like that at first, was she, full of rage and pride? No. Joy and mischief was what burst the seams of her, her infectious love of life.

'Oh God,' he says, to himself, to no one. He has believed so strongly, so *absolutely*, that *she* diminished *him* with her sarcasm and her punishments, her disappointment when he failed to pick up on her telepathic demands, her excoriating text messages and public undermining. He has held on to these beliefs with the tightness of grip that can only come from a fear that they might not be true.

But now, after two brief encounters with her, he is full of questions: what if meanness was her last resort? What if, having been walled up in silence, every brick laid by him, these aggressions were her only way out? What if he truly failed her? His own gran didn't change the locks the first time lazy, good-for-nothing Hugh spent all her house-keeping on booze, did she? Naomi didn't become mean overnight, did she?

It happened over time.

Perhaps... possibly... probably as a response to him.

'Oh God,' he whispers to no one. He has ghosted her. Even when they were together, he was cold, froze her out when she got upset. And after it went wrong and he left, he cut her dead.

Are his own crimes any better?

No, he thinks. No, they are not.

At the roundabout, he takes the turning to Lyme, his sense of having been right to leave slipping with every bend in the road. He has the impression he is sinking, collapsing internally. If he'd only talked to her like she asked him to. If they'd got help as she suggested, as she *always* suggested... and it dawns on him then, with an even heavier feeling pressing on the back of his neck, that he didn't, wouldn't go with her to see someone because he feared the therapist would take her side. That fear again: of being wrong.

How pathetic. How cowardly. How weak.

And now Naomi has his beautiful baby and will not let him into their life. It wasn't out of spite or revenge at all. She doesn't trust him, that's what this is. She doesn't trust him to be a good enough father. Somehow he will have to persuade her otherwise. If he can't, he will have to find another way. Because broken heart or no, she has no right to keep his child from him.

CHAPTER 13

Black-eyed and hunched-shouldered as the day he left that bloody woman, her grandson returns to the house. Joyce spies him through the crack in the living-room door from her vantage point at the top of the stepladder. He has forgotten to take off his boots. She has called, *Hello, is that you?* and he has not replied at all.

She rests the tin of masonry paint on the top step and descends slowly, holding on with both hands. The urge to run and comfort him is all very well, but the last place she wants to end up is A&E, especially at the moment.

'Sam? Samuel? Love?'

She finds him on the old chesterfield in the kitchen, head in hands. Naomi bloody Harper. She can feel it in her water. How she hates her, hates what that woman does to her grandson. Earlier this week, he was barely able to sit through dinner, gabbling excitedly about the grotto he and Miranda had found, showing her the photos on his phone, telling her how much he was looking forward to seeing Miranda's drawings brought to life. Now look at him: all that inspiration drained away. It is as if he has lost the strength to stand.

'You've seen her again then?' she tries.

He grunts.

'Didn't go well I take it?'

He shakes his head. Another grunt. He rubs at the back of his head. His eyes are bloodshot, that woman in every crimson filigree.

Joyce plucks the damp dishcloth from her overall pocket and rubs the flecks of paint from her fingers.

'I met her,' he says, his voice small. 'Just for coffee. I had to know.'

'And?'

His eyes fill. 'He's mine. The baby. Tommy. He's my son.'

'Right.' She sighs. 'Right.' Waits. Feels a little dizzy. 'My God, she's a piece of work.'

Sam covers his eyes with his hand. 'At first she denied it. But then she came clean.' He takes his hand away and meets Joyce's gaze once again, his brow creased, worried. 'I hurt her. Worse than I ever imagined. She's had to do it all on her own. In the middle of a pandemic. It must've been terrible for her, terrible. No wonder she—'

'She should've told you, love. I can imagine it's been hard. But she should have told you the moment she found out. She had no right, no right at all to—'

'But I get it,' he interrupts. 'I dropped her like a stone. I pretended she didn't exist.'

'You weren't to know!' Gingerly Joyce peels off her overalls, inside out so as not to get paint on the floor tiles. She folds them and places them on the old kitchen table before sitting down next to him. 'I've seen her moves, don't forget.

She's a tricky one, very tricky, and this is straight out of her handbook.'

'But you don't know what I was like. I was very... I wasn't easy either. I hurt her before I even left.'

'Hurt her how? Physically?'

'No! But I didn't talk. I was... a wall, she said.'

'You gave her the silent treatment? What, on purpose?'

'No! No, I would never... I just didn't know what to say sometimes when she was pissed off at me. Sometimes I was preoccupied with some problem at work or engrossed in a painting or a book or something. Sometimes I just wanted to be left in peace, you know? I never tried to punish her, but I think... I think she felt like maybe I was ignoring her. Or like I didn't take any notice of her.'

'Oh for God's sake, that's not enough of a reason to keep your flesh and blood from you!' But, she thinks, it's enough of a reason to make a woman cross. Joyce knows what it is to be ignored. Once the courting was over, living with Hugh was like living with a potato. A drunk potato. She told him as much when she threw him out, lines she'd rehearsed while she waited for him to come stumbling home one last time. *You've had your chips, Hugh Moore*, she said. *Now bugger off*. He didn't laugh, but boy, she did; she laughed for weeks. But she doesn't like to think of her own grandson treating his partner like that. 'It's not good to ignore a woman, love,' she adds. 'We need a bit of attention now and then. I'm not excusing her, mind. Dreadful behaviour.'

'Maybe I wasn't ready to see her side of it, you know? And there's something different about her now, there really is. I can't explain it. Now she's a mother...'

'I know. I know, love. Two sides to every story and no one's all bad, even her. It still makes my blood boil though.

No decency. No sense of right and wrong.' She makes herself calm down, pats his hand. 'So what's next?'

'She doesn't want me to see him. The baby.'

'*What?* Oh for heaven's sake, she can't do that!'

He holds up a hand: stop. 'I know. I know that.'

'I'll give Paul Thompson a ring. He's not family law, but he'll know who to ask.'

'No. No lawyers. I know you're trying to help, but let me handle it, OK? Let me... let me stand on my own two feet. She stormed off, but she always used to do that, and I'm thinking if I just leave her, she'll calm down and hopefully we can sort it out.' He meets her gaze, pleading with her.

'I suppose amicable is always best, if that's what you want. But if she doesn't do the right thing, we'll have to fight her. If that woman thinks she's going to keep your son from you, it'll be over my dead body.'

CHAPTER 14

Dear Sam,

So now I've confirmed your suspicions, as they say. I almost didn't. I only made up my mind at the last second. Funny how shocked you looked, considering I was telling you what you already knew.

So now here we are.

I wonder what you'll do now.

I wonder what I'll do now.

I think I'm still in shock. Are you?

This is definitely a letter now.

It's Monday, by the way. Typical you, to go silent on me for the rest of Saturday and the whole of Sunday, leave me to get more and more unsure about what I've said and done, whether it's justifiable or even understandable. That's abusive, do you know that? No, of course you don't. Well, I'm wise to your mind games. They won't work, not anymore. And I'm going to make sure you don't get too close too soon to little Tommy.

I've just changed him actually, put him down for his

nap and cleaned up after him, put a wash on, caught up with myself, managed to grab a piece of cold toast and a lukewarm cup of tea. I bet you spent your Sunday going for a lovely long walk, didn't you? All the time in the world. Take some nice photos, did you? Get out your watercolours? Or maybe you spent the weekend planting seeds in little pots to line the windowsill in the conservatory. Sorry, orangery. Maybe you've already discussed our situation with Joyce. She'll have told you how terrible I am, what a bitch I am for keeping your child from you, how dare I, am I right?

I don't blame her.

Bet you didn't see that coming. But I don't blame her. Really. As I keep saying, I'm learning to reflect. Dawn helped me so much. I know what I said at the pub was bad. I know people do and say bad things when they're angry, and I know I have a right to be angry, but it was still wrong of me to have a go at you in public like that.

But here's why I got the rage.

I have a right to see him, you said.

How quickly you claimed that right. So entitled, when you think about it, not that anyone would get that about you unless they knew you like I do. Funny, it's not in your star sign at all, but seriously, what did you ever do to give you the right to be his father? Slept with me, is that it? That's how it is for men, I suppose. A guaranteed orgasm and a nice warm bed. No periods to put up with, no cystitis, no pills to remember, no swelling, no sickness, no sore breasts, no weight gain, no stretch marks, no milk leaking down the front of your T-shirt in the middle of Morrisons, no sleepless nights, no crazy hormones, no wondering who the hell you even are anymore, what day of the week it is... I could go on.

I know I sound bitter, and you probably stopped reading that list halfway through, but all you have to do is read it when you should be trying to imagine what it's like to actually live through every single thing on it. You enjoyed me for years. Physically, I mean. I kept myself nice for you, didn't I? Always tried to ring the changes in and out of the bedroom, always bought the birthday cake, booked the restaurant, the night out with friends, and then, without any warning, you tell me you can't stand me being angry all the time. Did you ever stop to wonder why? Or if there was something you could do about it? Did you ever think you might have caused it? And then you walk out without so much as a backward glance.

That's what you did, Sam. Actually.

Out of interest, how does that count as a claim on Tommy?

Now. This is going to surprise you, but that's Pisces to a T – full of contradictions. I've had a good long think about it. After seeing you on Saturday, I can tell how much you want to be involved. I know you always wanted kids. And I know Joyce will be calling her lawyer, if she hasn't already. I'm not stupid. So tell Granny Joyce to calm down. I'm not going to keep Tommy away from you, OK?

CHAPTER 15

Sam, I've been thinking things over. I know I said you couldn't see Tommy, but I was hurt and angry and I suppose I wanted to punish you. I'm sorry. For all that I've fantasised about doing it, I didn't enjoy it. Can we meet this evening? I'll ask Jo to have Tommy. The Harbour, 8pm?

When Sam receives this message, he is engaged in the rather mundane task of lifting the old concrete flags at the Higher Mill job. It might be minor fantasising on my part, but I think I remember him straightening up like he'd heard a gunshot just as I was leaving to pick up Betsy, one hand flying to his back pocket. I remember reflecting at the time that he lived with the constant possibility of an emergency call from Joyce – she was an absolute bugger for trying to lift things or power up tools or climb places she shouldn't.

Except, of course, I didn't realise then that it wasn't just Joyce who was on his conscience now.

So, there he is, slipping his hand from his work glove, pulling the phone out of his pocket and seeing that message. Breath catching, he goes to the app and reads it a second time, a third. The breath leaves him in a gasp. She is going to let him see his son. He feels his mouth break into a wide smile. Replies instantly, gloves hanging from his back pocket like filthy, boneless hands.

Hi. I understand, dw. I've been thinking a lot about how things must have been for you and I'm sorry too. I was going to contact you at the weekend but thought you might need space, but then I worried you'd think I was going silent, which I wasn't, I promise. I'll never do that again, and if I do, just say the word and I'll stop. And yes, 8 at the Harbour. X

On the way home, Sam calls in on Miranda to update her on the day's progress.

'It's on the latch,' he hears her call down the hall.

She is at the small kitchen table, supervising Betsy, who is eating pasta with a dessert spoon.

'Hey, Bets,' he says, passing a hand over her soft hair. 'That looks delicious.'

She holds up a piece of broccoli. 'This is a tree,' she tells him.

Miranda catches Sam's eye and they share a smile.

'An oak?' Sam asks. 'Or a beech? Or actually, is it a chestnut?' He is careful to match Betsy's seriousness with his own.

For a split second, she stares at him as if he's lost his mind.

'It's not really a tree,' she explains. 'It's boccoli.' She puts the whole thing – leaves, branches, trunk, the lot – into her mouth.

'Great tree-eating. Sorry, broccoli-eating.'

'And pasta.'

'And pasta, yes.'

'And pesto.'

'And pesto. Of course. Silly me.'

Miranda's kitchen is tiny but cosy. There are fairy lights pinned around the back door to the yard, and Betsy's paintings and drawings are Blu-tacked all over the walls.

Miranda offers him a beer.

'Actually, no,' he says. 'I'm meeting Naomi later, so...'

Miranda's eyebrows rise; her face pinks. 'Right. Listen, you could have FaceTimed if you're going out. Or called even. You didn't need to—'

'No, no, it's fine. I'm not meeting her till later, and I was passing, so...'

'So you're... are you two—'

'Turns out I have a son.' The words rush out. He feels the heat they make in his face.

'*What?*' Miranda's mouth falls open. She stands up, makes to open the fridge but misses the handle and swipes at fresh air. 'You have a *son?*'

He grins. He can't stop grinning. 'Remember I said she had a baby with her the other day? Did I say that?' He meets her eye, but she shakes her head and looks away, deeper pink now climbing her neck. 'Maybe I didn't, but anyway, she did, and he looked like me – well, my colouring – and I just got this feeling, you know? Anyway, yeah, so at the weekend I asked her if he was mine, and at first she said no, but... yeah. I'm a father.'

'You're a *father?* And she didn't *tell* you?'

'No, but with lockdown and everything... and it didn't exactly end well, you know? And I suppose I didn't... I mean, I didn't contact her *at all* after I left.' He studies the tabletop, brushes a small cluster of crumbs into a pile, makes himself look up.

Miranda gives a slow nod, as if she's a bit shocked. He worries he's disappointed her. She's always telling him he's a good bloke: *you're too nice for your own good, Sam Moore*, is how she says it. He likes it when she says that, worries now that she won't think it anymore.

'Joyce reckoned it was kinder to let her rely on her friends and get over it in her own way,' he says. 'Obviously I would've called if I'd known she was pregnant, but I didn't. I had no idea.'

'Sure. Sure, I'm not... I mean I'm not... not at all.' Miranda has opened the fridge successfully now and is pulling a bottle of Peroni from inside. She holds it up and raises her eyebrows – *sure you won't?* – but he shakes his head.

'But don't let me stop you.'

'I won't, don't worry.' She flips off the top with the bottle opener that's screwed to the wall. 'So is tonight, like, a date?'

'Ah, no. It's not like that. No. No way. And listen, don't tell anyone, OK? I'm only telling you. Joyce knows about the baby, but I told her I was meeting the boys for a few beers. She'll just worry otherwise.'

'Maisie's got Thomas the Tank Engine,' Betsy says.

Sam switches his attention to her and widens his eyes. 'Has she? Who's Maisie?'

'She's my friend from nursry.'

'OK. And do *you* like Thomas the Tank Engine?'

She nods fast. 'Mummy says I can have Thomas for my birfday when I'm four.' She holds up four fingers, for clarity.

Again Sam widens his eyes to show how impressed he is. 'Well, aren't you lucky? And do you have a train track?'

She nods more violently this time. 'Mummy makes my fig of eight.'

'Fig*ure* of eight,' Miranda says, peeling the lid from a tiny yoghurt and putting it in front of Betsy along with a teaspoon. 'So the trains can go round and under the bridge and over the bridge. Good girl eating all your pasta. Lots of lovely vitamins.' She strikes a muscle-man pose.

Betsy grins, picks up the teaspoon. At the first mouthful of the dessert, she closes her eyes in apparent bliss.

Miranda turns to the sink and begins to wash out a small saucepan. 'Always have to do the pesto pan by hand,' she says, scrubbing at it. 'The dishwasher bakes it on. Then there's green specks over everything. Tell you what, you only make that mistake once.' She laughs, places the pan upside down on the drainer. Wipes her hands on her jeans, then rests them on the edge of the sink for a moment. She does not turn to face him.

The air is strange. Sam is not sure why. 'Are you OK?'

She turns then, but her smile is weird. 'Of course! And I won't tell, don't worry. Who would I tell anyway? I barely go out!'

Sam wonders if he should have told her sooner, when all he had was suspicions. He probably should have. Since his schoolmate Si left for Ireland, Miranda is the closest thing he has to a best friend. The lads are great, but...

But she's asking him about the job now, and he comes to his senses. They have completed the new paving, he tells her, and the plan tomorrow is to set the stilts in concrete for the decking.

It is only as he leaves that the subject of Naomi comes up again.

'I'm so pleased for you, mate,' Miranda says when he stops in the doorway. He has the impression she has got over whatever it was. 'I hope it works out. Just...' She pauses, her nose wrinkling.

'Just what?'

With some effort, she meets his eye. Hers are a tawny amber colour, like autumn. 'Just be careful, that's all. Don't want to see you get hurt again.'

'Oh, don't worry. I'll keep my wits about me.'

CHAPTER 16

OK, so I *may* have invented the bit about tawny amber – not the colour, but him noticing in that moment and not thinking muddy pond or mouldy lentils or something. You can't blame a girl for hoping. And as we got to know one another and his shyness fell away, he did look into my eyes more and more when he spoke to me, as I did into his, so he can't have found the sight of them completely revolting.

Wedgwood blue, in case you're wondering. His.

Sam arrives at the Harbour a little before eight. They are only serving drinks outside still, but there are heaters on the balcony. It being a Monday and not tourist season, the place is empty. He orders a pint of Otter and bags the table directly under the heater.

Naomi arrives only five minutes late, dressed in a thick khaki parka coat, navy-blue scarf and matching beanie hat. At the sight of her, he stands abruptly, knocks the table and sends a splash of ale onto the zinc top.

'Hi.' He reaches a tentative hand towards her upper arm

and aims to kiss her on the cheek. The kiss doesn't land and neither does his hand, but she doesn't swerve to avoid him, so he presses on, asks her what she'd like to drink.

'Diet Coke.'

'Diet Coke! Right you are.'

When he returns, they say cheers and she says she'd join him in a real drink but she's driving, and he can't help but notice that this too is new: she never drove drunk but she would always have a couple, which probably put her a little over the limit, especially as she barely ate anything.

Politely, rather formally, he thanks her for coming over to Lyme.

'I'm bored of Bridport,' she says. 'To be honest, I barely go out anymore.'

Miranda said the same thing earlier; it glances on their reason for meeting. An uncomfortable silence falls.

'So, do you want to start?' he asks, determined to learn from his mistake last time and be open to conversation instead of trying to take control. From experience, he knows it's better to let Naomi lead.

'Listen, I'm so sorry,' she says. 'About everything.'

He feels the chair thump against his back. He has never heard her say sorry before, not like that, not in all the time they were together.

'Don't be,' he says, but she holds up a hand.

'No, it's important. I need to apologise. I should have told you about Tommy. I was going to, but then the weeks went on and I think I was in a bit of shock. I had a lot of anger, and before I knew where I was, it was the twenty-week scan and by then Jo and I were like this little unit, you know? We even talked about raising it together – did you know she can't have kids? And then it felt too late to tell you because I should've told you sooner and I guess I just put my head in the sand. It was too much. I've never been that maternal, you know that, and my mum wasn't... I mean, she's not around anymore and I just found it so, so hard.' Her eyes gloss. She blinks. 'Yeah, it was hard. It was... a lot.' She drinks, her eyes darting to the boatyard, to the sandy beach beyond.

'You don't have to explain.' He holds up his hands. 'I get it. The way we left things wasn't... It was bad. I'm sorry for my part in that. And I'm sorry I didn't call you. I thought if I called, you'd think... I mean, we both needed to recover.'

She nods, her gaze fixed on the tabletop.

'So,' he says into the silence, 'maybe I could have him on alternate weekends?'

She startles, as if what he has said is outrageous. Immediately he feels himself fill with a kind of panic. He has done what he promised himself he would not do. He has ploughed in like an idiot.

'Not if you don't want to,' he adds quickly. 'I just thought I'd start the ball rolling.'

'We really are here on business, aren't we?' She smiles, but the smile is sad. 'And here's me looking my best.' She laughs, but again her laughter does not match her sad expression.

'You look great,' he says too quickly. 'You always look great. Really. You look lovely.' He reaches for her. This time his fingers land on her forearm. It is only a moment, but he feels that familiar electrical surge. He lifts his hand away, feels for the edges of the chair seat.

'I can't let you have him at weekends,' she says. 'Sorry, I just can't. Maybe one day, but right now I have to think of him. You left, you see, and it really was without warning. I can't put Tommy through that.'

'I get it. I probably told you my mum never let my dad do anything other than visit.'

'Was that for the same reason? That she worried he'd leave?'

He nods. 'And she was right; he left London before I was a year old. I don't remember him. I did think about trying to find him once I turned eighteen, but I never did. But I'm not like that. I won't leave Tommy. I want him to have a father, and I want that father to be me. A hundred per cent. A million.'

She blinks rapidly, appears to be composing herself. When she speaks, her words are shaky. 'You have to understand... I can't just give him up like a Pilates class and suddenly be on my own from Friday night to Sunday night. That wouldn't be fair. It would be traumatic. So for now, if you want to see him, it'll have to be in the week. Maybe Wednesdays or Thursdays?'

'Sure. I'll ask Miranda if I can work four days, at least for a bit. She's got a kid herself, so she'll understand. Hopefully.'

'I can drop him off on the way to work. And we'll have to call you my friend for now, OK? You'll have to be Sam. I know I'm being a bit overkill and I take what you say about not leaving him, but I don't know that, do I? I just need this to be on my terms.'

She is fragile, so much more than he thought.

'That's wise,' he says – slowly, carefully. 'Whatever you need. I'll ask about getting time off and let you know tomorrow.'

'Cool.' Her eyes meet his over the top of her drink. Her fingerprints on the frosted glass look like pawprints in snow. How beautiful she is; it makes his heart hurt.

The heater dies and he presses it again, its glow casting

a warm light, making a kind of aura around her. They smile at one another, and he feels like they've reached a new understanding. In front of the little balcony, an older couple walk by. Arms linked, they move in a kind of harmony, as if they are one, or as if one has grown into the other as mistletoe grows into a tree.

Mistletoe, he thinks. The most romantic plant there is.

CHAPTER 17

I was wary when Sam asked me for a day off a week. It was all going so fast, and although he didn't know it, Joyce had told me in confidence about the viaduct. As far as she was concerned, if Naomi could drive him to do something like that once, she could do it again. And yes, maybe part of me felt jealous that he was falling for her. For her and not me. When he told me about the couple who had walked past their table and used the mistletoe analogy, I knew he'd projected himself and Naomi onto them: the future he was already envisioning despite himself. I just nodded and smiled. What else could I do? I was his friend; it wasn't my job to pee on his bonfire. Except I remember thinking afterwards: mistletoe isn't romantic at all. It's a parasite that sucks all the nutrients from its host tree, weakening it slowly over time.

He reassured me that nothing would change. Darren could supervise on Wednesdays – he'd been keen to take more responsibility for a while. Sam argued that there'd be a saving if I only had to pay him for four days, which of course meant less money for him. He said he'd bring

Tommy with him sometime and introduce him to the guys when things got more settled. Reluctantly, I agreed.

He never did call in with the baby. Never even told the guys what was going on. It was as if, from that moment on, he was elsewhere.

Joyce too is tense when he tells her the plan. There'll be a loss of earnings – she says this out loud. She tells him he has no experience of babies, asks him how he will cope. Is he sure this is what he wants?

'Yes,' he tells her. 'It's what I want.'

The following Wednesday, Naomi takes the day off to show him the ropes. A little after nine, the doorbell chimes low in the kitchen and he and Joyce almost leap from their chairs.

'Crikey,' Joyce says with a chuckle. 'We're on pins, aren't we?'

He walks into the hallway, aware of his gran following at a distance like a bad sleuth. He opens the heavy wooden front door and there she is: sky-blue kitbag over one shoulder and baby Tommy in his primary-coloured car seat in the other hand. She looks small, smaller for standing on the gravel drive, himself on the porch step. He is infused with the feeling that she belongs to him in some way, that she is somehow part of his DNA.

'Hey,' he says, as casually as he can. 'Come on in.'

'Thanks.' She steps inside, her head bowed a little. When she looks up, he sees her glance at Joyce, a flicker of something he can't name crossing her face. Caution perhaps. A kind of fear.

'Hello, Naomi, nice to see you again.' Joyce's tone is a little crisp. She approaches slowly, her hands out in welcome or a gesture of defence, it's hard to tell. 'So this is the little fella, is it?' She leans over the baby, unable to stop a smile from spreading across her face. Tommy's eyes are almost violet, Sam thinks, here in the shadowy hall, but he gets no further with the thought, because quite unprompted, the baby smiles gummily at his great-grandmother, causing all three adults to exclaim in delight.

'Did you recognise your Granny Joyce, Tommy?' Naomi says. She is tentative, appears to be fighting to make herself look directly at Joyce. 'Or maybe Great-Granny? Or Great-Grandma? Sorry, I don't know what you prefer.'

'Well, let's not have Great-Granny for a start,' Joyce says, attempting to cover the sharpness with a kind of half-laugh. 'I feel ancient enough as it is. How about Nana? Or Nonna, like the Italians? Nonna Joyce. Then it's neither one thing nor the other. How would that be?'

Naomi's shoulders lower a fraction. 'Nonna Joyce. That's so cute.'

She puts Tommy's seat on the floor and crouches down to unbuckle him. Lifting him out, she brings her face close to his. 'Tommy, this is Nonna Joyce,' she sing-songs. 'She's your great-grandmother on your daddy's side.' The tips of her ears are red, the line of her parting white. Her neck is so fine, fine enough that Sam could almost circle it with one hand.

She stands, still cuddling the baby. Finally she tears her eyes from him and appears to offer him to Joyce. But Joyce throws up her hands.

'Very kind of you, love,' she says, looking flustered. 'But let him go to his daddy first, surely?'

'Oh. Sorry.' Naomi blushes and Sam feels desperately for her. They are strangers again really. Strangers who know each other well.

'I'll let you two get organised.' Joyce turns and heads towards the back of the house, hobbling slightly and pushing the heel of her hand to her hip.

Naomi watches her for a moment.

'Has Joyce hurt herself?' she asks with concern. 'She looks like she's limping.'

'Just gets a bit stiff,' he says. 'A little unsteady on her feet sometimes if she's been in one position too long.'

She appears to consider this before smiling and placing the baby into his arms.

'There,' she says. 'Thomas Joshua Harper, say hello to Sam.'

Harper. Not Moore. Not even Harper-Moore. He says nothing. It doesn't matter, not for the moment. They can talk about that a little further down the road.

Tommy is heavy, heavier than Sam imagined, and warm, oh so warm against his chest. His head smells of soap and milk and something mildly medical – antiseptic perhaps. Sam turns the child towards him and gazes into his blue eyes, sees himself, tiny, reflected. This is a miracle, he thinks. Nothing short of an actual miracle. He does not voice the thought aloud. Wonders if he can speak at all.

'Hello there, little fella,' he whispers after a moment, shifting the boy again in his arms, unable to keep the grin from his mouth as he speaks.

'You can talk to him normally, you know,' Naomi says. 'You don't need to whisper.'

'Sorry. I was afraid I'd frighten him.' He brings the baby closer, until their noses are almost touching. 'I'm your daddy. Yes I am. Can you say daddy? Da-da? Can you say da-da?'

Naomi laughs, breaking him from his trance. 'Look at

you. You've gone soft already. But we said Sam for now, remember? Sorry.'

'Oh God, no, *I'm* sorry.' He feels the heat creeping up his neck. When he tears his eyes away from his son's, he sees that Naomi is studying him like a cat on a wall.

'It's OK,' she says. 'It doesn't matter too much. It's just for now. If we forget, we forget.'

'Thanks. It's all such a lot to get used to.'

Naomi has written Tommy's routine on a piece of paper, which she hands to Sam once they are in the kitchen. Taking it from her, he feels under scrutiny from Joyce. But whenever he looks towards her, she appears not to be watching them.

Naomi unpacks her kitbag, which is full of nappies, bottles, baby wipes and little jars of organic food she has prepared herself.

'I even cook now,' she says. 'I batch-cook actually. Get me.' She giggles.

'Amazing.'

The bag opens out and becomes a changing mat.

'Heavens,' comes Joyce's voice from over by the stove. She is watching them after all. 'All mod cons.'

'All the gear,' Naomi jokes, though her voice is smaller than usual. 'You know me.'

Yes, I do, Sam thinks. I do know you.

While Sam heats the bottle, Joyce tells them she'll leave them to it and disappears. Immediately, the air relaxes, as if the room is exhaling. Naomi shows him how to test the temperature of the milk on the back of his hand, tells him to shake it really well to make sure there are no hot spots.

'Shake it like a Polaroid picture?'

She laughs easily at his reference to a song they both loved. 'Or an espresso martini,' she says. 'Oh my God, do you remember Jo puking that time?'

'Hard to forget.'

They laugh together, their eyes meeting for a split second before they return to the serious business of Tommy's care. Naomi sits next to Sam on the couch while he gives Tommy a bottle. He tries not to think of her astride him on this very sofa, naked but for his shirt, which she had thrown across her beautiful freckled shoulders, as if that would have been enough to protect her from embarrassment had Joyce returned from bridge club at the wrong moment.

Tommy sucks at the plastic teat, his eyes never leaving Sam's. *Who are you?* Sam thinks, imagines his son thinking the same thing.

Naomi leans in close enough that he can smell her perfume. 'You're a natural.'

After the feed, she shows him how to wind the baby, both of them screeching in delight when Tommy emits an almighty belch.

'Crikey,' Sam says, giggling. 'That's like Simon after six pints of Otter.'

'You should hear him at the other end. Even my dad couldn't fart as loudly as baby Tommy.'

Sam laughs, though Naomi is suddenly serious.

'Is something wrong?' he asks. 'How is your dad, by the way?'

She closes her eyes and shakes her head. When she opens them, they are filmed with tears.

'We lost him,' she whispers. 'To COVID.'

'*What?* Oh my God, Nomes, that's terrible.' He pulls her to him, an impulse as natural as breathing. No wonder she has changed so much. Her edges have been not so much smoothed as sand-blasted. Life has humbled her. And while it's perhaps true that she needed a little humility, he would never have wished it to be gained like this.

Together they stay like that in the silence: himself, his baby son on one shoulder, his ex-partner enfolded in his free arm. For that moment, they are an imperfect, fractured almost-family.

The front door slams. Sam springs away from Naomi, who looks at the floor and blows at her fringe. Joyce's footsteps echo on the hall tiles. Unsure of what to say, how to be, he is saved by a squirting noise followed by a bad smell. On his shoulder, Tommy coos, his breath hot on Sam's neck, as if he weren't in any way responsible.

'Poo!' Sam says. 'Whoa, that stinks.'

Naomi throws back her head and bursts into loud laughter. 'Lesson number three! How to change a nappy.'

'Hello, chaps.' Joyce is coming through the wide square doorway to the kitchen. She is wearing her red jeans, trainers, her red hexagonal glasses. Her hair is spiked with wax and her cheeks are pink with exertion. 'I braved the hill.'

'Wow,' Sam says. 'You went *out* out?'

'All the way down to Langmoor Gardens, if you don't mind. I'm going to build up until I can get down to the sea and back. As far as the fish shop, at least. Then I can get my scallops.'

'Naomi's about to train me in the art of waste management,' Sam says.

Joyce wrinkles her nose. 'I think I'll play the great-grandmother card. I can make coffee though.'

While Joyce heads for the range, Naomi lays the changing mat on the old oak table. 'Is it OK to change him in here?' she asks.

'Yes, yes, of course.'

She talks him through it. When his fingers are clumsy, she only laughs. When he gets it right, finally, she tells him he's done really well. He has a flashing image of her, mouth contorted with rage: *I can't believe you fucked it up – again.*

He can't remember what *it* was. He never can. There were so many *it*s.

'Remind me how you take your coffee, Naomi,' Joyce calls.

'Actually, I'm going to give you guys some space,' Naomi says, picking up her coat. She meets Sam's eyes, hers tender. 'You can put him down for his morning nap now. I'll fetch his travel cot from the car, and his sleep suit.' She places a warm hand on Sam's arm before leaving him and Joyce in the kitchen.

Joyce blinks at him, her eyes large behind the lenses of her specs, her smile vanished now that Naomi is out of the room. 'Are you comfortable with that? Was that the arrangement?'

'Yes! Don't worry. She's going to go away for two hours. Like a trial shift. If it goes OK, I can have him all day next week.'

She nods brusquely, her mouth puckered tight. 'Righto. I'll pour your coffee once she's gone, else it'll go cold.' Stiffly she returns to the stove.

Naomi is back, a huge cuboid hanging from sturdy straps in one hand, a quilted baby-blue thing in the other.

'Lesson four,' she says. 'How to put up a travel cot without losing a finger.'

Fifteen minutes later, Tommy is settled in the travel cot, in the spare room that they've decided, to Sam's suppressed delight, will be his nursery when he's here.

'I'll see myself out,' Naomi says – that warm hand again, this time on his shoulder. 'Any worries, just call, yeah? I won't go far. But you'll be fine. You're a natural. I'll see you in two hours.'

Quietly Sam reiterates her instructions for Tommy's lunch, and she nods and says, yes, that's it, perfect, then gives him a wide smile and a little wave.

In the silent dimness, he listens to his son breathe. He feels capable. Trusted. When they were together, she was always snatching things from him, low mutters escaping from pursed lips – *oh for God's sake* or *I can't watch* or *honestly, it's too painful* – before performing whatever task it was correctly. But now he has passed all the tests she has set for him, with flying colours.

After a moment, he kneels on the floor and rests his head on the old carpet before lying flat on his stomach. He will pull up this carpet, he thinks. Sand the boards. The mesh sides of the cot allow him to watch his son: the bud of his tiny mouth; his papery, shell-like nails; his whipped, downy hair.

His breathing stops. For a moment, Sam's heart clenches. But then Tommy releases the warmest, sweetest, gentlest breath.

'Miracle,' Sam whispers, fingertips pressed to the mesh. There are no words for what he feels in his heart. To be a father, to lie on the floor and watch his son sleep, is the most everyday thing and yet so extraordinary it makes his breath catch in wonder. Nothing must be allowed to spoil this, he thinks.

Nothing must be allowed to take this away.

CHAPTER 18

Through her bedroom window, Joyce watches the sporty red Golf edge past her MG, pull out of the drive and recede behind the bay hedge.

She is eighty-four years old and has no idea how she feels. Her gut tells her something is up, but guts have memories, in this case bad ones. Hope tells her that bad memories are all this uneasy feeling is, that the feeling is outdated and unfair, a bit like revulsion for, say, prawn cocktail based on it upsetting your stomach once. But even as she tells herself to put aside her fears, her mind fills with the more concrete image of her grandson, not so long ago as all that, going to the viaduct in the battering rain towards that terrible purpose, standing on the precipice and almost...

She shudders.

Naomi was pleasant enough. But we can all be pleasant when it's in our own interests. No less pretty either. What was going on between her and Sam when she, Joyce, walked into the kitchen? Had they been kissing? Are they back together but keeping it secret? As well they might after all that drama. There was definitely something in the air. Please God not a return to the soap opera, she thinks: the constant arguments, the blame – blame thrown at *her* sometimes, even by Sam. *Naomi says you ignored her. Naomi thought you were cross with her yesterday. Naomi said you were a bit sharp with her earlier.* These minor accusations, these thousand cuts, as they say, after Joyce had cooked roast dinners, picked them up from West Bay after a hike, after she'd washed their towels, their sheets, after Naomi had let Sam wash up without moving a muscle to help. Generosity is a funny thing. Boundless until it is abused, when it mutates into something that reduces you, makes you resentful in ways you don't want to be, snappy, curt, mean. The very last time she saw Naomi, the girl asked if she and Sam could take her car for a spin. Casually, as if it were no big deal. Her precious, vintage, perfectly preserved MG RV8! As if it were some rusty old Datsun! Cheeky beggar.

'Sorry, no,' Joyce said. And walked away before she spoke out of turn. Before she found herself changing her mind.

Maybe help is all the girl is after this time. A bit of money too. Maybe. Though if Joyce knows anything, it's that it won't stop there. It never did anyway, before. But fair enough; kids are expensive, especially these days.

And oh, Tommy's a smasher! That spun-cotton hair! That gummy smile! Those enormous blue peepers looking up at her! Her: Nonna Joyce! Nonna Joyce, if you don't mind! Despite everything, she chuckles to herself, feels a warmth spread through her. Babies do that. Make all the troubles of the world melt away. One gurgle, one giggle, and hardened cynics turn to mush.

She pulls on her cashmere cardigan, the reason she's made the pilgrimage up two flights of stairs. She's feeling the chill this spring in a way she's pretty sure she didn't last year. Her hip aches, but there's no way she's going to start popping painkillers. So far, she's resisted the tyranny of the pill box, despite the doctor telling her she should really take statins if she wants to bring down her cholesterol. No way, José, she told him. I'll eat porridge before I start that nonsense.

She hates porridge.

On the way back down, she clasps the handrail. Getting old is the pits, it really is. Still, she's not dead yet. And while she's here, she's going to make sure she enjoys that little lad. If Naomi wants a spare pair of hands and some extra cash, fine, but Joyce will be watching her very closely, very closely indeed. She has things she wants too: namely time. She'll buy Tommy his own little watering can, teach him to paint a wall, wire a plug, you name it. There'll be none of those computer games in this house, Xboxes and what have you. No way. Pumpkin carving at Halloween, paper chains at Christmas – she wonders if you can still get the pastel-coloured strips with the sticky bits to lick. Simnel cake at Easter, little Tommy standing on a stool when he's old enough, chubby little fingers in the sweet batter. The young go on about mindfulness, ha! Joyce's generation invented mindfulness. They just called it taking pleasure in your chores and your hobbies, the seasons and their festivals, instead of moaning on all the time about living your best life.

Yes, there's so much she wants to show this little smasher. Who knows, if she's lucky, she might see him in a little school uniform.

Hopefully.

Downstairs, Sam makes them both a flat white with his milk whizzer thing.

'He's asleep,' he says in the same way you'd announce you'd won the lottery. 'I can't believe how quickly he went down. She's done that by sticking to routine, you know. Nomes reckons routine's really important.'

'Old-fashioned that. I can't disagree. Your mother didn't agree with routines. She fed you whenever you so much as squeaked, put you to bed when you fell asleep. Didn't do you any harm – it was just more work for her, getting her bosoms out every five minutes.'

Sam smiles at her. 'She was a good mum.'

'She was. A good daughter too. Hippy. Suppose I deserved that, being such a capitalist.'

'I'm sorry.'

'Don't be. It was never about the money itself, mind, more about showing bastard-features I was better off without him. Which I was. But then you came along and I had to rethink.'

'Sorry.'

'What're you saying sorry for? Your mother dying was the worst thing that's happened to both of us.' She lays a hand on his. 'But having you come to live with me was the best thing, so...' She pats his hand, makes herself stand. 'Are we allowed to take him outside when he wakes up?'

'Don't see why not.'

She studies him a moment. Sees happiness shining inside him like a torch in a tent. Remembers taking him camping, on the Isle of Purbeck, in Devon, Cornwall, all over. She was in her sixties! But the energy he took, he gave her back with interest. He is the reason she's stayed so fit.

'You're happy, aren't you?' she says.

The light is in his face now, the full beam of it on her.

'I am,' he says. 'I really am.'

CHAPTER 19

Dear Sam,

So you survived your first day! I won't lie, I was surprised by how good you were with him. When I told you how I did things, you didn't make me feel like I was being bossy, like you used to do when we were together, like I didn't have the right to ask you to do things properly or explain how they were done. You stuck to his routine, and you were so good when I told you how to change his nappy, telling me I was the best teacher, that I was being so patient. Instead of grunting or saying OK, OK, like I was nagging, or giving it large with the silent resentment vibes.

And when you handed him back to me, it was like you were parting with gold or something. I can't believe you're so attached already. You always had a soft side. Hopefully you'll take him every week now, and that will be bonding without being too much for me. I have to say, even though I know I have to be careful, from my side it was great to get a real break, even for two hours. Next week you'll have him all day. I wonder how you'll manage.

What I love about writing to you like this, without you here, is that I can ask you questions and then fantasise about you answering the way I want you to. Like, what did you feel today when you half held me in your arms? I can ask that and then I can imagine you replying: I felt love, babe. I realised I was a fool to leave you.

Maybe I'm not fantasising. I definitely picked up a vibe. My horoscope said: Ignore emotional undercurrents at your peril. I'm not ignoring anything. I'm still going to be really careful about how much time you and Tommy spend together; there's still a lot of trust to be built. And I have to be sure you have real feelings for me before things go any further – if things go any further.

As for Joyce, she made a good show of seeming pleased to see me, but she was watching me like a hawk. Has she told you to be careful? Has she told you to watch yourself? I bet she has. I'm not criticising her; it's just a bit frustrating. Everyone deserves a second chance. That's all I'm asking for. She has such a strong influence on you, but you need to think for yourself now, cut those apron strings. For us. For baby Tommy.

CHAPTER 20

The following Wednesday, Sam waits at the sitting room window, cup of coffee in hand. A little after 8.30 a.m., his breath catches at the sight of Naomi's car pulling into the driveway.

'Hey,' she says when he opens the front door. She is dressed in her work clothes: a skirt and blouse, suit jacket and ballet-style shoes. She even has her lanyard on: *Lyme Regis Medical Practice* repeating on the ribbon around her neck.

'Are you coming in?'

'I've got to get to work, sorry.' She proffers the kitbag. In his car seat, Tommy is staring at everything as if seeing it all for the first time.

'I've made organic vegetable and chicken,' he tells her, taking the bag, not quite managing to hide the pride in his voice. 'Finely pureed, no salt! I used my soup whizzer thing. And I've bought some rusks, the same ones you left last week, oh, and a teething ring, a changing mat, nappy bags and nappies.' He doesn't tell her he's ordered a cot from Argos, some bedding, that he's started work fixing up the bedroom they chose last week. Despite their excellent start, it's still early days and everything feels too precarious. But hopefully, when Naomi sees the room finished in a few weeks, she will be ready to understand how serious he is.

She smiles and shakes her head in what looks like wonder. 'Wow,' she says. 'I'm impressed, Sam Moore.'

'I haven't got any formula,' he says, scratching at the back of his head. 'I went to buy it, but it was so complicated.'

She only laughs – not the slightest hint of an eyeroll at his incompetence. The sharp heart of her chin lifts. 'No worries.' She nods towards the kitbag. 'It's all in there, so just take what you need. I'll write down a list of things, like the right brand of formula and the organic ready-made food he has when I don't have time to make it, OK?' She takes a step back then stops, fixes him with her gaze, her cheeks a little flushed. 'I really am impressed though. No joke.'

They stare at one another, tentative smiles tugging at their mouths. She is not wearing her hat today, and her brow is soft, her hair mad with curls and her eyes kind – as they have been almost the whole time since their paths crossed again.

The moment passes. Embarrassed, Sam shakes his head. 'Well, have a good day at the office!'

She pulls a silly face, turns, her gait light as she makes her way back towards the Golf. Once she's opened the car door, she stops and raises her hand in a wave.

'I'll be back just after four. I've changed my hours since... well, you know.' She rolls her eyes and laughs again. 'Bye, guys! Be good!'

A rev of engine, a blast of exhaust, and she's gone.

'Well, little fella,' Sam says to his baby son, whose eyes are as dark and deep and blue as he remembered. Such unblinking trust! It is... it's quite scary actually. The physical safety of this tiny being is his responsibility – at least for the coming hours – and that's not all. The other thing he must protect at all costs is this little human's psychological welfare. His precious head. His innocent heart.

In the kitchen, Joyce claps her hands and leans forward, face etched with glee. She takes the baby from Sam and holds him to her chest, her eyes closing. She lifts him up and down, sing-songing her words to him as she moves him expertly onto her good hip and walks, limping a little, around the room.

'Hello there, my love. Hello there. Say hello to your great... to your nonna. Say hello, Nonna Joyce, say Nonna Joyce. Non. A. Joyce. Hello! Hello, hello, hello.'

Tommy reaches up and pulls at her nose. Emits a small cooing sound.

'Did you see that?' Joyce cries. 'Need to clip his fingernails though – he'll cut me to ribbons. Yes, you will, little one, yes you will.' She nuzzles Tommy's nose and makes a *brrr* sound. She gasps, pulls back, goes in again:

'Ah – brrrrr.'

Tommy giggles.

'He laughed!' Sam can barely contain himself. 'You made him laugh! Do it again!'

Later, and with Joyce's help, Sam figures out the sling that Naomi has left so he can walk about with Tommy strapped to his chest and keep his hands free. He is heavy though! Sam makes a mental note to buy a larger baby carrier, one to go on his back so he can take Tommy hiking. For practice, he and Joyce wander out into the back garden. It is so vast that there is no need to venture to the park for now. They walk up to the dense copse of firs at the very end of Joyce's land, then back and round to the front of the house, to the low bay hedge, the sea a live and ever-changing panorama. Then back for another lap to allow Joyce to achieve her step count for the day.

'These are bluebells,' Sam says, pointing as they stroll. 'And these little fellas are red campions. You've got your black bamboo over there, your hydrangeas, daphnes, pennisetum; that's wild garlic over there, the one that looks a bit like rhubarb is your mighty gunnera, then these chaps over here will blow like fireworks come summer. Echiums. Ech-ee-ums. Echiums.' He turns to Joyce. 'Do you think he'll remember all that?'

Joyce nods. 'We'll soon make a horticulturist of him. He needs some Moore family culture to water down the Harper blood.'

'Joyce! Don't be a snob.'

She huffs. 'You know what I mean.'

Sam lets it go. As long as Joyce is polite to Naomi's face, that's the best he can hope for, at least for now.

The day passes more easily than either of them has anticipated. Tommy has his mid-morning milk and nap, eats his lunch, has his afternoon nap, all at the exact times Naomi stipulated. Sam is keen to stick to her rules. She is his mother, after all, and knows best. The baby's needs are not hard or demanding, but they are constant. By the time Naomi arrives, Sam realises he is really tired. At the sight of her, Tommy begins to cry and squirm.

'Toms! Mate! You're making me look bad.' Disappointed, and fighting a feeling of mild betrayal, Sam meets Naomi's eye. 'Honestly, he's not cried once all day, I swear.' He is expecting Naomi to ask what the hell he's done to the child, but as she has done so many times lately, she merely laughs.

'Hey, baby!' She folds him into her arms and kisses his head. 'Hey, baby-boo, have you had a good day? Mummy's boy, aren't you? Are you a mummy's boy?'

'Are you... are you coming in for a bit?' On the doorstep, Sam shuffles from foot to foot, hoping she'll say yes.

But she shakes her head. 'I'll get him back now. He needs his bath and story time, don't you, darling? Hey?' She kisses Tommy again and returns her gaze to Sam's. 'How's he been?'

'As good as gold.'

'Good. That's really good.'

'It's hard work though. Nice work. I mean, I loved having him.' He blows at his hair then, just in case there's any room for misunderstanding, adds: 'I'm already looking forward to next week.'

'That's great! It was nice knowing he was with his dad. The childminder's lovely and everything, but it's... it was just nice.'

He nods, smiles. 'I know what you mean. It was nice for me too.'

She moves to go.

'What's her name by the way, the childminder?'

Naomi blushes and looks at her shoes. 'Cheryl.'

'Ah,' he replies, understanding. 'Cheryl.'

She raises her head. Her eyes are screwed up in apparent mortification. 'Sorry.'

'Don't be. You've already apologised for that.'

'I know, but...'

'Don't worry about it. Seriously.'

She nods, her eyes bright. 'But we're doing all right now, aren't we?'

'Of course. Of course we are. We're doing great.'

'And you don't still... hate me or anything, do you?'

'Of course not. I never hated you.' Heat climbs his neck. 'And... and this'll be great for Tommy. If you need me to have him at the weekend, just, you know, shout.'

'That's kind, but let's take it one step at a time, shall we?'

The heat reaches his face; he feels himself blush. 'Sure, sure. Sorry. Getting ahead of myself.'

'Maybe in a few weeks?'

'Sure. Yes. That'd be great.'

Smiling, she turns to go. He waits on the stone doorstep, feet cooling through his thin socks. She clips Tommy into the back seat, closes the door, gets into the driver's seat. She moves carefully, as if everything she does impacts the baby.

As she pulls out of the long, wide driveway, he sees her in silhouette, waving.

He raises his hand. 'Bye, Nomes,' he whispers. 'Bye, Tommy.'

CHAPTER 21

Dear Sam,

So you've done your first full shift with Toms and now you're ready to take him for a weekend. I must admit, I did have a little laugh about that in the car on the way home. You have no idea how hard it is to look after a baby full-time, but I'll let you off. There was no malice in it. That's the thing about you, Sam. You never mean any harm; you just do it by accident. Usually it's what you don't do or say. Do you remember that time I had about four inches of my hair cut off, and when you got in from work I asked you if you noticed anything and you looked around like a cornered criminal and asked if I'd varnished the coffee table? I was literally standing there looking completely different and you didn't even notice. When I got upset, you told me I was overreacting instead of just putting your arm round me, telling me I looked nice and saying sorry. You did stuff like that all the time and it used to really hurt my feelings. But Dawn helped me see it's not intentional. It's not personal.

I should have laughed, shouldn't I? Me, varnish a coffee table? As if!

Anyway, I'm pleased you enjoyed having Toms. And when I agreed that you could have him one weekend sometime, you couldn't hide your feelings, could you? Your eyes literally lit up, and that's a good sign. You see, we were close once, and I just know we can be close again.

CHAPTER 22

On a Saturday in late May, Joyce is standing at the kitchen sink mixing filler for the crack in the wall of the nursery. The varnish on the floorboards has dried, and once the walls are painted, they'll be most of the way there. But she isn't thinking about that; she's thinking about the absence of drama this last month. So sure was she of it coming, the lack of it is stark, as if it's a solid thing in and of itself – like a table suddenly missing from a room, the indentations in the rug creating the expectation that it should by rights still be there. The strange lightness in the air is such that she half expects the ornaments to start levitating off the sideboard. No wailing recriminations, no slamming doors, no swearing to make a sailor blush – all of which only makes her own breath audible, her footsteps loud, the clang of her tools in the kitchen sink deafening.

Naomi has not put one foot wrong. Like clockwork – no, like *Swiss* clockwork – she drops Tommy off each Wednesday morning. Here again, this almost tangible *nothingness*: no belligerent lateness. No utter disregard for the timings and plans of others.

In this conspicuous peace, Joyce and Sam have eased themselves into a lovely routine. As she said to Miranda on the FaceTime the other day, 'I count the days to little Tommy's visits, I really do. And when Naomi comes to take him away, it's like she's taking one of my limbs with her. But Sam says we can't push for more, not yet.'

'And what about Naomi? Is she any nicer?'

Joyce couldn't help but laugh. 'Do you know, I barely recognise her. The haughtiness is gone, the guilt trips, all the little barbed comments disguised as jokes. And she doesn't do that coy wheedling thing anymore, not so far as I've seen. I thought she might have wanted to punish Sam for leaving, you know? For being absent during the child's early months. But no. She seems to have moved past it.'

No punishments. Another troubling absence.

As for Sam, she thinks now, he is happier than he has been since he left Naomi – ironic, since the happiness has come precisely because Naomi is back in his life, albeit in a different form.

Not for the first time, Joyce wonders whether there's anything physical between them. She remembers the one and only time she let hopeless Hugh back into their red-brick semi-detached villa off Clapham High Street; he was back in her bed before he'd dropped his bags, only for her to kick him out two months later when the mask of reform slipped and his promises went up in sweet, cloying marijuana smoke. But just because Hugh never grew up doesn't mean to say that Naomi hasn't. And after what Sam told her, it's possible that *he* needed to grow up too, learn to communicate from time to time instead of brooding and huffing like a horse stuck in a stable.

She stirs the filler. It's a bit stiff, so she adds more water, curses herself for being too lazy to fetch her glasses to read the proportions on the side of the bag. Another stir; the mixture is easier this time. She lifts the bucket out of the sink and turns to make her way upstairs, realising in that moment that her glasses are on her head.

'Fool,' she mutters, grasping the banister with her free hand.

Whatever has happened, happens or might happen between those two, what's beyond doubt is Sam's devotion to that little boy. The other Saturday he drove to Exeter and returned with a mobile toy for the cot. He bought a sleep suit, a night light that plays a lullaby and rotates, showing a circus scene with acrobats tumbling, and a frame backpack that doubles as a makeshift high chair.

'The things they have nowadays,' Joyce said. She did not ask how much it all cost.

In the nursery, he is sanding the repair on the window frame. He has worked every evening and most weekends, determined to have something to show Naomi when she comes this Wednesday. Joyce joins him, begins to fill the crack in the back wall, the two of them working in companionable silence. Maybe it was this silence Naomi couldn't stand, she thinks, tries not to, thinks again. Maybe she couldn't stand Sam's ability to lose himself in a project and not have to talk for hours on end. In that sense, Joyce and her grandson are peas in the proverbial pod.

Saturday turns to Sunday, then Monday. Sam works late into the night, black shadows deepening under his eyes. In bed, Joyce falls asleep to the muted babble of Radio 5 Live from down the landing. In the morning, she is about to inspect the nursery but stops herself. He will want to show it to her himself.

Sure enough, she is popping a couple of jacket potatoes

in the range that evening when he calls her from the top of the stairs.

'Joyce? Gran? Nonna?'

Wincing at the soreness in her hip, she makes her way slowly up to the mezzanine, pausing to get her breath before continuing up to what they now call Tommy's room.

She knocks at the door. 'Dorset Council building inspector.'

Sam opens the door, clearly beside himself with proud delight. 'Welcome!'

She steps inside, feeling her mouth drop open, her hands meet at her chest, her fingers interlock.

'Oh my,' she whispers. 'Oh my heavens.'

The room is perfect, the paintwork pristine, the cot in the centre, bedding carefully made and fluffy as egg whites, a large floppy-eared rabbit on top, the mobile toy attached to the side and turning slowly; in one corner an old Ercol chair from Joyce's first London flat, painted to match the room; in the other corner the old tallboy she last saw chipped and covered in cobwebs in the garage. The Roman blinds she ran up on the Singer last week have been fitted to the window, and a pale blue paper shade covers the light bulb.

'When did you finish the tallboy?' she says. 'How did you get it up the stairs?'

'Very slowly and with great difficulty.' Still grinning, he walks over to it and turns the little key, now a shiny silver rather than a rusty brown.

'I barely recognise it! I was going to chuck it out. Did you change the key?'

'Fitted a new lock. I had paint left over from the walls and half a tin of varnish, so I just thought, may as well, you know?'

He pulls open the drop-down door of the main compartment, which used to house the spirits and mixers back in the day, a million years ago. Instead of the drinks, there's now a changing mat, which he has attached to the inside so that it flattens when the door opens, making a chest-high changing bed. On either side are smaller compartments where he has put cotton wool balls, a pot of nappy cream, wipes.

'Welcome to the changing station! Upcycled!' He closes the drawbridge door and bends to the drawers below. 'And we can put his spare clothes here. And shoes once he can walk. And, you know, anything else he needs.'

He stands up, switches on the lamp on top of the tall-boy, sending circus acrobats tumbling round and round, and on the wall, larger, fuzzier figures roaming like shadows on a cave.

'Your mum would be so proud,' she manages to say. 'It's beautiful, love... Oh, Sam, you've done a grand job. I just hope Naomi appreciates it.'

'There's no way she'll let you have him at weekends?' Joyce asks him over dinner.

He shakes his head. 'She's still wary. I know our break-up had been coming for a long time for me, but I think for her, it was sudden. I should've told her I was unhappy.'

'Don't blame yourself for all of it, love.'

'She even suggested we go to couples counselling, but I...' He shifts in his chair as if he can't get comfortable.

'I didn't know that. About the counselling.'

'No, well... I suppose I never gave her a chance to...'

'Do you wish you had?'

He shrugs, doesn't look at her, drives his fork around his plate after a lone cherry tomato. 'She always said I was a coward, and maybe I was. And now the baby's here...'

'You wish you were back together?'

'A bit. Maybe. I know Nomes can be stroppy, but maybe I should have been more... I dunno, stronger? A man. But don't you think she's different?' When he looks up at her, it's as if he is a boy again, handing her his school report.

Joyce takes a mouthful of her supper – the mackerel Sam picked up from Dave at the fish shop on his way home, which she has griddled and served with the jacket potatoes and her home-made tomato and bean salsa; dynamite, if she says so herself.

Sam is still waiting for her answer, his fork hovering. He does have a point, she supposes. Naomi *is* different. There's no denying it. Or is it simply easy to behave well when you're not living the nitty-gritty of day-to-day life together – who buys the toilet roll, who does the shopping, who puts the hoover round? Outside the grind, we can all hold on to our best selves. We can be dazzling.

'Motherhood certainly seems to suit her,' she says carefully. 'And if she's not the maternal type, as you say, then she's right to keep working. She doesn't have her mum anymore, does she? And her sister works?'

'Think so. I've not asked.'

'And her dad... poor bugger. No family to help her through the long days.'

'I always said I'd be a stay-at-home dad.'

'And now you've done a few days of childcare, you still think that, do you?'

He nods, not picking up that she's teasing him. 'I love looking after him. Love going in to him when he wakes up from his nap. His little face. I love it when she's here too. When she's with me and Toms, we feel like a family.'

'I can see that. And I'll not be here that much longer.'

'No! I meant with you too.'

She laughs. 'I'm only pulling your leg.' She gets up, gestures for him to pass her his empty plate. 'So you're keen to try again, is that what you're saying?'

'I think it is, yeah.'

'So ask her out to dinner.' The words escape her without passing through her brain.

'Are you serious?'

'All I know is, when you were with her, you were more unhappy than you'd been since we first got here. Having seen her in action, I blamed it all on her, of course I did. You're mine, you're my blood, aren't you? But if you're beginning to feel like it wasn't all her fault after all and you're ready to talk things through, then maybe... maybe you've both grown up a bit. Follow your heart, I suppose I'm saying. Life's too short not to. If you want her back, let her know. If she doesn't feel the same, you'll still have the little 'un, and in time you'll see him more. It's not as if there aren't lots of families like that. I did all right with your mother. Your mother did all right with you. And we had a lot less than you've got going for you.' She can't quite believe she's just said all that when Naomi still makes her feel uneasy. But Sam is a grown man, and it isn't down to her to warn him away from the woman he either loves or thinks he loves. If she does, she risks losing him all over again.

She slides his plate on top of her own. 'How's Miranda, by the way?'

'She's fine. Good, yeah, why do you ask?'

'No reason. Have you talked to her lately?'

'Not really. I've been racing home to get the nursery finished. Maybe I'll ask her to dinner.'

'Miranda?'

'No, Naomi.'

CHAPTER 23

Before you ask, no, I didn't make that bit up about Sam thinking Joyce meant ask me out to dinner. It wasn't wishful thinking; Joyce told me the next day and chuckled away at the misunderstanding. I responded with a hollow laugh and said something like: *Sam? Ask me out? You've got to be joking!*

Easier to hide your feelings over FaceTime, and by then she'd moved on to telling me all about how Sam had fixed up the nursery, what an amazing job he'd done, and my heart shrank with every word. *Brilliant*, I said, and *Wow*, and all the things you say when you're pleased. But I wasn't pleased. As well as gutted, I was worried. He was getting in too deep, too fast, after everything he'd been through, and, of course, the isolation of the pandemic. I suppose I didn't trust his judgement. But then I didn't trust my own. I'm not above jealousy; no one is, not when you love someone. Not when deep down you wish they were yours.

But there I go again, jumping in. Let's go back to Sam, who is waiting for Naomi to come home from work so that he can show her the labour of love he has created for their son.

The doorbell chimes through Joyce's big old house a little after the kitchen clock's spotted woodpecker rat-a-tat-tats four o'clock. Nervous anticipation leaping in his chest, Sam almost jogs to answer the door.

Out on the driveway, Naomi looks up expectantly, her expression darkening a fraction when she holds out her arms for Tommy, only for Sam to step back.

'Come in a second,' he says. 'I need you to see something.'

'Sam. I really don't have—'

'It'll only take a minute. Literally. Come on.' He holds the door wide.

Her shoulders drop, and, head low, she steps into the house.

'Come up,' he says, handing Tommy over when he starts to wriggle.

'Hey, Tom-Toms,' she croons, kissing his head and rocking him in her arms. 'Hey there, little babba.'

'Leave your shoes on,' Sam says, itching to get upstairs. 'Carpet's old as time anyway.'

He walks ahead, senses her on the stairs behind him. On the landing outside the nursery, he throws open the door and stands back to let her inside. He has left the circus lamp on, the blinds closed to get the full effect. The room looks magical in the dim, dancing light. At the sight, Naomi's mouth drops open just as Joyce's did.

'Sam,' she whispers, stepping slowly inside. 'Oh my God.'

He draws up the blind, letting in the late-afternoon sun. 'I made this out of my gran's old cocktail cabinet,' he says, opening the drop-down door. 'Remember it was in the garage? Anyway, I saw these in John Lewis and thought, I could make one. It's a pretty similar shape and size.'

She nods, her eyes wide with what looks like amazement. 'Oh my God.'

'Look! You've got all the gear, all handy.'

She is shaking her head, her eyes shining. 'I can't believe it. I can't take it in. You've done all this yourself?'

'Joyce helped. Nonna Joyce.'

'It's amazing, absolutely amazing.' She has crossed the room and is standing so close he can smell her perfume. It takes him back to her before. He almost leans down to kiss her, but she places a hand flat on his cheek. 'I don't know what to say. I can't believe it.'

He stays perfectly still. He does not want her to move her hand from his cheek, does not want the three of them to break apart, not even by a centimetre. 'I thought if you saw it, you'd know I'm serious. About Tommy.'

She smiles, but her expression is sad. 'Is it all about Tommy? Only Tommy?'

He meets her gaze, sees hurt.

'No,' he says. 'It's... Actually, I was wondering if we could go out to dinner? If I could take you out?'

'On, like... like a date? As in not just mates?'

He nods.

She shifts Tommy to the opposite hip. 'But you know it wouldn't be like a first date, don't you? It's a big thing to ask. For us, I mean. You'd have to be sure.'

'I am sure.'

She breathes deeply, her out-breath shaky. For a moment he thinks she is going to say no.

'OK,' she says. 'I'll see if Cheryl or Jo can babysit.'

'Friday?'

'OK.' The smile becomes a grin. 'I'll come to Lyme. I don't mind driving. But I really do have to go now.'

She flies out of the room, almost bumping into Joyce.

'Well?' Joyce says. 'What d'you think?'

Naomi giggles. 'Oh my God, it's amazing!'

Together they head towards the stairs. Sam goes ahead but is barely at the mezzanine when he hears a loud cry followed by a horrible protracted thud. Joyce's glasses bounce past his feet. He swivels round. Sees Joyce: torso and arms stretched down the stairs, the rest of her still on the landing.

Naomi is standing over her, hand clapped to her mouth, Tommy on her hip. 'Oh my God, Joyce, are you OK?'

'I'm fine!' Joyce remains still, as if she can't figure out how to begin getting up.

Sam rushes up the few stairs. Crouches carefully beside Joyce and takes her gently by the shoulders.

'I must've tripped on something,' she says.

'I'm going to turn you slowly, OK?' He half lifts, half turns her, slowly, slowly, taking all the weight he can. It is not much; she is birdlike compared to ten years ago. With her lying against him, he pushes her gently upwards until she comes to sit at the top of the stairs. When he is sure she is stable, he takes his hands from her back but leaves them almost touching her, just in case. 'Are you OK?'

She nods but appears dazed.

He glances up at Naomi, who buries her face in Tommy's head and sniffs loudly. He feels his mouth open. But nothing comes out.

'No harm done,' says Joyce, but her voice quavers.

'I'll get your specs.' Sam dashes to the mezzanine and

grabs the glasses, hurries back and hands them to her. She puts them on. He watches her for signs of poor coordination. She might be concussed; her retina might have detached; she's probably broken a rib at least.

She blinks. 'I think I'll just sit here for a moment. You two do what you need to do.'

Naomi takes a step nearer to the stairs. She glances at Sam, seems unsure. 'Do you want me to stay?'

'No, it's OK. You go.'

'Call me later, OK? Let me know?' Looking down at Joyce, she adds, 'I'm so sorry you fell, Joyce.'

Joyce holds up a hand. 'Accidents happen. I'll be fine.'

Once he has seen Naomi out, Sam races back up the stairs, but Joyce is no longer on the landing.

'Joyce? Gran?'

'Just going to soak for a bit.' Her voice comes from the bathroom.

Outside, he leans his forehead against the door. 'Are you sure? We should get you checked out.'

'Sure I'm sure.' Her voice is small. 'I can wiggle my fingers.'

'I know, but—'

'And my toes. I'd rather avoid the hospital if I can, thank you.' Her voice firms. There is no pushing against that particular tone. 'Bit of a shock, that's all. If you could bring up a glass of brandy and leave it outside the door?'

'Sure. Coming up.'

He leaves her to fetch the emergency Remy. As he pours a large measure into her best Edinburgh crystal, he notices that his own hands are shaking. She's climbed up stepladders and onto chairs, often balancing heavy tins of paint. She's never fallen in all the time they've lived together.

But she isn't walking as well as she used to.

She is not as indestructible as she once was.

CHAPTER 24

Dear Sam,

When you showed me Tommy's room, I almost lost it. And your face! Looking at me like a dog waiting for a biscuit. I was blinking back tears, I really was. And when you asked me out for dinner, how could I say no? It was what I've been hoping for, but it had to come from you. I know I have to be careful. I cannot mess this up, can't let you think it's what I want more than anything. And I do want it, more than anything.

Anyway, apart from Joyce's fall, I think things have been really great. You and your gran are so in the swing of it now, aren't you? You're both so loved up too, which is great, because I so want this to work. My mum's parents didn't talk to her for the whole time she was pregnant, but then, bam, the moment I came along and my granny held me in her arms everything was forgiven. That's the power of babies. I hope Tommy can have that power over us.

He's awake now, so I'll have to leave this for today. There's his bottle to heat, the park to walk to, and I need to pick up some more nappies and formula. We can't all sit around doing up old furniture. Only joking!

But before I go, I will say that you doing that nursery nearly finished me. I'm falling in deeper every time I see you. I'm so glad we found each other again. I don't think I could go back now even if I wanted to.

CHAPTER 25

That Thursday morning, on the way to the job, Sam tells Miranda he's taking Naomi out to dinner.

'I should book something,' he says, half turning to her as he drives. 'Where do you think? Where's good?'

'Not sure,' she says, shaking her head. 'But didn't you used to be in the doghouse all the time for not being romantic enough? Millside, somewhere classy like that? On the other hand, you don't want to overdo it in case she thinks you're pressuring her. The Rockpoint?'

'I've tried. Fully booked. We used to go to the Harbour a lot, but it's shut. Too many staff off isolating. The Pilot Boat's being refurbished.'

'Why don't you ask her what *she* wants to do?'

'I don't want to look indecisive.'

Miranda shakes her head. 'She's got you second-guessing yourself already.'

'It's not like that,' Sam protests. 'I just want to show her I'm serious, and maybe, if we talk, she'll realise I'm better at... well, at talking about... you know... stuff.'

'So you definitely want to get back together? Be a couple again?'

'I just... With the baby here, I want to be sure. I'm beginning to think... I was weak, I think.'

'Sam!' Miranda opens her mouth as if she's about to say more but closes it again, tight.

'Do you think I'm being stupid?'

'It's none of my business. If you guys think you can make it work, you should go for it. Just... don't let her tell you off. Don't apologise for every little thing. You're a good bloke. The best. Don't forget that.'

Across the cab of the van, he glances at her, sees she is looking at him intently.

'She's not like that anymore,' he says. 'Honestly she's not.'

Miranda returns her gaze to the windscreen and throws up her hands. 'OK,' she half sighs, shoulders rising then falling. 'OK.'

They park up outside the Higher Mill project. Darren and Lee are already there, bringing the tools out of the garage. Miranda is sliding her tape measure into the pocket of her rain jacket.

'Mi,' he says. 'Are you pissed off with me?'

She lays a hand on his arm. 'I could never be pissed off with you, you twit.' She lifts her hand, opens the passenger door and throws her legs over the side of the van. 'Come on, let's see if we can get these bloody levels sorted.'

Sam hangs back, watches Miranda greet the guys with a wave. He can hear the back-and-forth rhythms of banter, though not the exact words. After a moment, he pulls his phone from his pockets and texts Naomi.

Hey. Where do you fancy going on Friday? Posh restaurant or pub? X

Hooked over his phone, he holds his breath. *Naomi Harper is typing.* He waits. The WhatsApp lands. He exhales in a long, shuddering rush.

Weather warm so fish and chips and walk along the seafront? Low-key. Is that OK? X

Naomi used to hate eating in the street. Used to hate eating anything fatty, come to that. If this isn't proof of how much she's changed, he thinks, what is?

CHAPTER 26

At seven sharp, Naomi is at the door, all smiles. Over the phone, she said she wanted to go out early as she gets tired; besides, she's still a bit nervous about leaving Tommy in the evening. It's strange to see her without her suit on and without Tommy. It's like looking at a photograph of her from before, something Sam has been doing more and more lately, scrolling through the deleted album he never quite deleted permanently. Tonight she is wearing her more usual attire of wide jeans and funky jacket. She has put on more make-up too, he notices, her eyes blacker, her lips pinker and shinier, and her black hair straight rather than the wavy style she wears for work.

'Do you like my hair?' she asks.

'Yes,' he says. 'Sorry, I was about to say. It looks really nice like that.'

'I don't have time to straighten it before work anymore.' She smiles. He feels a rush of relief.

As they walk together down Cobb Road, she tells him that Tommy is with her sister, and fills him in on some of the cute things he's done today. Sam suggests a drink at the

Royal Standard before they grab fish and chips at the harbour; she smiles and says, sure, sounds great. The pub is empty and they are told to take seats outside.

'I'm getting used to drinking outdoors,' Naomi says after they've ordered – a pint of Tribute for him, half a lager for her. 'It's more Scandinavian, isn't it? I'd like to live in Scandinavia. Finland or Copenhagen or somewhere like that.'

'You've been saying that since we watched *The Bridge*,' he says, and she laughs easily. Genuinely, he thinks. It feels good to make her laugh like that.

'Oh my God, I was obsessed,' she says. 'Do you remember I even started wearing my leather jacket under my coat? Like that would be enough to make me look just like her.' She laughs again, wipes at her eyes. 'I'm such a knob sometimes.'

He smiles and takes a drink. She is so lovely when she's like this. So good to be with.

'So, things seem to be working out?' he tries. 'With us?'

'You and Joyce have been amazing.' She falters, glances down at her lap before meeting his eye again. 'Listen, I need to tell you something.'

His chest tightens. 'OK.'

'I know I was difficult to be with.'

'No, I—'

She holds up a hand. 'Listen. I know, OK? I blamed it all on you, but I've been seeing a therapist and I'm starting to understand why I might have turned you away.'

'But I—'

'Sam! Let me say it, OK? I was moody. I was critical. I know I said mean things to you sometimes, and I was sarcastic and I slammed doors.'

'I'm the one who punched a window.'

She shakes her head. 'You did. But I was winding you up.'

'You did take me to A&E though.'

The smile they share is warm.

'Seeing that room you did for Tommy,' she says, 'it just reminded me how amazing you are at stuff like that. I took that for granted. I put you down, I know I did. I tried to get you to be someone you're not. I thought I wanted you to be tougher or more decisive or whatever, but since you left, I've realised you are who you are, you know? That's all we can be, isn't it? You're a bit of a pushover, and that's fine because... because you do things like make a changing station out of a piece of junk. I stopped seeing that. I'm not sure if I ever really saw it, to be honest. But I do now. And I'm sorry. There. That's my big speech.'

'I was bad at talking.' He coughs into his hand, adjusts his position. 'That's my big speech.'

She laughs, takes a sip of her drink, places the glass softly on the table. 'But I didn't make it easy, did I?'

'This is not all your fault.'

'I'm not saying it is. I'm saying I'm not blameless.'

'Well, I'm sorry too. I'm sorry I closed down. I dismissed you. Your feelings. I left instead of trying to sort it out. I should've faced you.' He reaches for her hand.

She clasps his fingers tight. 'I need to tell you something else. I sold the flat. Our flat. I know I didn't tell you that day but I was a bit caught off guard and I was still really angry. I had this weird idea that you had no right to know anything about my life. But yeah, I sold it.'

'It was yours. You had every right to sell it.'

'It's good of you to see it like that. My dad left me and Jo some money, and I put that together with the money from the flat and I bought a house. It's nice, a nice place. Modern, which I never thought I'd like. Grown up, you know? It's got three bedrooms and a garden. I wanted a garden for Tommy. Everything about my life is about him now, do you get that?'

'Of course I do. Of course.'

'It's funny, because I always hated the idea of kids. But now...' She sighs, her smile watery. 'Now, he's all I care about. Well, he's who I care most about, and it's a very short list.'

They are still holding hands. He planned to say so much, but now he has the feeling it has all been said, that they've agreed on something he can't quite reach but knows without doubt he wants. And when he leans in and kisses her on the mouth, she lets him, as he knew she would.

'I still love you,' he says. 'That's my other big speech.'

'Me too. I never stopped.'

Their eyes lock for a long time. He has the impression they are aware only of each other.

'What are we going to do?' he asks.

'I don't know, Sam Moore. What *are* we going to do?'

CHAPTER 27

The key rattles in the front door. Joyce checks the clock on the mantelpiece. Nine thirty, early to be coming in. Perhaps they've had a fight. Might not be a bad thing. Might remind Sam why he left in the first place. Because her grandson is the proverbial moth; that woman not so much a flame as a bed of embers, a glow you only see in the blackness, flaring against your wingtips when it's far too late.

A moment of silence. She is about to call out when she hears him singing – not words but da-da-das, his voice thinning as he bends to take off his boots, thickening again when he stands. It's a theme tune. She recognises it. Some detective series he told her to watch, set in Copenhagen.

The door opens. Sam comes in. He is not frowning, far from it. He is grinning like an idiot.

'You sound pleased with yourself,' she says, sliding her bookmark between the pages of her Kate Atkinson and placing it on the coffee table. 'You were singing away when you came in.'

'Was I?' He closes the door and leans against it, as if for

support. His smile is still wide and silly. Obviously the evening has not gone as badly as she hoped.

Feared. *Come on, Joyce.*

'It's nice,' she says. 'Nice to hear you singing again. I take it you had a good time?'

'Really good actually. We talked properly, you know?' He wrests himself from the door and comes to join her, taking the armchair, rubbing his hands together. 'You laid a fire.'

'I did.'

'It was bloody chilly this evening actually.' Sam stares into the flames, lost in his thoughts. 'We were frozen.'

'Fire'll soon warm you up.'

She does not add that she laid it to fight an attack of the blues that came at her from nowhere. The emptiness of this big old house in the evening came as a shock after so much time together – a bit like when he first left to live with Naomi. This last year, even when he's in another room, she's been able to hear the faint notes of his music, the burble of whatever podcast or nature programme he's listening to. Sometimes she just wishes this sodding pandemic would bugger off so she could get out there and fill her old lungs with the Sea Shanty Chanteurs, share a few laughs down the pub with her friends, swim in the sea. And now that little Tommy's here, well, she just hopes this thing will be truly over in time for her to take him down to the beach with a bucket and spade, buy him an ice cream, share a bag of chips. That's what she got stuck thinking earlier, feeling sorry for herself. She's done everything she's been told by that fool at Number 10, obeyed the rules like a soldier. Because it's been a war this. Nearest most people have been to one anyway.

Yes, she managed to get quite cross with it all.

But then she poured herself a large Amaretto and reminded herself, as she always does, of all those who've had it ten times worse.

Sam is still staring into the fire.

'It's early,' Joyce says. 'I thought you might have fallen out.'

'Not at all. She was anxious to get back to Tommy, that's all. She doesn't complain. She *never* complains.' He draws his gaze from the fire, looks at her, smiles.

Again, unease stirs in her belly – why, she has no idea. 'She does seem like a different person,' she says. It is less, much less, than she means. Because there's something odd about this transformation. Maybe that's what's bothering her. Motherhood changes you, yes, but not this much. And the changes are slow; they're cumulative.

'It's as if I'm getting to know her all over again.' He sounds joyous, not picking up on Joyce's misgivings at all. 'But at the same time, I know her inside out and back to front, you know? It's weird.' Again he looks at her, and she sees through him as if he were made of glass. Sees the scowling ten-year-old covered in scuffs and bruises from fighting in the playground, the lost boy uprooted from his home, the excited kid of a few months later who brought home a bunch of six daffodils and told her he'd grown them himself.

It is this last one she sees now. He is excited, dizzy, childlike. He is, she realises, in love.

Whether Naomi has changed or not, Joyce can't be the one to burst his bubble. He's a grown man. His love life is none of her business. To voice her fears would spoil everything she has built between them.

'And you believe this change in her, do you?' *Oh, take a bow, Joyce. Great restraint, I must say.*

But he only nods, no offence taken. Astonishing how guileless he is, how trusting. Worrying.

'Well, if you're sure,' she says carefully. 'Just, you know, as the Doors say: *take it easy, baby*. There's no rush, is there? No rush at all.'

CHAPTER 28

It was around this time that Joyce and I began to talk more frequently. She wasn't gritting her teeth or anything as she had been at the start, more quietly concerned. As for Sam, he talked constantly about the baby. And I mean *constantly*.

Me? I kept my feelings to myself obviously, along with the fact that I'd noticed he'd shaved off his beard. And yes, I wondered if Naomi had asked him to do that, what else she was asking him to do, telling him to do. But I didn't see too much of him, because Betsy and I both tested positive for COVID and had to isolate. I remember Sam dropped some groceries off at the cottage on one of the days. I didn't ask him to; he just improvised, buying all the things he'd seen me give Betsy – the organic yoghurts she liked, and a head of broccoli, which he picked out of the bag and laid on the front step, telling her as he backed away two metres that he'd cut it down in the forest. This moved me. As I said, he was such a softie, no matter what some of the more lurid press said about him afterwards. Even if *desperate local man* glided near the truth, he was not a *weird loner*, nor was he *reclusive*, nor, of all things, a *crazed troll*.

We had a quick chat at a distance. He told me he and the lads would get tested, though I told him my best guess was that I'd got it from my mate Tara.

'We walked five K really carefully,' I said. 'Then forgot and hugged goodbye. Force of habit. Anyway, we're not too ill. I just don't want to give it to my folks. Or yours.'

'Exactly. I'd die if I gave it to Joyce.'

She would, more likely, I thought but didn't say. I said something like: 'I think the government slogan should've been *It's Not About You.*' I laughed at my own joke.

'You should do the press briefings.'

'I should. Stay the hell at home.'

He laughed. 'Do you need anything else? I can stop by the pharmacy.'

'We're fine, don't worry.'

He hesitated, as if he didn't like leaving us. 'Text if you need anything.'

I made to close the front door before adding, as if in afterthought: 'Oh, listen, how's it going with Naomi?'

He grinned, and as my heart sank further and further, he told me that last night there'd been a phone call deep into the early hours, the sky beginning to lighten as she whispered down the line that she loved him still, there was nothing she could do about it, and he had replied, me too, I can't help it either, I've tried not to, but I do, I love you too, Naomi Harper, you are under my skin, lodged in my bones, running in my blood. And she laughed and said, not like you to be articulate in matters of the heart, Sam Moore, anyone would think you'd changed, and oh yes, he said, I have, I'm so glad we can talk, it's so much better this time, maybe we've been through a kind of catharsis, and she laughed and said, catharsis, what the hell does that mean,

Naomi's new place is small and modern, the front garden a neat rectangle of lawn, the tarmac driveway lined with orange physalis. He makes a note to tell her that the seed pods, Chinese lanterns as they are known, are highly toxic, even fatal. They will both have to be vigilant once Tommy starts to walk.

He presses the doorbell, nerves rising now. Checks his watch: 7.10 p.m. Perfect. It was Naomi who taught him that arriving ten minutes late was the polite thing to do. Too punctual and you risk finding the host still getting ready, too late and that's just rude. In one hand he has a bottle of her favourite Prosecco, in the other a bunch of pink tulips from the supermarket, cellophane removed and wrapped in pink tissue and brown paper by Joyce. Naomi can't stand super-market flowers – she says they are for cheapskates, but he didn't have time to call at the florist. This kind of thing used to set his nerves on edge – the fact that there were so many unwritten rules he didn't know about – but he is beginning to see that Naomi was always trying to help him get things *right.*

and he said, it means I love you, I love you, I just do, and then the sun came up and he thought he might explode.

He didn't say any of that. Sorry, that was me obsessing, sliding down the wall after he'd gone but stopping short of putting on 'Killing me Softly' and having a self-indulgent cry-along. What he actually said was that they were becoming close again, that they talked a lot on the phone.

'It's like Tommy's given us a new start,' he added. 'I'm actually going to hers tonight. For dinner.'

'Sounds like it's going great,' I said helplessly. More than anxiety for him, I'll admit I felt sad for me. When he was here with me and Betsy, it was always just so... easy. It was when I felt most happy, almost as if we were a family. 'So are you... are you guys back together?'

He'd just told me they were, for God's sake. In so many words. But I couldn't stop myself. I was shielding my face with my hand as if the sun was in my eyes. It wasn't.

'I guess so.' That lovely grin failed to be suppressed. 'Yes, I think we are.'

I can remember kicking at something that wasn't there on the front step. 'That's great. Good on you. That's great, really good.'

Sam told me later that as he walked away, he had the feeling I wasn't pleased but he didn't know why. Hardly surprising, he thought at the time. Miranda has only heard me say that things were grim with Naomi. Miranda doesn't know her like I do. She's worried for me. Good friends can be overprotective, he thought.

Miranda is a good friend.

The bright yellow door opens. His breath catches. She is wearing an off-the-shoulder top, the black line of either a bra or a camisole strap distracting him momentarily. The skin of her collarbone and neck shines in the porch light. Her eyes are smoky with black eye make-up, and her perfume drifts out to him. How, he thinks, how did I ever manage to attract this woman? As well as looking and smelling incredible, she is funny, clever, and now she is kind too. He wonders what she is thinking, whether she, like him, is thinking about their confessional words of love whispered to the hazy dawn.

Hopes she hasn't spotted the flowers aren't from a florist.

'You've shaved your beard off,' she says, grinning. 'Thank God! You look so much better – didn't I tell you you would?'

'Er, thanks. I brought you these.' He holds out the flowers. 'And this.' He hands her the bottle. 'I put it in the fridge, so it should still be cold.'

'Oh my God, well *done*! And it's my favourite. You remembered.'

I remember everything, he thinks. Though the bad stuff is fading like tail lights in fog.

Inside, the house smells of something spicy. Naomi never really cooked; she was always on a diet. So when she tells him she's made a lamb and apricot tagine, he fights to hide his surprise. The house is immaculate: smooth walls and skirtings, a dining table and chairs that look solid, expensive. There are paintings of landscapes, a field of flowers, an abstract in grey and cream tones, and on the mantelpiece, a framed photograph of Naomi and Tommy. The taste is more conventional than he remembers. More expensive perhaps. He wonders how she afforded it all... although didn't she say she'd been promoted? Did she? Her dad left her some money, she definitely said that. Her taste has evolved along with her. She has grown up, more than him, he thinks.

'It's so nice,' he says, though secretly he prefers the eclectic look of their old flat, the second-hand stuff she used to bring back for him to fix up. 'It's so... well appointed.'

'You sound like an estate agent.'

There is something of the old Naomi in her words, but when he glances at her, her face is warm. She was only joking; he sees it now in a way he realises he didn't before. *I was only joking!* she would say – constantly – when he was hurt by something she'd said.

Now, however, he joins her in the joke. 'Lovely open aspect and finished to a high spec.'

He takes in the two dark grey sofas, the brightly coloured scatter cushions, one embroidered with a queen bee in gold thread. The coffee table looks like it might be walnut. It occurs to him that he can't see anything from their old flat.

'I sold all our stuff,' she says as if she has read his thoughts, handing him a glass of Prosecco. 'I suppose I didn't want anything that reminded me of you.'

He shakes his head. 'I'm sorry.'

'Don't be. Come on – we've done our apologies.' She chinks his glass with her own and stares so intently into his eyes he feels himself blush. 'Here's to us. To you, me and little Tommy.'

'Can I see him?'

'If you're quiet.'

She asks him to take his shoes off, which he does, leaving them neatly by the front door. He follows her upstairs, both of them silent, their footsteps muted by a thick cream carpet. On the landing, she puts her finger to her lips and opens the door. He follows. Tommy is asleep in a large pine cot, arms up as if in triumph. He is so beautiful. A beautiful little chap.

'Dead to the world,' she whispers.

'Angel,' he whispers back, a little choked.

They are both leaning on the side of the cot, staring down at their boy. Like parents. Like a family. The room is warm and shadowy, Tommy's night light a soft pinkish glow. He dares to lay a hand on her arm. She responds, turning towards him, raising herself on tiptoes to kiss him deeply on the mouth. A tingling sensation spreads up from his feet. He pulls her to him and kisses her again, kisses her cheek, her neck, the hollow at her collarbone.

'We should eat,' she whispers when they break apart. 'I'm never up past ten these days.' She strokes his cheek before creeping out of the room. He waits, hears her soft footfalls fade down the stairs.

Tommy sighs. His lips smack, as if he is dreaming of milk. Sam takes in the sight of his baby boy: his high, rounded forehead, which he thinks now is like Joyce's; the golden brush of his eyelashes, his tiny mouth. He is too perfect. Sam feels the ache of it in his heart, an ache that is becoming more part of him every time he sees this little guy.

'Goodnight, kid.' He kisses his fingertips and touches them to Tommy's soft head.

Downstairs, Naomi is lifting a casserole dish out of the oven. There are cooking implements stuck to a magnetised strip beneath the cupboards, a cream fifties-style kettle and matching toaster. A framed logo on the wall says: *Home Is Where the Heart Is*.

Naomi would have laughed at something like that before. But she is not laughing now. She is telling him to sit down, asking him if he'd like a glass of red or more fizz. He doesn't want to admit that Joyce dropped him off at the end of the road, that he was half expecting he might stay, is still interpreting her remark about going to bed at ten. Does she mean with him? It didn't seem like that's what she meant. And sure enough, despite the delicious food and wine, their renewed pledges of love, the lazy trail of her fingertips down his arm, at half past nine she checks her watch and tells him she's sorry to be such a square, but she'll have to kick him out in half an hour.

'Don't you want me to stay?' he asks.

She looks at him, her gaze hardening a fraction. 'Is that what you thought?'

'Sorry. Not to presume, just, you know, from wanting to. I want to, I mean. I want to be with you.'

She smiles, and his heart unclenches. 'I want to be with you too. I do. But I can't just flick myself on like a switch, you know? Not after everything. I need time. And I need... I need guarantees, I suppose. How do I know you're not just nostalgic? Or just fancy the idea of having a family? Or just plain horny?' She laughs, but the laughter dies quickly. 'I know you love me. And I love you. I just... I've got to be so careful. Tommy and me... we've been through so much, and I can't...' She presses her fingertips to her eyes.

'I'm so sorry. And I get it. I never met a single one of my mum's boyfriends, didn't know she even had any until Joyce told me. I do love the idea of a family, but only with you and Tommy and maybe one day another little one, who knows? And I am remembering all the good times, but only because we had them, didn't we? We were good before we were bad, and I think we've both learnt to be good and stay good.

Better. And I get you need guarantees. More than a nursery. More than... than an upcycled changing station.'

He is on his knees before he even realises what he's doing. He takes both her hands in his. 'Naomi Harper, will you marry me? Let's do it, just you and me. No one needs to know. Nomes? Marry me. Please.'

She begins to laugh. Breaks one of her hands from his and strokes his hair.

'Nutter,' she says.

'Is that a yes?'

'It's a... Sod it, it's a yes.'

'You don't feel pressured?'

'No.'

'Sure?'

'Yes!' She giggles. 'But you're still not staying over!'

He laughs, kisses her knuckles one by one. 'OK! I'm going!'

'Go on, get lost!'

'I will. Look at me. I'm so going.' He stands, kisses her and walks out of the kitchen, calling over his shoulder: 'D'you know what? I don't even want to stay. Nah. Very happy to go home. In fact, I'm exhausted.' He fakes a yawn.

They are both laughing – a little hysterically.

On the doorstep, one hand gripping the front door, he asks: 'Are we mad?'

'Everyone is.' She kisses him. 'Let's be mad together. And let's make it work this time, eh?'

'Yes! This time we'll make it work.'

CHAPTER 30

Dear Sam,

I wanted you to stay tonight, honestly I did. But there are reasons why I can't let you in just like that. Like I said, I need guarantees, and boy, did you deliver! To be honest, things are moving faster than I thought they would, but then you're a typical Virgo male, aren't you? You love the chase, but I can tell you're coming from the right place. I know you love me – you just needed reminding of that, and deep down, I don't think you'll leave me, not again, not with Tommy on the scene now. I can see how your face lights up at the sight of him. And that makes me happy, because I need us to be a proper family. You see, when it comes to Tommy, I need to be so, so careful.

My therapist, Dawn, says boundaries allow us to love others while still hanging on to ourselves. Being Pisces, I struggle, but I have to learn to lay down my boundaries because I'm the one who was left high and dry. I'm nervous as hell, Sam. I think these last few weeks you've really come to understand how humiliating you leaving was for me, especially right at the start of lockdown. You couldn't have been crueller really. Talk about a double whammy. Ironically, I must be one of the few people in the world glad we all had to stay in. No gossip. No one looking at me and judging. No one dropping into casual conversation that they'd heard we'd split up, how was I managing, eyeballing the baby, waiting for me to explain so they could go home and warm their hands on Naomi Harper and how she was trash just like the rest of her family.

So I avoid Bridport. I take Toms over to Seaton or Beer. There's hardly anyone on the beach these days. And if one day I do see someone I know, I'll pretend I haven't seen them or that I don't recognise them. I can't be bothered with any of it. I want to move away really. Start again. There are other great places to live besides Dorset.

I wonder what will happen now you've asked me to marry you. I wonder if you'll book the register office or if you'll leave all that to me.

I'm waiting, Sam.

Surprise me.

CHAPTER 31

It is only once he's outside that he remembers he doesn't have the van. Only once he begins to walk down Naomi's driveway towards the path that he realises how tipsy he is. Naomi kept topping him up. Was she a bit drunk too? Her glass seemed always to be full, but he has no memory of her drinking, and now he thinks about it, an uneasy feeling rises in him. Has he made a fool of himself? So desperate not to lose her and Toms, he has gone and asked her to *marry* him. But now that the cold air has hit him, the hot elation is cooling by the second. Was she humouring him? Will she bat it off tomorrow as drunken silliness?

He stops. There's a bitter taste in his mouth; he's dehydrated. On the cul-de-sac, yellow windows make lanterns of the houses. Everyone is home. Home is where people feel safe these days.

He walks on. It takes him twenty minutes to reach the bus terminus, and when he gets there, he sees he has another twenty-five minutes to wait. He thinks about calling a cab, getting it to drop him off on Cobb Road so Joyce doesn't catch him wasting money. But doesn't.

By the time the bus arrives, he is shivering, sobering up, the sleeves of his jacket pulled over his hands, chin tucked into his shirt collar. The road back to Lyme dips and rises, the countryside hulking black shadows, more cardboard silhouettes. The road is like his mind, he thinks, a little drunkenly. Dipping, rising, his thoughts dark and flimsy.

By the time he descends at Holmbush car park, he has resolved to prove himself to Naomi. He must man up, solidify, become... *substantial.* He can't lose her, not this time. He can't lose the family that has fallen into his lap like a late-autumn plum – sweeter for thinking the tree was bare. He will buy her an engagement ring. He already has her ring size from when he bought her a silver ring from the gift shop on Coombe Street, providing that finger is the same width on her left hand. What else can he do?

Think, Sam.

She mentioned once that him doing Wednesdays saved on childcare.

He hits his forehead with the flat of his palm. 'Childcare!'

He hasn't even thought about the cost and is filled with new admiration for her, for never once mentioning the expenses she has had to take on alone. He has never really had to think about that stuff, and he curses his ignorance. He will rectify this tomorrow. Whatever comes of his tipsy proposal, they should share the costs of raising Tommy equally. That way, even if she changes her mind, she won't be able to extricate herself so easily. She won't be able to cut Tommy off from him ever again. She won't be able to stop him from seeing his son.

At the house, the living-room lights are on. Joyce stays up late, later since lockdown. She has only just begun to see her friends occasionally in the daytime, outdoors and at a distance, but still she stays strong – good-humoured, stoical, her absence of self-pity a constant lesson to him.

She is reading. The sweet-almond aroma of Amaretto reaches him as he bends to kiss her on the cheek. Marvin Gaye sings quietly from the CD player.

'Nightbird,' he says. 'It's nearly midnight.'

'I was FaceTiming Harriet. The choirmaster, you know? She's wondering about getting us back practising again. Socially distanced sea shanties, she says. She sings socially distanced sea shanties on the seashore.' She chuckles, then raises her eyebrows, searching his face. 'You look a bit... troubled.'

'No, I'm good.' His heart is beating faster. It feels for some reason like what he has to tell her is bad news. 'I've... I've asked Naomi to marry me. And she said yes.'

In the magnifying lenses of her glasses, Joyce's eyes round, fishlike and strange. 'You've asked her to *marry* you?'

He nods, powerless to stop the grin that is spreading across his face despite the look of shock on his gran's. 'And she said yes! At least, I think she did.'

'What do you mean, you think she did?' Her tone is incredulous. And a little hard. 'Either she did or she didn't, love.'

'She did,' he says, flustered. 'I'd had quite a bit to drink, but she definitely said yes. I mean, I wasn't drunk, just... No, it was clear. She was surprised, I think, but she seemed pleased. I just had this horrible thought on the way home that I'd ring her tomorrow and she'd have no memory of it.'

'Why on earth would you think that?'

'No idea.' He shrugs. Sometimes Naomi didn't remember things, things he was pretty sure he'd said. But that's not why. Is it?

Under the bay window, the old cast-iron radiator bangs.

Joyce always switches the heating off half an hour before she goes to bed. She says she likes to listen to the sighs and grunts of the house falling asleep, but they both know it is because she is frugal.

'Are you... are you pleased?' he asks.

She is blinking as if she has something in her eye, and when she speaks, it is to the fire. 'It's not for me to say, love. If you're happy, I'm happy, but isn't it a bit *soon*?'

'Probably. But it's like we've never been apart in some ways. Except that, having been apart, we've both had the chance to reflect. So in a way it's better than the first time.' He reaches for her hand, squeezes it. 'We don't need a party. I'm not going to wait until all the restrictions have lifted. I mean, who knows? They're talking about another lockdown come winter and I've... I think I've realised what I want the rest of my life to look like. I'm going to book the register office tomorrow.'

Joyce puts her free hand over his, smiles when he places his own on top. But says nothing. From the speakers, Marvin Gaye asks them what's going on, over and over.

'I'll still come and see you all the time.' The words feel sad and somehow final, and he rushes to temper them. 'Naomi was saying over dinner that she's sick of Bridport. Maybe I can persuade her to move here. We can try for another baby, a sister or brother for Tommy! Another great-grandchild for you!'

'Oh, love! Slow down.'

He laughs. 'Sorry. You're right. I do need to chill out. She said yes, but she's still... she's like a cat that won't come out from under a chair or something.' He glances at Joyce, longing for her to speak again, but she seems lost in contemplation, staring at their hands on his leg. 'I'll miss you. I'll miss us living together. This last year...'

She withdraws her hands from his and reaches for her nightcap. 'Oh, you've been held back far too long by this damn bug. It's time you started living again. Living your life! And if you're sure...'

'I'm sure. One hundred per cent. It's going to be so different this time, totally different. I have a good feeling about this.'

But does he? As he climbs the stairs to bed, his gut clenches with something old, something he can't name. Insecurity, he thinks. Naomi is being so careful, as if afraid. Fear too. Is he picking up on his own fears or her fears about him? The other night, she reminded him of the time he put his fist through a window during an argument. There was another time when she wouldn't stop shouting, going on and on about something he'd done or, more likely, hadn't done. He slammed his hand against the kitchen cupboard door and just... roared at her. And she stopped dead. She stopped shouting and seemed to shrink, backing away from him, making him feel instantly guilty. She hid herself in their room. He had to talk to her through the door, apologise over and over, persuade her to come back out.

Is it *himself*, this familiar uneasy feeling? His fear of her ability to make him behave in ways he has never behaved with anyone else? Perhaps. Was he... in those moments was he *abusive*? He would never have hit her, never. But she didn't know that. And she didn't *make* him shatter the glass pane with his fist. No one can make us do anything. We are responsible for our own actions, that's what Joyce always says. He needs to calm down. He needs to hear her better, learn to talk rationally about the kinds of problems all couples have instead of feeling persecuted, going into himself and finding only the inarticulate rage of victimhood. When Naomi is cross, he needs to listen. And now that she has agreed to marry him, he must do everything in his power to take her fears about him away. He has to get her to look at him and see only safety, her future, her home: Sam, Naomi and Tommy. And if it all works out, the children yet to come. Her family. His family.

He opens WhatsApp and writes:

Am so happy you said yes. I'll organise everything. We can have a party once the world returns to normal, if that's what you want. But in the meantime, I'm going to start paying my share for Tommy. Let's agree a figure. I want you to know I'm a safe bet. I'm here for ever. I love you. Always did, always will. S xx

CHAPTER 32

Joyce stares into the fire, now no more than one glowing, blackened log. The air cools at the back of her neck. There is no way she can sleep now, not after what he has told her, no way, José. She pulls the throw from the arm of the sofa and wraps it around herself. It is an effort, her shoulders stiff; she can't reach back like she used to. Can't touch her toes either, though she can't remember when she stopped being able to. Ageing: there's no stopping it, no controlling it.

There are so many things she can't stop. So much she can't control.

CHAPTER 33

Wednesday comes. Naomi messages to say she's taking the day off, to celebrate their engagement, so Sam is even more excited than usual. He has spent Monday and Tuesday keeping the news under wraps from the boys. He can't risk telling anyone. Naomi is as fragile as a blown eggshell. He doesn't want people she hasn't seen for over a year coming up and congratulating her before it's even official; she'd run a mile.

She arrives a little later than usual and dressed in casual clothes. He greets her at the door, kissing her deeply on the mouth and holding her tight.

'Hey,' she says, and pokes him playfully in the chest. She does not mention their engagement.

'Hey, you.' Nor does he.

Joyce, however, does.

'I believe congratulations are in order?' she says as they enter the kitchen.

Naomi giggles and nods, blushes adorably. 'Yeah.'

'Well, congratulations.' Joyce smiles but does not

approach Naomi or make any kind of move towards a hug or even a peck on the cheek.

Sam feels a small cloud of resentment bloom in his chest but says nothing. Besides, Naomi is giggling again, saying only: 'Aw, thanks. Thanks, Joyce.'

The silence that follows lasts a beat too long. Sam suggests they take Tommy around Langmoor Gardens, and Naomi agrees. Once out of Joyce's orbit, he can feel her relax a little, and they chat easily as they stroll, sitting together on a bench to give Toms his milk, then wandering out of the gardens at the top of Broad Street. Toms falls asleep in his buggy. They walk together down the hill, grab a takeaway coffee from the Whole Hog, continue slowly down and double back along Marine Parade, meandering past the harbour, around the chalets, and back up Cobb Road to the house.

As they step inside, Joyce appears in the hallway and announces she has made vegetarian fajitas for lunch. Sam takes this as a peace offering, though there has been no official declaration of war. They make polite conversation as they eat. No mention is made of the wedding, which hovers somewhere between a taboo and an open secret.

After lunch, Joyce remarks how sunny it is and says she's going outside to plant vegetables. Instead of seeming pleased at being left alone with Sam, Naomi offers to help. It is all Sam can do not to gape open-mouthed at her and say, *What? You? Get your hands dirty?* And when he glances at Joyce, he can see she too is taken aback.

'If you'd like to,' she says, the trace of a smile in her voice. 'Follow me.'

While Tommy dozes in his pram in the shade, the three of them work. Naomi borrows a pair of Joyce's wellies, not even caring that they're old green Dunlop ones and don't go with her outfit.

'Ta-da!' she says, mock-posing outside the shed, making Sam and Joyce laugh.

Armed with the spade from the tool shed, she digs like a Land Girl. Joyce lifts the plugs of compost carefully from the pots, lowers them into the damp ground, the roots white and strange in the black soil. Sam fills the holes, presses the earth firm around the tender stalks. He has a sense of the three of them locked together in the work; the concentration they share in this simple task eases him. The sun shines warm on his neck. He feels someone watching him, and when he looks up, Naomi is standing over him, one hand resting on the spade. Their eyes meet. She smiles, and he wonders when, when in his whole life, he has been as happy as in this precise moment.

Joyce leans back from her kneeling position, pulling the gardening gloves from her hands.

'I think it's time for a brew,' she announces. It takes her several attempts to stand, but she is good-humoured, tells them she's set solid.

Alone with Naomi, Sam tips her face to his and kisses her.

'I'm so happy,' he says.

'Me too. I could get used to this.'

Joyce returns a while later, mugs clanking on the tray gripped tight in her knobbly hands. When she passes Naomi her tea and calls her *love*, Sam tries not to notice the flutter of hope in his heart.

The three of them sit on the old bench drinking tea in the sunshine and eating the Victoria sponge Joyce made this morning.

'I could get used to this,' Joyce says, and for the first time directs her smile at Naomi, who covers her mouth with her hand.

'Didn't I just say that?' she cries to Sam, her voice filled with glee. 'Didn't I just say that, two minutes ago? I literally said, I could get used to this!'

CHAPTER 34

Towards four o'clock, Joyce is tidying away the gardening tools when Naomi taps her on the shoulder. From her face, Joyce can see she's asked something, but the words are inaudible over the roar of Sam using the sit-on mower over on the main lawn.

'I should probably be getting back,' Naomi says loudly, thumbing over her shoulder. 'He has his tea at five.'

Joyce tries to straighten, presses her hands to the ache in her lower back. 'I've already defrosted some chicken and vegetables for him.'

'Are you sure?'

'Of course. Unless you want to skedaddle? You can take it with you if you like?' The lawnmower stops; Joyce's last question comes out too loud, making both of them laugh.

When their laughter stops, Naomi gives her the warmest smile, and Joyce feels herself thaw. She has put on a good show of friendliness towards the girl, but now the smile she returns is genuine. Naomi has worked so hard this afternoon: not once complaining, not even when she stumbled and got mud on her lovely trousers. She and Sam are so natural together, like an old married couple, and if they think she didn't see them kissing from the kitchen window, they've got another think coming. There have been moments when she could scarcely believe this was the same pouting manipulator she met years ago. There have been moments when she hasn't trusted this change. And as for the wedding, well, it's a rush, but it's a rush she'll have to go along with if she doesn't want to face a very lonely old age indeed.

And in all of this, hasn't Naomi brought with her the gift of new and precious life?

'I'll go and heat it up.' Naomi turns to head towards the house but stops and turns back to Joyce. Something hesitant flickers across her features, as if she is about to ask for a favour. 'Would you... would you like me to tidy up here while you feed him?'

A flush of pleasure rises warm in Joyce's cheeks. 'I would, love. I would indeed.'

She takes off her gloves and places them on the ground next to the Tomorite, the slug pellets and the garden wire. She digs in her pocket for the keys.

'Big one is the shed,' she says, handing them over. 'Little 'un is the back door. When you're done, just pop them—'

'Under the big geranium pot?'

Joyce smiles. 'You remembered.'

Joyce is already testing Tommy's food against the back of her hand, sitting beside the high chair that Sam bought off eBay and repaired, when Naomi appears, sudden and stealthy as a cat.

'Are you all right for a second?' she asks. 'I was just going to gather my stuff.'

'Of course. Off you go, love.'

Joyce spoons the mushed-up food into Tommy's mouth. She can hear Naomi upstairs, her light footsteps, her keen, swift movements. The next moment, the back door creaks open and she calls out to Sam that she's heading off in a few minutes. Guiltily, nosily, Joyce stands up so she can see out of the back window. Sam and Naomi are embracing, her head resting on his chest.

A shout breaks into her thoughts. Tommy is staring at her, indignant.

'Sorry, little man! Nonna not concentrating? Nonna is knackered, I can tell you that much. Nonna will be having a deep soaky bath, yes she will, yes she will, a deep soaky bath with bubbabubbabubbles!' She leans in and rubs her nose against his; he squeals with delight then opens his mouth for another spoonful. 'Nonna loves little Tommy, doesn't she? Doesn't she? Little Tommy is the light of her life, yes he is, yes he is.'

'You're so good with him.' It is Naomi. From the garden to the kitchen in seconds. She strokes her son's head, kisses him tenderly. 'You love your nonna, don't you, Tom-Toms? Eh? Love your nonna to the moon and back, don't you?'

Yes, Joyce thinks, studying the girl a moment. It is time to let go of old hurts. It is time to forgive. It is time for a new start – for all of them.

CHAPTER 35

That night, Sam is sitting up in bed reading *A Man Called Ove* when there's a knock on his bedroom door.

'Who is it?' he calls out with a smile, laying the book on his lap.

'Lady Margaret Thatcher, ghost of.'

'Enter.'

Joyce limps in, stiff after the afternoon's hard work. She is wearing her dark pink silk pyjamas with a paler pink scarf and is holding something in her hand, something small. She hobbles over to the bed and sits down next to him, the mattress barely registering her birdlike weight.

She hands him a midnight-blue velvet jewellery box. 'You'll be wanting this.'

'What is it?' But he knows what it is. Knows what it means. Already he can feel heat climbing his neck, his face, and when he opens the box, it is as he has guessed. A single diamond, clasped in a platinum claw on a platinum ring. He knows the details of this ring because Joyce has shown it to him before, and when she speaks, it is to reiterate what she said years ago.

'I said when you met the love of your life,' she says, 'I said, didn't I, that this would be yours to give her. I told you that, didn't I?'

'You did.'

'Well, now you've met her, and I don't think I'll be going on Tinder any time soon.'

'Joyce,' he says, plucking it from the velvet mount.

'It might need resizing.'

'Thank you. Thank you so much. Not just for this, but, you know, for all of it.'

'Don't be daft. It was always yours. You just needed the right woman to wear it for you.'

Excitement seizes him; he checks his watch. 'It's only half past ten. I should drive round there right now.'

She chuckles. 'Break in and leave it on her pillow like the Milk Tray man.'

'Who?'

'The Milk Tray... forget it. An old advert, fella dressed in black, breaks into the lady's house and leaves a box of chocolates on her pillow.'

'Ah. Actually, no. I think I need to respect her boundaries.'

Joyce lowers her chin to her chest, bottom lip pushed up against top. 'Boundaries? What happened to romance? Bit of spontaneity, surprise? You can borrow the MG.'

You never surprise me, Sam. You never just book something and whisk me away.

Old words, rising like mist.

'You're right,' he says, throwing his legs out from under the duvet. 'Sod boundaries!' He kisses her on both cheeks. 'Don't wait up!'

Half an hour later, in pyjama top and jeans, he parks Joyce's MG on the road outside Naomi's house. He is about to get out but finds himself still in the car, one hand on the door handle. Now that he's here, he feels a lot less sure than he did when he set off. At the sight of a pale grey Volvo he doesn't recognise on the drive, his chest tightens. It is late, so late, and he has come here without asking.

He gets out, walks the short length of pavement to the driveway. Downstairs, faint orange lines glow between the blinds.

He backs up, throws his eyes up to a bedroom window – no more than a yellow sliver between drawn curtains. It is after eleven. Naomi told him she always turns in by ten. If she's in bed or preparing to go to bed, this is an invasion of her space. Actually, it's an invasion of her space regardless of what she's doing. He should have texted. Joyce's suggestion that this would be a romantic gesture is old-fashioned. Turning up in the middle of the night and breaking into women's houses is not what men do anymore; he doubts they ever did. By today's standards, the Milk Tray man was a stalker, a creep. This was a bad idea.

He is about to walk away when the front door opens.

But it is not Naomi.

'Can I help you?' It is a woman with reddish hair who looks about the same age as Naomi.

'Oh,' he says. 'Sorry. Sorry to disturb you. I was just...'

The woman is looking at him suspiciously. Something is off here. Something is wrong.

He raises a hand. 'I was looking for Naomi, my... Sorry, I've just realised it's much later than I thought. Sorry.' He is already backing away, but the woman appears to relax, her posture loosening against the door jamb.

'Naomi's out with her sister.'

'Oh.' The word is a sigh. The woman at the door is the

babysitter. Of course. The Volvo is hers. God, he's a paranoid idiot. 'Gotcha. Sorry. I'll get out of your hair. Sorry!'

'Shall I tell her who called?'

'Sure. Sure, yeah. It's Sam. Sam Moore. Actually, just Sam. She'll know who it is. Thanks. Sorry for the interruption. Goodnight.'

He drives home cringing. Puts the radio on loud to try and drown his thoughts, but up they swim to the surface. Naomi will get the message from her babysitter, but she won't understand why he's come over so late, will have no idea he came to give her his grandmother's engagement ring, something of such deep significance, a tangible emblem not only of his love but of Joyce's acceptance, a welcoming of Naomi into the family. No, all she will know is that he was loitering outside her house late at night, didn't text, didn't even ring the doorbell.

What the hell were you thinking? she will say. *You can't just turn up in the middle of the night like that – that's so weird.*

Halfway home, unable to keep his breathing steady, he pulls into the forecourt of a service station. Makes himself calm down. Thinks about calling Miranda to ask her what the hell he should do, but no, it's late, too late – he doesn't want to wake her or Betsy. Breathe, Sam. Get it together. You just need to pre-empt the babysitter's message, head it off at the pass. Should have done that the second you got in the car.

But when he pulls his phone from his jacket pocket, his heart shrinks. There is a message from Naomi already.

Cheryl said you stopped by at 11?? Am out with Jo. What did you want?

'Oh God,' he says aloud. 'Shit, shit, shit.' Cheryl, of course. He should've put two and two together.

Sorry! he writes. *I wanted to give you something, but it's OK, it can wait. Romantic gesture fail, lol. Love you. Xxx*

Transfixed by anxiety, he waits. Seconds pass. His guts twist.

'Please reply,' he whispers, phone held close to his face. Almost yelps when he sees the rolling dots. Ten seconds pass. Twenty. Forty. The dots vanish. He waits. The dots return, ebbing like waves. Finally the message flashes up, but it is short, so much shorter than the wait promised.

OK. See you Wednesday.

'Is that all?' This, he shouts – shouts at the phone, alone in the dark shell of the car, gripped by a spike of almost overwhelming rage.

There is no kiss. There is no humour, no warmth. No *speak tomorrow*. No *goodnight*. No asking what the gift was or why he would drive half an hour to her door in the middle of the night. There is not even any anger, no *what the hell?* No *that's a bit weird, Sam, don't you think?* There is only this... this businesslike response, as if he has called by in the late afternoon to drop off a book he has borrowed and, finding her out, left it on the porch.

Another spike, as fleeting as the last: resentment. He drove all that way. He is still in his pyjamas, for God's sake. He is hardly a stranger, after all, and she replied curtly without even wondering what the romantic gesture might be. He was wrong about the anger too – there is anger all over that reply, of course there is. It is an all-too-familiar punishment: the cold shoulder.

Staring at his phone in his hand, it is like trying to decode a thousand-year-old message carved into a stone tablet. He remembers a similar confusion: the time he brought the wrong flavour crisps back from the supermarket. Naomi had asked for lightly salted, but when he got to the shop, there was only salt and balsamic vinegar, Thai chilli or chicken and thyme. He stood for whole minutes, frozen by indecision. Surely salt and vinegar was the nearest to lightly salted? Salt in the title? No? Or was chicken and thyme better, less sharp, equally savoury? Chilli? No. Yes. No. Too spicy? He can barely believe the way his thoughts ran so out of control back then, is aghast at the person he was, fretting over... what? A packet of bloody crisps! And even now he can remember the dim sense that feeling like that over something so small was wrong, that something in him had broken, though as yet it had not occurred to him that Naomi herself was the architect of this damage.

His knuckles whiten on the steering wheel. No. That is not who she is anymore. It is not who *he* is. It is not even an objective take on what has just happened, nor what happened years ago. He was too sensitive, still is. Naomi always told him that. Obviously he used to feel hurt when-ever she said it, but of course he could not protest without proving her right. Instead he swallowed down his injury like blood in saliva after a hard right hook to the jaw.

But he has grown up a lot since then. They both have.

The night of the crisps, when he got home having finally plumped for salt and vinegar, she pulled a face and told him she didn't like salt and vinegar, that the Thai chilli would have been better, but oh well, it was too late now. She sat in silence and watched him eat the crisps. Did not take even one, sipped her vodka and Diet Coke through thin lips.

So what? She was cross, that was all. People are allowed to be cross. She didn't shout and scream, didn't wrestle him into a headlock. The nausea that rose in him under her cold gaze was an overreaction; he can see that now. And she was entitled to her feelings too. It wasn't against him *personally*. He should have been stronger. He should have *soothed* her, should have stood up to her. He is a man after all. Women need strong men, not indecisive, oversensitive fools.

But he wasn't strong. He didn't tackle it. He left. And in leaving caused her so much damage, damage he now has to heal. His job is to make her feel safe again, and instead he has called on her house in the middle of the night like a weirdo, frightened her off just when things were better than they have ever been. She will feel watched, checked up on.

How did he ever believe himself some romantic hero? How, before, did he ever believe *himself* the wronged party?

I hate what you turn me into with your big trampling feet.

'Fool!' He bangs the steering wheel with the flat of his hand. 'Fucking idiot!'

Sure, is all he can think to reply. It is a fraction of what he longs to write. Wednesday is a *week* away; there is no way he can cope without seeing her before then. What about the weekend? Friday? Tomorrow? He can't ask now. He needs time to make up for his mistake. He adds a kiss and sends the message. But when he writes a second text with *PS I love you*, he finds he hasn't the courage to send it.

He restarts the MG. Tomorrow he will book the register office. Decisive action. He can meet her from work and... No. No! Get a grip! Commitment, yes, but with space. He can maybe take her out on Saturday night, offer to pay for the babysitter as well as a restaurant, if they can find one open, yes; and the money for Tommy, they can get that organised too. He will dig himself out of this. She has shown him how much she has changed; it's up to him now to prove to her that the change is on both sides.

CHAPTER 36

Dear Sam,

I won't lie, I felt a bit freaked out when you came round in the middle of the night. And when you replied to my message, I showed Jo and she said, Oh my God! Seriously, though, Sam, what the hell? You don't drive to a woman's house in the middle of the night without warning. That is weird, honestly. I never thought you'd do something like that – you used to be so respectful.

When I got back, Cheryl told me you didn't even say why you were there or whether it was urgent or anything. She said she found you loitering around the front door. You can't do that. I don't want her thinking I'm with a lunatic.

I'm curious though. Why did you drive over? Booty call, maybe? All this sexual tension driving you a bit bonkers? I think the women in those period dramas were on to something, you know. No one keeps anyone waiting anymore. I know I never have. But it's amazing how much control it gives you. And now I'm thinking maybe I always gave myself too quickly, you know, before? Maybe that's why men never appreciated me enough, treated me like dirt. Maybe that's why you left – maybe I should've held back more.

If I wait, will it bond us together more deeply in the end? Will it make us a closer family?

CHAPTER 37

The next morning, he texts Miranda to tell her he'll be late at the site, and, as soon as nine o'clock comes, calls Lyme Regis Register Office. He explains he wants a small, intimate wedding. The friendly woman on the phone tells him he can book the Guildhall; they can be married overlooking the bay. It will be three to four hundred pounds for the ceremony, plus a further fee for the registrar. If he wants something even smaller, he can contact the Dorset Registration Service and arrange a ceremony at their offices in Dorchester. This will cost him much less.

'It's not about the money,' he says. 'It's more about the privacy and... We would want it to happen as soon as possible.'

'All right,' she says but falls silent.

'End of June?'

'End of June, we could do you a Monday. Fridays are all booked. Wednesdays a bit hit and miss. A Monday any good to you?'

'Would I need witnesses?'

'You'd need two witnesses, but we can provide those for a fee.'

He tells her he'll get back to her, calls Dorset Registration Service. Another friendly woman tells him it will be forty-six pounds to be married and that the ceremony would take place in Dorset Historic Centre in Dorchester. Witnesses are thirty-four pounds each. Again, he thanks the woman and tells her he'll get back to her.

He closes the call and sighs. It's so hard to know which type of ceremony Naomi would prefer. He wanted to return to her with something concrete, to make up for last night. He would book the Guildhall immediately, of course he would. But it might be overkill. When they spoke about it on Wednesday, Naomi said she wanted something super private. Dorchester would be exactly that, plus he might even be able to find a hotel for the night.

But then the Guildhall is so much nicer, so iconic... and he could book a hotel somewhere nearby – maybe even see if they can get a room at the Pig on the Beach over in Studland.

A hotel. Thick white bedlinen, champagne, room service. Himself, peeling Naomi's dress from her lovely shoulders, placing his lips on her collarbone.

His breath staggers. They have yet to spend a night together or share anything beyond a kiss.

And in that moment, a flash of inspiration comes to him.

'Yes,' he whispers to himself. 'Yes.'

While the thought almost makes him wince in frustration, Naomi might appreciate it if they did things the old-fashioned way, like... like a courtship. For two people who already know each other intimately, it would prove his respect for the boundaries she talks about, plus it would give their wedding night a real sense of anticipation. It would make their first night together extra special: a fresh start, almost a rebirth.

Hell, it would be almost like the first time.

(Except he would know what he was doing a bit more.)

It is not indecisive to ask Naomi what her preference is. It is considerate. He is simply involving her in the choice. Yes. Right. Good. A good pretext to call her. He will call her later, after work.

'Nomes,' he says. 'It's me.' His stomach feels hollow. He has not been able to eat very much this evening.

But, 'Hey,' is all she says, her tone familiar, warm, as if no disaster has occurred, no disaster whatsoever.

'Sorry about last night,' he says. 'I shouldn't have come over without texting.'

'Oh my God, yeah, what was that about? Sorry, I was a bit worse for wear.' Still her tone is neutral. Amused even.

He sighs, so hugely she asks if he's OK.

'I was worried I'd upset you. I know you said about boundaries, and that was—'

'What? Don't be silly. I mean, I'd prefer it if you let me know first, obviously, but I wasn't *upset* – it's not a big deal. I was a bit hammered when you texted, you know what Jo's like, and my tolerance is shot these days. Did you say you had a gift for me or something?'

She is not angry. She never was. He has wound himself up into a state, but now he could dance, he could, and in fact he does, there in his gran's hallway. 'I do have something for you. Something a bit special actually. In fact, can I come over later? I could try again.'

'I'm intrigued,' she says, giggling. 'Jo's here at the

moment and I've just asked if she wants to stay for dinner, so...'

'Maybe at the weekend then?'

'Sure. I can't really afford a sitter, not twice in one week, but you could come over on Saturday? Do you mind?'

'I can pay for the sitter if you want to go out?'

A pause. 'That's so sweet, but the whole mask thing gets me down, and half the places are shut with people isolating. We can order a takeout if you like? I can let you pay for that. Cheeky Indian? We love a cheeky Indian, don't we?'

He laughs. 'Deal. We can discuss money for Toms. You're good at that stuff, and there's... there's something else I need to run by you too.'

He closes the call, feels boneless with relief. Saturday night, they will sort out the practical side of things, really take things forward. Even if she asks him to stay, he will say, *No, let's wait. Let's wait until we're married like they did in the olden days, like characters in a novel by...*

Jane Austen! He hasn't read her himself, but he knows from Joyce that *Persuasion* is the one set here in Lyme Regis. It's the perfect gift for the perfect proposal, which he will repeat, properly this time.

'Perfect,' he says aloud. 'Just perfect.'

CHAPTER 38

On Saturday, late afternoon, he calls in at the bookshop on Marine Parade, where the nice assistant whose name badge says *Tamsin* tells him he's made a good choice before dashing to find him the paperback. As she rings up the purchase, he tells her it's for his ex-girlfriend, that they are back together. Tamsin smiles and replies that this makes the book extra perfect because it is about a second chance in love, which makes him glow to the roots of his hair.

He arrives at Naomi's at six, loaded with two large bottles of Singha beer, the book and the ring. Naomi is wearing loose black velvety trousers and a casual grey sweatshirt that falls off one shoulder. She has pinned up her hair and he kisses her on the neck.

'You smell amazing,' he says, in that moment resolving to pick up some of her favourite perfume: Chanel No. 5, which she once told him she wore because it was Marilyn Monroe's favourite. It'll have to be a small bottle. There's not much left in his account after buying the cot and all the other stuff. He might have to borrow some cash from Joyce.

'Good timing,' Naomi is saying, leading him into the house. 'I was about to take Tommy up for his bath, but you can do it on your own if you like?'

'Cool.'

In the living room, Tommy is sitting on his play mat surrounded by bright plastic toys. At the sight of Sam, he raises his arms and groans to be picked up.

'Hey there, little chap.' Sam lifts him, kisses his cheek.

When he looks at Naomi, she is smiling at him. 'I brought beers,' he tells her, handing her the carrier bag. 'A-a-and... dinner is arriving at eight. I ordered tandoori lamb chops and steamed rice for you, chicken jalfrezi and Peshwari naan, which you will nick half of, for me. Poppadums, all the chutneys and a side order of sag aloo. Did I miss anything?'

She laughs. 'Oh my God, you really remembered! Do you want a beer now?'

'I'll just have one,' he says. 'I've got the van.'

'Oh.' For some reason, she looks disappointed. He follows her into the kitchen, where she fetches glasses from the cupboard. On his hip, Tommy drives a truck round his chest, making a brum-brumming sound. Sam closes his eyes a second. I am with my future wife, he thinks. My baby son is driving a plastic truck over my chest. It is nothing, but it is everything.

'Are you OK?' he asks.

'It's fine, I just...'

'Did you... I mean, did you want me to stay?'

'I do, I *really* do, I just don't want Tommy waking up and finding you here. I'm not changing my mind at all, but he's still my number one. I mean, he always will be – you do understand that, don't you? I'd expect him to be your number one too. More important than me even.'

He nods. 'Yeah. I guess. I hadn't thought about that. I love both of you. In fact, can you hold him a sec?'

'Sure.' She takes Tommy from him. 'He weighs a ton, doesn't he? Sam? What are you doing?'

He's kneeling – for the second time – that's what he's doing.

'The other night,' he says, gazing up at the flyaway strands of her hair dancing against the setting sun, 'when I drove over, I wanted to give you this.' He digs in his pocket, pulls out the box and opens it.

Her free hand flies to her mouth. 'Oh my God!'

'This was Joyce's. She gave it to me after you left on Wednesday and I'm giving it to you. Nomes, I know we've had our ups and downs, but it would make me the happiest man on the planet if you would agree to marry me and wear this ring as a symbol of my love and my intention to make you and Tommy my family for ever. What do you say?'

'Oh, Sam.' She bends to kiss him and he rises to meet her lips with his own. When he pulls away, he sees that her eyes are filled with tears. 'Of course I'll marry you, Sam Moore. Already said so, didn't I?'

'I suppose it's taken me two goes to believe it.'

She lays a hand on his cheek. 'Funny old Sam.'

'Ah! But what would you say if I told you I've already called the register office? If we marry on a Monday, they can fit us in at the end of next month.'

Her mouth drops open.

'You said you wanted something small. The only thing you have to decide is whether you want the Guildhall or the offices up in Dorchester. Unless you prefer here in Bridport?'

Her hand floats up to her forehead then down to

Tommy, who she shifts over to the opposite hip. 'Sorry, it's just... Let me... let me think about it, OK?'

He fights to keep his face from falling.

'Hey,' she says. 'I'm not saying let's not get married. It's just quick, that's all. I mean, we've only just got back together.'

'But we've already done the getting-to-know-you stuff. This last year I remembered only the bad parts, but being with you again, I... I was just trying to show you how decisive I can be, that's all. I want to arrange it all. That way you'll see I've changed too.' He is not so sure about this last claim, but at least now Naomi is laughing, all trace of unease draining from her features.

'Oh my God,' she says. 'I'd love to see that.'

He laughs too, delighted to have not screwed up smack in the middle of trying to repair his last mess.

'Tell you what,' she says. 'Let's get this fella to bed and we can chat over our takeaway, OK?'

'Deal.'

He follows her upstairs into the bathroom. Like the rest of the house, it is freshly painted – in this room a delicate orange blossom. The towels match. Even the soap matches.

As Naomi runs Tommy's bath, Sam sits on the loo and sets about easing the baby out of his clothes. He talks to him all the while, explaining everything in a soft voice as he has seen Naomi and Joyce do.

She tests the water with her elbow, nods to him that it's OK, and he lowers Tommy into the shallow bubbles.

'You've made everything so lovely,' he says. Wonders what the master bedroom is like. But now is not the moment.

'... the house was like this when I moved in,' Naomi is

saying, 'but my focus has been Tommy. Every penny, everything has gone on him.' She looks around her. 'Not a colour I'd choose, but it's warm and I quite like it now, so I ordered matching towels.'

'It's perfect.'

Later, when Sam holds his son, gazing into his eyes as he gulps down his milk, when he lowers him gently into the cot and places the flat of his hand on his little chest, feels the warmth of Naomi's hand on his back, he feels a deep sense of peace.

Once they are back downstairs, he raises the subject of maintenance. After protesting a little, Naomi whips out her laptop and, with the apparent ease of a computer programmer, sets up a joint account.

'If we're getting married, rather than you doing a direct debit, it makes more sense for us to put money into a joint account. Also, no offence, but I don't like the idea of you giving me money like I'm a charity case. We have equal responsibility so we should pay equally. And this way, anything he needs we can take from this account without it being, like, *I bought him this* and *you bought him that*. If we run short, we can top it up as we agree or whatever. So, like, his childminder fees can go in here, for example.'

'And I'd like to set up a savings account for him, for when he's older.'

'Good idea. We can have that as a joint too. That way, if I've got any spare, I can put it in there as well. Not fair if it's just you. Or I can do a direct debit from my account.' She meets his eye and grins. 'We can really look after him, can't we?'

And any more that come along, Sam almost says but stops himself. One step at a time.

A little later, after they've eaten, he gives her the book and tells her what the girl in the shop told him.

'Ah, thanks,' she says, but a little disappointingly, she lays the novel to one side and picks up her iPhone. 'Let me show you this banking app – it's so cool. I'll put it on your phone too and I'll show you how to do the thumbprint thing. Can't believe you're still using a passcode.'

'My hands are often dirty,' he says. 'Even in gloves. It's just easier.' But he is pulling the phone from her hand and throws it aside so he can kiss her. The kiss intensifies and he feels her respond. Himself too, as she lets him run his hands over the smooth lines of her body. At the waistband of her jeans, his fingers find the silken flesh of her belly, her warm back, and she sighs, her lips pressed to his neck. He has not touched her like this in so long; she is ridiculously soft, and as he traces the curve of her waist to her hip, sense almost leaves him.

'Shall we go upstairs?' Any resolve to wait until they're married is gone.

She shakes her head. 'I love you, I do. And I really want to, but...'

'That's OK.' His voice is high with suppressed disappointment. 'Honestly, it's OK.'

'Are you all right?'

'Of course! Actually, I was thinking we could have, like, a courtship, like they did in the olden days? That's partly why I bought the book.'

She smiles – the breath of a laugh. 'You're so funny. But that might be cool.'

'We could even... I mean, we could even leave it till our wedding night, if you want?' He can't believe what he's just said, as his blood is still settling.

Her eyes widen. 'Oh my God, like we're olden-day sweethearts! That's such a cute idea!'

'That's what I thought.' He swallows hard. Feels like he did when he first got to Lyme Regis Primary and gave Simon his best Top Trumps card so that Simon would be his friend: part elation, part crushing sacrifice.

CHAPTER 39

Joyce gives him two thousand pounds towards Tommy's care, telling him to think of it not as maintenance but as the christening gift she would always have given him: nursery furniture, say, or a silver bracelet, or commemorative china.

'Joyce! Are you sure? Thank you so much.' He is glad of it. He has barely any money left.

Naomi shows him how to scan the cheque and pay it into Tommy's account, all on his phone.

'There,' she says. 'Easy-peasy! You can use your thumb now, which is easier when you're at home and saves you having to remember a passcode.'

She puts his thumbprint into her phone too, in case of emergencies, and puts her thumbprint into his.

'Now that's romance,' he jokes, attempting to conceal how much this reassures him. They are still going forward. Maybe they can get married soon. But he doesn't ask. Best not to push.

Naomi takes a week off and comes to the house every day, leaving before Tommy's teatime, always putting his needs before her own. Sam takes the week off too, even though the garden project is in its final stages, and together he and Naomi go walking, Tommy in the backpack Sam bought. They hold hands, find secluded spots to kiss, hands running beneath each other's clothes when Tommy is asleep. Sam can still remember the shock and delight of Naomi letting him into her bed on their first date. Still blushes at how quickly it was all over, at the delicious memories of Naomi teaching him, guiding him over the weeks that followed. This almost teenage fumbling in the woods is so far from how they were before. But as she reminds him, a return to innocence is the point.

Sometimes Jo babysits, sometimes they pay for Cheryl. Sometimes they eat at Naomi's; sometimes she comes over and together they cook for Joyce. Naomi never complains like she used to about spending time with Joyce. In fact, it is often she who suggests it, expressing worry that Joyce might be lonely. Naomi has got used to nights in, she says. She prefers them these days. Besides, the pubs and restaurants are still struggling to stay open; too many staff down with COVID. Thank God Sam's job is safe and Naomi is a key worker. We are so lucky, they say. Others have it much worse.

At the end of July, Sam finishes the Higher Mill job. He and Miranda meet with the delighted client, who hands him an envelope of cash – a few pints for the boys, he says, for a job well done. Sam shows him the underground grotto, shining his torch into the tunnel, explaining that it used to be a floodgate for the mill race back in the day.

As they drive away, Miranda teases him, tells him he's a big kid, that the client glazed over with boredom. Seeing him laugh, she carries on, really roasting him, until they are both helpless with giggles.

'Honestly,' she says, wiping her eyes, 'I think you might be an actual Enid Blyton character.'

In the easy silence that follows, he longs to tell her how things have moved along with Naomi but for some reason can't find the words. Miranda hasn't asked how it's going, and when she gets out of the van, she says only that she'll be in touch with more work in the next few days. A big project, she tells him. She'll need his magic touch. When he asks her if she wants to come out later to celebrate the end of the job, she says no, that she's tired, but to have a drink for her.

He finds he is disappointed.

That night, he and the lads go for pizza at Poco's and a few beers at the Harbour Inn. It is warm, almost balmy. In good spirits, Sam drinks more than he means to. When Darren asks him about his love life, he shrugs and says, yes, he's met someone, that it's getting serious. He doesn't mention Naomi by name because when he and Naomi split, Darren shook his head and said, *Best way, mate. She's trouble, that one. Her and her sister.*

By the time he staggers up the road, it is midnight: later than he intended. The air is cool; the alcohol hits and some part of him is aware that he is drunker than he's been for a long time. At the top of the hill, the house is silent and dark. Even in his woozy state, this strikes him as unusual. Joyce always waits up. She likes to hear about his evening, doesn't sleep until she knows he's safe home.

He steps inside to a silence that feels off-key.

'Hello?' he calls into the hall. Something is not right. The hair on his forearms rises.

He switches on the light. Nothing is out of place, but still his skin prickles. 'Joyce? Gran?'

It's cold. That's what it is. Colder than it should be, a draught coming from the back of the house.

Steps quickening, he makes his way along the hall. The back door has been flung open. He steps out into the garden, stops dead. Listens, head twitching like an owl's.

A creak. The shed. The angle of the door is wrong. He approaches slowly, sees that it is unlocked, drooping a little.

'Hello?' His heart beats faster. 'Anyone there?'

He throws open the shed door. There is no one inside. The tools hang from their hooks, neat in the outlines he traced out for them with indelible marker pen. He looks closer. The spade is missing. The sight fills him with fear. He casts his eyes about, but there is no sign of it. Pulse thrumming in his ears now, he runs back to the house.

'Joyce!' He dashes up the hall, throws open the living-room door. Here, it is still warm. His gran's pink wrap is on the sofa. He picks it up and presses it to his face. It is not cold. It smells of Coco perfume, of sweet almond, of her. Out of the corner of his eye, he catches something off and turns to see the television on the floor, smashed as if dropped. The DVDs are scattered around it. The shelf above is half empty.

Burglars.

A sob catches in his throat. Moving faster than ever in his life now, he takes the stairs three at a time, races for his gran's room, bursts in.

The wardrobe doors are open, clothes strewn on the floor. Her dressing-table drawers are open. One has been pulled out, lies upside down on the padded stool. The bed is made. She has not been in it.

'Joyce?'

He sees her feet first: toes towards the carpet. The angle of them is strange, wrong.

'Gran!'

CHAPTER 40

It is after eleven. Joyce yawns hugely. She should go to bed really but wants to wait for Sam, ask him about his evening out. She turns the page of her book, smooths it with the heel of her hand.

A bang.

She gasps, hand flying to her chest. 'Good Lord.'

Senses pricking, she freezes, head cocked towards the door.

After about a minute, it comes again: *bang*. A long sigh leaves her.

'Daft bat,' she mutters. It'll be the back door. Clatters against the indoor wall sometimes if there's a draught. She's pretty sure she locked it though. Didn't she? Yes, locked it and put the key on the little hook by the coats. Definitely.

Sam then. Forgotten his key. Taken the bunch from under the geranium pot?

She stands up, listening hard.

'Sam?' she calls. Her voice is high, tiny.

Doesn't call out again. Some deep gut feeling argues against it. Sam would have seen the lamp on in the front room. If he'd forgotten his key, he'd have rapped gently on the window like he always does. He'd have called to her, grinned at her cheekily through the pane. If he had his key, he would have called to her the moment he was in the house.

Footsteps. In the hallway. Clear as a pin.

They are short, quick. They are not Sam's.

Heart racing, she switches off the lamp. Moves across to the armchair. Crouches low behind it. Her legs ache, her hip screams at her to stand back up. She shifts, half falls onto her bottom. Her coccyx hurts with the urgent pain of injury. She's done herself a mischief. Bugger.

The footsteps have stopped. The silence is thicker now. In the grate, a log pops, almost makes her cry out. Footsteps again – in the kitchen, tap-tap on the harder floor, light. Two people, or someone young, moving fast. Muttering. Whispering. Whoever it is, it isn't her grandson.

The squeak of the kitchen door. Then the footsteps come again, muted now by the hall carpet. Closer. Close. She peeps around the edge of the armchair, her whole body trembling with fear. In the slit of light under the sitting-room door, shadows move. Stop. Still she cannot tell if there is one person or two.

The door handle rattles. She shrinks back, closes her eyes. Her teeth are chattering. Please God, let her be hidden behind this chair. The shushing glide of the door across the carpet. She holds her breath.

'There's a fire,' someone says – low, almost husky. A teenage boy possibly. 'She's definitely in.'

The door sighs, clicks closed.

Joyce's breath leaves her in a long rush. Her heart is beating fast. Sweat pricks at her hairline. Whoever it is, they've gone for now. But from what they said, it's someone who knows her, knows this is her house. She is panting, one hand to her chest to calm herself. Rage floods her then. Someone's teenage boy is in her house. Someone's kid, off the rails, up to no good. Pam from Chanteurs – her lad is a wrong 'un, always smoking weed in Langmoor Gardens with his muckers. Came to the house once asking about odd jobs, a malevolent look in his eye.

She wonders about getting up, calling for help. No, not yet. She'll stay here and wait it out. At least until Sam comes home. Does the intruder know Sam is out? Has he been watching the house?

Oh, Sam. Sam, love. Come home.

The base of her back throbs. Her hip. Her shoulders. She has to move before she sets solid. Inch by inch, she lifts herself up, gripping hard on to the back of the armchair. Listening, listening, listening. Every move silent, ears trained, she creeps back across to the window. Outside, no sign of a car, only Sam's van and her MG.

She edges towards the door. Presses her ear to it. She can hear her own heart banging. Beneath it, thinks she can hear movement upstairs. Not footsteps exactly, only the less identifiable thumps and rustlings of someone else in the house. Consciously she slows her breathing. The grooves of the brass doorknob press into the palm of her hand.

The landline is in the hallway. No. No way – too exposed. If he were to come out of a room, there'd be nowhere to hide. Her iPhone? Upstairs, on her bedside table; she can see it in her mind's eye. She did a Sudoku last night before she went to sleep but hasn't even turned the phone on today. The iPad is in the kitchen, but even if she dares go that far, she's not sure she knows how to call the police from it, if it's even possible.

A crash. From a front bedroom – hers, she thinks.

Into the hot hollow of her hand, she lets out a soft cry. She should run – now, out of the front door. Run down the drive and to Eric and Martha next door, ring their bell, shout through the letter box. She could run pretty fast, she reckons, sort the damage out later. It's only a short way. But no. Safer here, here where he's already looked. *Take what you want*, she communicates to him silently. *I don't care about any of it.* The engagement ring has already gone to Sam and Naomi. The rest is junk anyway. *Take it. Take the lot.*

Footsteps drum down the stairs like a rat across the attic. Joyce's throat blocks. Seconds pass. The house falls into a new and heavy silence. She has no idea where he is. Ear to the door. The air stills. The silence alters, settles like dust. Still she listens. The carriage clock chimes half past eleven. She waits. And waits. It chimes quarter to midnight.

Breathing fast and shallow, she opens the door. The house is empty, she's sure of it. But still. She returns to the fireplace, drains her glass – for courage – and lifts the poker from the cast-iron set. Steeling herself, she makes her way out into the hallway.

Silence. Dark. She takes the stairs slowly, listening, listening, listening. This terrible, terrible listening. On the mezzanine, she waits. Outside, through the picture window, the garden is hulking black shapes. There is no breeze. Even the tips of the firs are still.

Aching all over from sitting on the floor, from standing for almost an hour as the sitting room cooled, she climbs the next flight. On the top landing, she stops, limbs juddering violently now. With the end of the poker, she pushes open her bedroom door. Steps silently forward. Feels around the jamb for the light switch. The switch clicks but no light comes. The bulb must've blown. Heart thick in her mouth, she edges forward. Peers around the door into the gloom.

The room is empty. With a rush of determination, she reaches the bedside and turns on the lamp. In the slow-growing light, the outline of her dressing table sharpens. It has been ransacked, the drawers open, one overturned on the stool. The room is full of shadows. They will have taken her phone. Of course they will. She will get into bed and close her eyes tight and wait for the sound of her grandson coming in through the front door. He will check the house as he always does, will find the back door open. If the burglar has left a mess downstairs, she won't tell him what she has suffered. She will say she must have smoked too much, slept through the whole thing. He'll fit an alarm. Sad, that they'll have to do that. This is her home; it has always felt so safe.

Fingers tightening around the poker, she creeps further into the room. Something then. Something. A whisper. Human breath? The air is loaded. Her own terror, perhaps, heart still hammering, legs still trembling.

She reaches the far side of the bed. Her phone is there after all. But the curtains are drawn. She did not draw them. Hasn't been upstairs, not since after lunch when she went for a bath. She dressed in the bathroom. She did not return to the bedroom at all.

A movement in the folds of the curtains. She raises the poker over her head.

'Out you come,' she says, her voice small but loud enough. 'Out you come, come on. I won't hurt you, but you need to get out of my house.'

The curtains sway. Open. A girlish lad, or a laddish girl, steps from behind them, head slightly bowed. She doesn't recognise him.

'Sorry, miss,' he says.

'Get out,' she hisses. 'Go on. Off you go, before I call the police.' She adjusts her stance, feet wide. He will not intimidate her, not here. This is her house. 'Off you go, go on.' Her voice betrays her, high and warbling with fear.

The lad takes a step towards her, holds up his hands. There is something feminine about him. In his earlobe, one diamond stud. It's so hard to tell nowadays.

'All right.' He still has his hands in the air, an expression of ironic amusement on his smug little face. 'Calm down. I'm going.'

You're a disgrace, she thinks, but she is too frightened to speak, has no idea how she spoke only seconds ago. Her legs have started to shake uncontrollably; the poker is becoming heavy, too heavy. The lad has not moved. His smile widens, becomes a grin, and this makes her even more afraid.

'Please go,' she manages, but he is not looking at her. He is looking over her shoulder. A creak on the floorboard behind her; something lands hard on the back of her head, the thump of her shoulder then against the floor. Blackness.

She opens her eyes. The room spins. A big shoe... shoes... circling, dancing, inches away from her nose.

'Is she dead?' It's the lad's voice.

'She will be.' A voice she... Does she know that voice? 'I've trashed the telly, opened a few drawers in the kitchen. It looks pretty convincing.'

A bang, far away. The front door.

'Joyce? Gran?'

Sam. He is here at last. Thank God.

'Fuck,' the lad says.

The shoes are still there, sometimes many, sometimes two. They are waiting for her to die, waiting to see if she needs helping along. She makes to grab an ankle, but her arm doesn't move, doesn't do what she's told it to. The shoes move, out of sight.

Sam's voice, calling her name. *Sam. Oh, Sam.* Fast footsteps fade.

She closes her eyes. A dark kaleidoscope. The shoes. The voice. Dear God.

CHAPTER 41

Blood beating in his temples, Sam pulls out his phone, dials 999.

'Ambulance,' he says, fighting to keep his voice clear. 'My grandmother's been attacked. We've... I think we've been burgled.' He places his hand to Joyce's back, feels an almost imperceptible rise, keeps his hand there as he gives the address. 'Alive? Yes, yes, I think so... No forced entry. The back door was open.' His eyes acclimatise to the darkness. 'I think she's been hit,' he half sobs. 'Head injury, oh God, come quickly. Come quickly, please.' He puts his shaking hand gingerly on Joyce's head. Sees a blackish patch at the corner of her mouth. The woman is telling him the ambulance is on its way, to try not to panic, to stay with her.

'There's blood,' he says. 'There's blood at her mouth, I think. She might have been hit with something and then fallen... Yes, I'll try, I'll stay with her, yes... Yes, of course. I won't move her... Talk to her? Yes. Yes, OK.' He closes the call.

'Hey.' His voice is a tremor. 'It's me, Sam. The ambulance is on its way and you're going to be OK – you're going to be all right.'

She stirs, groans. He returns the flat of his hand to her back. 'Don't move. Stay still if you can. It's going to be OK – soon have you up and about.' He pulls the duvet from her bed and covers her, eyes the pillow, but the woman said not to move her so he leaves it.

Joyce groans, louder. He has the impression she's trying to speak.

He lies down next to her, ear to the carpet so he can see her face. Her forehead is beaded with sweat, her eyelids low but not closed, her mouth open, her breathing a laboured rattle. Her nose is bloody and wide. Broken, he thinks.

'Hey.' He reaches under the duvet, finds her hand. It is clammy, hot. He holds it, feels a response – weak but there. 'Hang on. You're tough as boots, aren't you? Toughest woman I know. Ambulance is on its way. I'm right here, I'm here with you, soon have you up those ladders, come on, don't close your eyes now, open them, can you open them, that's it, keep them open, don't go to sleep, Joyce, OK? Stay with me, come on, keep your eyes open, those upstairs windows won't paint themselves.' He laughs, tears coursing now down his face.

Joyce's mouth moves but all he hears is a strained noise.

'What? What're you saying? Eh?' He pushes his ear to her mouth, feels her breath against his ear, hears her whisper: 'Naomi.'

She gasps, her eyes widen – huge, round – meeting his for a second. Something unreadable in her gaze, something troubled flickers, before she exhales a long, rushing sigh.

Her eyes close.

. . .

Joyce is not breathing.

'Joyce?' he says. 'Joyce!'

Naomi, she said. Just that. He squeezes her hand. 'It's OK. Naomi's fine. Naomi's at home with Tommy. You just hang on in there, OK?'

She is not breathing. His nose is running. He can't see. He presses against the blanket, puts his arm around her. But he can no longer feel the rise and fall. He pushes his face to hers, but no warm breath comes against his cheek.

'Joyce?' he whispers, his throat aching. 'Don't die. You can't die. Joyce. We need to see Tommy in his school uniform. Joyce? Joyce!' He pulls her to him, rubs her back. 'Hey. Hey, hey, hey, keep warm now. Joyce? Don't close your eyes. Stay with me, come on. Come on, Joyce. They're coming. Hang on, please hang on.'

The doorbell rings. He can't leave her. But he must.

'Joyce? I'll be right back.' He lets go of her hand and runs out of the room, down the stairs, his chest filled with heat. Opens the door, is alarmed to see two paramedics, both dressed in hazmat suits: a woman and a young lad, he thinks, no more than twenty.

'She's upstairs,' he says.

'She went quickly,' the woman says, gently replacing Joyce's wrist on the floor. 'It's good you were with her, that you talked to her and held her hand. I'm so sorry.'

She is sorry. Joyce went quickly. It was good that he talked to her.

She has died then. Joyce has died. Sam has known this and not known it since she communicated with the very last of her breath her dying concern for the mother of his child.

Naomi, she whispered. Naomi, who she came to love in the end just as he does.

The paramedics tell him they have to go. They tell him not to move her. The police are on their way, to stay calm. They have to attend to another call, they say. They are overrun. They'll see themselves out.

Sam sits down next to Joyce and takes her hand. He will look after Naomi and Tommy, he tells her. He will make her proud, she will see. He is going to marry Naomi and raise a family, here, in this house, with all their happy memories. If their second child is a girl, he tells her as quiet police sirens become louder, he will call her Joyce.

CHAPTER 42

'Can I call my fiancée?'

'Of course.' The family liaison officer goes into the kitchen while another police officer sits beside him on his gran's old chesterfield sofa and asks to take his statement.

'What time is it?'

'Just coming up to two.'

'Two? Oh my God.' Time has vanished, hours evaporated.

Naomi's phone rings out, rings out, rings out. He looks up at the officer, who is younger than him, with a fluffy, patchy beard he'd be better off shaving for the next few years. That this thought would come to him now strikes him as bizarre. Not bizarre, no. It is Joyce. It is what she would have said afterwards, once he'd gone.

'Mr Moore? Sam?'

'She's not picked up. She goes to bed at ten.' He pauses to accept hot, sweet tea from the female officer, whose name he has already forgotten. 'She has to get up early for work. She's with our son. We're getting married...'

'That's OK,' the woman says.

Maddy, that's it, he remembers now. DS Maddy Cordell.

'She'll see you've called once she wakes up.' Her voice is soft, almost a whisper. 'Now, if you can tell my colleague Stuart what happened, in as much detail as you can remember.'

Stuart. The guy is called Stuart. Stuart and Maddy. He nods: he's sorry, he's a little distracted, he'll get on with it now.

'I came home just after midnight. I thought Joyce... I thought my gran was in the living room, but she wasn't and then I saw the television was all smashed so I... I began to panic...'

He tells them as best he can. No, there was no one else here, at least he doesn't think so, not when he got here. No, he didn't go into the kitchen, has not been in any other rooms since he got back. He was waiting with Joyce, keeping her company, you know?

'I didn't want her to be alone. Or cold. Even though she was... I mean, I knew she was...'

Maddy tells him it's OK, to take his time. He nods and sips his tea, takes the tissue offered to him, wishes Naomi had answered the phone. He wishes she were here so she could hold his hand and share this ocean of sadness, this abyss that is pulling him towards it, pulling him in. He wants his boy, wants him in his arms. He wants his family. He needs them.

'Can you tell us how you came to discover your grandmother?'

'Sorry. Yes. I was in the living room? I saw she'd left her scarf and her shot glass. She has... she has a nightcap, you know? Amaretto. She loves it, loves almonds. Sorry, I'm only remembering that now. And come to think of it, she hadn't cleared away her ashtray either. She has a... roll-up. So yes, so, I... I checked the garden, I think. The back door was open. I could feel the cold air. That's how I knew it was open. Anyway, yes, I went out. I... Wait... I checked the shed. And the spade. The spade was missing.'

'The spade,' Stuart repeats.

'All the other tools were there. They have their own individual hooks, you know? But the shovel wasn't... it wasn't there.' Dimly Sam is aware of Maddy leaving them, her voice talking to someone on her phone out in the hallway. *Check the shed*, is all he hears.

Refocusing, he tells Stuart he ran upstairs as fast as he could, found her bedroom trashed, his grandmother all but unconscious on the floor. No, he has no idea if anything has been taken. He could check the safe, yes, but they would have needed the combination. No one knows the combination apart from himself and Joyce. No one even knows where the safe is.

The phone rings. It is Naomi.

'Sam,' she says, her voice sleepy. 'Did you call me on purpose, love?'

He breaks down. 'Oh God,' he says. 'Something terrible has happened.'

'Sam?' She sounds suddenly awake. 'Oh my God, are you OK? What's happened? Can you tell me?'

'It's Joyce. She's been...' Murdered, he thinks. She has been murdered. He has not yet had this thought, but now here it is, and he will never not think it, never not know it. 'She's dead,' he whispers. 'There's been a burglary. She must've disturbed them, oh God.'

'*What*? Dead? Joyce? She can't be. How can... Are you *sure*? Oh my *God*.'

'I was out. I just got back and she was...' He glances up

at the liaison officer; she smiles sympathetically. 'Can my fiancée come over?' he asks her; she nods. 'Can you come?' he says down the line.

'Of course, darling. Just let me call Jo, OK? Toms is still asleep. Just... hold on, OK? I'll be there as soon as I can.'

He closes the call, smiles doubtfully at Stuart. 'She was asleep. She's calling her sister to come. For the baby, you know?'

The police officer nods, takes the rest of his statement. At a certain point, his mobile rings. He answers the call and a moment later leaves the room. More police have arrived at the house; Sam can hear them in the hallway.

'Why are there more police?'

'That'll be forensics,' Maddy tells him.

Forensics. My God.

Stuart returns, asks Sam if he has anywhere he can stay tonight.

'I'd rather stay here. I can sleep on the couch. I don't think I'll sleep anyway. I don't want to be away from her. I can't leave this house.'

'What about your partner's place?'

He shakes his head, no.

'That's all right,' Maddy says. 'I'll be here for a good while anyway. I can stay if necessary. Let me freshen that tea.' She lifts the mug from his hands, moves away on soft soles.

Stuart is sitting back down, pen and notepad in his hands. 'You think this person came in through the back?'

'Yes. The door was wide open. Joyce must have forgotten to lock it.'

Stuart scribbles notes. 'And are there any spare keys to the back?'

'Under the plant pot by the shed.' The shed. The missing shovel.

'Gotcha. Plant... pot... by... shed.'

'They could have taken the key from there,' Sam says. 'It's not very well hidden.'

'We can check that.'

They go over it a further two times. Stuart tells him they're just trying to build a picture, but Sam has the feeling he is being tested, that they are trying to catch him out.

'And your gran had no enemies as such?'

'She's in her eighties, you do realise that? She's not a Mafia boss. This isn't some organised hit.'

'And you're her only living relative?'

'Yes. Why? What is this?'

'OK, Sam. This is hard, I know. It's tiring.'

It is. He feels tired. The whole thing is pointless. The burglars will be miles away by now. Burglars. Murderers.

'Look,' he says, 'you've got fingerprints and I've told you everything I know over and over. I can't do this anymore.'

'All right. We'll need you to come in and give a formal statement later, OK?'

'OK. Whatever you need.'

More tea. Where is Naomi?

The doorbell chimes. Sam almost jumps from his seat. The clock on the wall says 3.30 a.m.

'That'll be my fiancée.'

'Stay there.' Maddy leaves the room, returning a moment later with Naomi, who is in pyjamas and slippers with a coat over the top.

'Oh, darling.' She sinks onto the sofa next to him and holds him tight, whispering into his hair that she's sorry, so sorry, you poor, poor lamb.

He lets himself weep onto the soft fabric of her pyjamas, breathes in the fresh scent of her – soap and perfume mixed with her lovely skin, her clothes.

'I wasn't here,' he sobs.

'And she was already... she'd already gone when you got here?'

'Yes. No. She tried to talk, but she was too... She'd gone.' He can't speak for the racking sobs that have overtaken him. Vaguely he is aware of Naomi asking questions, telling the police that she can't stay long but that she'll come back with the baby.

The sky is lightening. Naomi is asking him where the key for the safe is.

'Sam, the police are asking. It's in the cellar, isn't it? I can go down with Stuart. Just tell me where the key is.'

He tells her it's a combination, tells Stuart the number.

'Do you know what's in there?' Stuart asks.

'Er... just cash, I think. A lot of cash.'

'OK. We need to check it.'

'Of course.' Sam stands up, holds on to Naomi's arm. 'Can you bring Tommy? I need to see him. I want him here. Can you bring him? I'll do the safe.'

'OK,' she says, stroking his hair. 'I'll give him his breakfast then come straight back. I'll call work, tell them I'm taking the day off, OK?'

'Thank you. You're so good, thank you.'

She kisses him, holds him tight, tells him she loves him, that she's here, that it will be OK. He lets her go. When she leaves, he is shockingly, instantly bereft, like part of his physical being has been removed.

Stuart coaxes him down into the basement. It is cold and smells strongly of coal from the pile at the bottom of the chute. He punches in the number, a combination of his and

Joyce's dates of birth, pulls out three A4 envelopes with cardboard backs.

'Wow,' says the cop, eyebrows rising. 'How much is in these?'

'I'm not sure. A hundred grand? Two hundred maybe? I'm not sure. I know she ordered hundred-pound notes from her bank, wrapped in the little paper slip things. She liked new notes, you know?'

'Didn't she have an account?'

'Yes. She's got shares, accounts, but she always kept some cash. For emergencies. But it's not been touched, so...' He closes the safe, muddles the numbers. 'Whoever it was didn't know about it.'

'Yeah,' says the cop, nodding. 'It's looking like burglars who panicked. The key has gone from under the plant pot, by the way; my colleague checked. You said the spade was missing. They haven't found it on the premises. We really need to find it. And the keys.'

'You're saying... you're saying that's the murder weapon?'

'I'm saying we need to find it. Your grandmother sustained a bad head injury, which is looking like the cause of death, though I can't confirm. And yes, this is a murder inquiry.'

CHAPTER 43

Dear Sam,

No matter what you find out about me, I'm not a psychopath and I do care about you. But Joyce was the fly in the ointment, and I needed things to move on. I could hardly take a chance on her living another ten years, could I? She had to be dead by the time we got married.

I actually figured out how I was going to do it the day we did the garden together. Funny, because that morning my horoscope said: New information will light your path.

And it did. That's the thing, you see. When you read your stars, you know what to look for. So when Joyce told me where the keys to the back door were, I thought: that's it. It wasn't new information as such. I knew where the keys were from before, but I'd completely forgotten, hadn't I? But as soon as she said it, I was like, yeah. That's it.

Because the thing I'd already realised was: I'm not going to be able to make it look like an accident with you hovering around all the time. I realised that when I tripped her up. I thought she'd go rolling down the stairs like they do on the films, but she just sort of stumbled and reached like she was saving a goal or something. She didn't even break a wrist. Aren't old people's bones supposed to be brittle?

You didn't really believe that was an accident, did you? I saw the way you looked at me when she fell. I mean, in the end the moment passed and I thought, well, I might get you to believe me maybe once more, but even with idiots, you don't get many chances before people start suspecting. People start putting two and two together and thinking, hang on a minute, how come Naomi Harper was always the duty manager when those nurses went home in tears or when those complaints came in about staff rudeness or whatever? Or how come the till is always short on a Saturday, oh, hold on, isn't Naomi Harper the Saturday girl? Or weren't Naomi and Jo Harper in the girls' loos that time the towel dispenser caught on fire?

And I can't have that. I've got to be perfect. I've got to be a changed woman.

I have to tell you, it is so tiring being nice – biting your lip, not reacting when people are rude to your face like Joyce was to me. You feel like the Barbie doll at the end of Toy Story, you know when she's on the luggage thing and her face is hurting from smiling all the time? That's how I feel. Honestly, when I get in the car and relax, it's like when you take your shoes off after work, do you know what I mean? You're like, aaaaah.

Knowing where the keys were lit my path, so to speak. Not just the back-door key but the shed key too. And that's where all the tools are, isn't it? Some pretty heavy-duty stuff in there.

All I had to do was pick my moment. And when you

said you were going out with the boys, I thought: that's it. That's my chance.

The thing is, Sam, I'm not even sad. Joyce'd had enough life. She told me that herself that time we were planting the veggies. She said she was starting to get a bit wobbly on her pins so it was only a matter of time. If I hadn't helped her along, she would probably have ended up in a home, and they look after them way too well in there. Harry – that's Cheryl's other half - his mum was in one and he said they did her hair and her nails every week, gourmet food every day, all the tea, all the cake. She lived way longer than she should have. I mean, when you think about it, it's no wonder they don't do the decent thing and shuffle off. If I was getting my nails done once a week, I think I'd hang around too. For a lot of them, life is better than they've ever had it. It's almost anti-nature, really, when you think about it. Like artificial life support, do you know what I mean? Joyce would have hated it. She was so independent. And those places are so expensive; they literally chug through all your inheritance. I couldn't have watched that happen, no way. It was you who said that when you know what you want for the rest of your life, you want that life to start as soon as possible, right? Yeah, I'm pretty sure you said that, babe.

You, not me.

So anyway, I'm just waiting for Tommy to wake up and thinking how great it is that now I know the number for the safe. I've put it into the notes on my phone for safe-keeping – safekeeping, get it? Honestly, though, I'm so glad I dashed over in the role of sympathetic fiancée. That was the one thing I couldn't figure out: how the hell I'd get you to give me the number without it being obvious, and then, bingo! I knew the safe was still full of course.

Burglary was never the intention; we just knew we had to make it look like that.

You're probably wondering how anyone could summon up the courage or whatever to do something like that. Hit someone with a spade, I mean. Well, I'll let you into my little secret. It's rage, babe. It's amazing. It's like cocaine or something. It's better than coke actually. I'm not seeing my therapist anymore, but it was her who told me I had a lot of anger. She told me to write you a letter, which is what I'm doing, so you can't say I didn't follow her advice, can you? She didn't mean send it or anything – she just meant as a way of getting my feelings down and helping with the rage. I never saw the point. Not a big writer, am I, and it wasn't like it could change anything. It's too late for that. But I'll admit, whenever I update my little letter, I can feel my shoulders coming down. Literally, my hands get steadier with every word.

But, saying all that, writing a letter is nothing compared to swinging that spade and watching old Joycie hit the deck. Judged me for years, she did. She wasn't judging me then, was she? Not looking down her nose anymore, is she? Wishing her grandson had found someone better than skanky old Naomi Harper. I tell you something else, when you rang me to tell me she hadn't made some sort of miraculous comeback, it was all I could do not to shout Yesss down the phone. Thank God she did the decent thing. Honest to God, I was worried sick waiting for your call. How I managed to pretend I was asleep I will never know.

You'll be wondering why all the rage. Well, since you're asking, I suppose it's because I never got to the bottom of why – why you left, I mean. You, Sam Moore, leaving me, Naomi Harper? You were so punching, mate

– anyone could see that. It just doesn't even make sense. You weren't supposed to do that, Sam. I mean, who do you think you are? Especially when you never really told me you weren't happy, and even more especially when you knew you were leaving me to face lockdown completely on my own. I didn't think you were capable of doing something like that, honestly I didn't. It just felt like you were throwing everything away, and for what? To go and live with your granny?

Classic Virgo, you see? You have to fix things, don't you? And of the two of us – me and Joyce, I mean – I suppose she was the creaking gate, wasn't she? No offence, I just mean as in old. And you always said I was the strong one. I reckon you thought if you said it enough times, you'd convince yourself it was true. Maybe it made you feel better. Maybe it was your way of talking yourself out of the guilt. If I was strong, you could leave. If Joyce was vulnerable, that made it OK.

Look, I know we were having problems before. I get that, I absolutely do, but I just thought we could have made it work without you having to physically move in with your actual grandmother, do you know what I mean? You put me in a completely impossible position, Sam. How could I have moved into your gran's place when she doesn't even like me? She never liked me. I know if you were here you'd say that's not true, but I know you know it is. What was it Princess Di said – there were three in the marriage? My point exactly, Diana.

I'm going over old ground. We already had this fight a thousand times the first time we were together. But just so you know: after you left, I kept reliving the moment over and over and over again, when you just turned your back and walked out. It was like you didn't care, Sam. Like *you'd never cared, not really. So yeah, that's where the rage comes from.*

I still have flashbacks actually. Pisceans worry too much about everyone else's happiness, and that's why people take advantage. Dawn said you might be a... What was the term? Ah, that's it, I've just looked in my therapy notebook from last year, which I keep in my little bedside table. Dawn said you might be a 'covert passive-aggressive narcissist'. I was like, a what now? That's why I had to write it down. She explained it all. She said you started to find fault with me towards the end of our relationship because you were in the 'discard phase'. She had to explain that as well. It means you'd already moved on to your next energy source so it was better for you and the story you were telling yourself if I was the one at fault.

That made a lot of sense when she said that. Joyce was your new energy source, do you see? I mean, she was your old energy source, but basically you wanted to go back to her but you had to make it look like a mercy mission. Good old Sam sort of thing.

Because the thing is, you need to be adored. That's what Dawn said, in so many words. I mean, that's what she was getting at. And only your gran can give you the adoration you crave.

'That's right,' I said. To Jo, later, not Dawn. 'Sam never could stand criticism.'

And Jo agreed.

I know you tried to be kind about leaving, with the flat and everything, and I do appreciate how generous that was. But at the time it felt worse somehow. I can't explain it. Like you couldn't even stand owning a flat together if it meant having to deal with me, even in a business arrangement, even for a second. It felt like you just wanted to laser me out of your life like a cancerous mole or something. You were literally throwing money at the problem and that problem was a human being. Me.

That's what you people do, isn't it?

'I need to leave for my health.' Do you remember saying that to me? Can you imagine how that felt? Like I was a disease or a parasite or something? Like I was an actual mental illness? Then you just disappeared. Literally nothing, no word at all. No texts, no calls to see if I was OK, no WhatsApps. Nothing.

Who does that? Who treats another human being like that? Let alone someone they supposedly loved?

Anyway, we don't need to stress about this stuff anymore. Joyce is out of the picture and our relationship has two people in it now, not three. Well, three, not four, I should say, if you count Toms. I'll give him his breakfast and then I'll be back to play my part.

I hope they've taken her away by then. No offence, but I can't stand the thought of her still in the house, even if she has, you know, passed on or whatever. I was about to make sure of it when we heard you coming in. As I say, I'm not a psychopath, I was building up to it – it's not an easy thing to do, even when you're off your head on rage, even when she was most of the way there. And it's hard to make it look like someone must have bumped their head twice. I was trying to figure it out, hoping she might just go on her own, you know? But we were running so late. We only planned to be in there ten minutes, but we couldn't find her, could we? We had to lie in wait for her. And then you came back and we were like, holy shit! When we heard you go out the back door, we just legged it down the stairs, out the front door and down through Ware Cliff. We were killing ourselves. It was hysteria, but *we didn't stop running till we reached the car park. By the time you rang, I'd had a nice long shower and was ready to miss your call, so to speak.*

So, it's plain sailing from here. You'll be upset. I get that. You'll need your family around you more than ever, and I'm banking on that. Quite literally. Because I'm your family now. Me and Tommy. We're all you've got. I know I said it was too soon to get married, hun. But:

a) reverse psychology always did work well on you, and

b) when I see you hurting the way I know you will, well, I'd have to be cruel not to marry you then, wouldn't I? I'd have to be cruel not to do whatever you want me to.

Which is great, because basically you'll be doing everything I want you to.

There's nothing like a tragedy to make people realise life is short. You have to grab your opportunities with both hands. You have to seize the fucking day. And that's all I'm doing. We don't all have wads of cash to inherit, babe. We don't all have mansions handed to us on a plate.

CHAPTER 44

When I got to that bit of Naomi's letter, I couldn't continue reading for a long time. Poor, poor Joyce. Part of me still can't believe it, still can't believe it of Naomi, even given what happened later. As Darren said the other day, the Harper sisters always were a menace. Their father too. And this is probably a good time to tell you that Naomi's father didn't die of COVID; that was another of Naomi's lies. He died after he staggered, inebriated, out of his chalet and ended up falling into the harbour at West Bay.

What really winds me up is that even when people found out what Naomi did to Joyce, after it all came to a head, they *still* talked about Sam as if he were the criminal! I mean, I know what he did was wrong, but the headlines were so offensive, the rumours just that – rumours, not one word of truth. He did what he did because he was out of his mind, and anyone who can't understand that is a psychopath as far as I'm concerned.

After Joyce's death, Sam and I had limited contact. He was off work obviously, grieving and in shock. I tried to visit, but she – Naomi – answered the door and told me he was resting, that he wasn't up to seeing visitors, that he'd be in touch. So I called. Over the phone, he'd talk about what had happened, cry down the line sometimes, but then sooner or later he'd always have to ring off, and I just knew in my bones it was because Naomi had caught him talking to me.

I know he gave a recorded statement at the station, and that once Darren and the boys had provided alibis, he returned home.

So, to the facts of the case as known at that time:

An autopsy finds that Joyce died of a heart attack either as a result of the blow to the head or of shock. The head injury is a blunt-force trauma consistent with a common or garden spade or similar, but the spade is still missing, along with the spare keys to the shed and the back door.

A pair of witnesses who claim to have been 'talking' late at night in the undergrowth at Ware Cliff – I'll leave that for you to unpick – say they saw a young skinhead lad dressed in a black hoodie and black jogging bottoms running laughing down the steps of the track that leads from Ware Cliff to the holiday chalets behind Monmouth Beach. The police strongly suspect that this is their killer intruder. They release an E-FIT image of a young lad with a crew cut, his eyes black, soulless.

The intruder tried the shed, took the spade thinking to break a window but then spotted the keys. They weren't exactly well hidden, and even if they were, under the plant pot would have been the first place anyone would look.

The working theory is an opportunistic burglary gone wrong. There is one set of fingerprints and trainer prints, which don't match Sam's, Naomi's or Joyce's, which suggests a lone intruder, possibly after drug money, since there is nothing of note missing. The intruder was looking for ready cash or, failing that, cards. You can pay up to a hundred pounds contactless now – enough to buy booze, enough to get cashback at a supermarket till. Finding no trace of intrusion into the cellar, the police conclude that the thief was unaware of the safe and probably didn't know the house or its occupant.

The story makes the front page of the local news, a smaller article in the later pages of the nationals. A week later, Joyce's body is released and I help Sam to write her obituary via email. I make posters appealing for information with a beautiful photograph of Joyce that Sam sends me. She is sitting on the bench next to the veggie patch drinking tea, gardening gloves and a trowel on her lap. Me and the lads put the posters up all over town. Sam tells me he cannot read the papers, go online or go out, even to hike. I get the impression he is depressed, or simply holed up with Naomi and the baby. I don't get as far as him being coercively kept prisoner.

Naomi tells Sam she's taken another week off and brings Tommy with her every day. She tells Sam she can see how much comfort he takes from his little boy. She cooks, cleans and waits on him as if he were ill with a kindness that astonishes him. She will not, however, stay at the house. She is too spooked, she says. For his part, he cannot leave.

'Stay here,' Miranda offers down the phone. 'Bets'd be thrilled to have you.'

'I can't,' he replies. 'I wish I'd never left the house in the first place.'

'It's not your fault.'

'It feels like it is. I just... I just want to stay here for the moment.'

With Naomi, he is listless, almost mute. He expects her

to become angry, but she confounds him with her patience, her seemingly bottomless empathy, her sensitivity.

'I understand,' she says, over and over again, sometimes putting forms in front of him to sign, sometimes asking to borrow his thumb for the app. 'One hundred per cent. You're not yourself, babe. Don't you worry – you just take your time.'

He sleeps a lot. When he speaks to Miranda, he likes the sound of her voice, the normality with which she asks if he's OK, if he needs anything.

'Naomi has it covered,' he says. 'She's doing the shopping, the cooking, everything.'

Miranda fills him in on any funnies that Betsy has said that day, as well as the progress they're making on a luxury villa over in Colyton. It helps take his mind off things.

Naomi takes care of the funeral arrangements, shows him a photo of the coffin she has chosen, the flowers, the supermarket delivery for the wake. She lifts everything out of his hands as if to her it weighs nothing at all, and he is grateful.

'We should sell the house,' she says one afternoon when she has managed to persuade him out for a walk. 'I can take care of the whole thing. It'll sell in minutes; a property like that, in that location.'

'But I thought we could live there. We could, you know, raise our kids there?'

'Oh my God, no, Sam. I can't live in the house where Joyce was... Are you seriously saying you could?'

He shakes his head. 'I suppose not, not now you say it like that.'

'And it needs hundreds of thousands spending on it. Tens of thousands at least. It'll be a lovely project for someone who doesn't have bad associations with it. Everything needs updating – kitchen, bathrooms, everything. You don't want the kids growing up with draughty windows, do you? Dodgy electrics, inefficient heating? No, we need something modern, something clean – like my place but bigger. Here in Lyme if you prefer, or we could look further out. Tell you what!'

She squeezes his arm, excited now. Part of him bristles at her good mood. It is only nine days since Joyce died. But she is doing this for him, he reminds himself, to try and raise his spirits, give him something else to focus on, and he loves her for that. Of the two of them, she has always been the more forward-driving.

'Go on then,' he says. A smile fights to turn up the corners of his reluctant mouth.

'If we sell Joyce's place quickly, then when we get married you can move in with me. You know we said we'd do things the old-fashioned way? Well, you could carry me over the threshold when we get back from honeymoon. That way we can bank the cash and really take our time choosing. And when we find the perfect place, we won't be in a chain, so we'll have an advantage. It's so competitive round here, especially since the pandemic. Everyone wants to move to the coast now, don't they? And we'll be in pole position. It'll be a lot less stressful, trust me. I can ring round the estate agents, get them to notify us first, tell them we're in a position to proceed immediately. It'll give us the edge.'

'You're so good at all that stuff.'

She giggles. 'Me and my spreadsheets are a force to be reckoned with. And you're too shaken up. You're vulnerable. I can help you by organising things for our future. You don't have to worry about any of it, OK? Not one thing. My stars said, "Start as you mean to go on" today, so that's what I'm doing. You just focus on getting better.' She stops, kisses him on the mouth. It is the first proper kiss since before that terrible night, and it makes him want to cry, to curl up in her arms and let her take over.

'You're wonderful,' he says, hugging her tight. 'You do know that, don't you?'

Because she is. She has stepped in like a guardian angel when he was at his lowest, and when he tells her this, she laughs and says he doesn't even know what else she's done yet, that she's been saving it for a surprise.

'What? What surprise? What have you done?'

She looks up at him, her head to one side, and plucks something from his sweater. 'Joyce wouldn't have wanted you to be sad, Sam – you know that.'

'I do. I do, but—'

'She had a good life. A long life.'

'I know. It's just—'

'Sam, listen. Listen to me. D'you remember when we were gardening that time? Well, she told me that now she'd met Tommy, her life was complete. She felt like she could go quite happily.'

'She said that?'

'Totally.'

'I didn't know she felt like that.'

'Well, now you do. She said that knowing you'd finally got the family you wanted meant the world to her, the absolute world.'

It doesn't sound like Joyce, doesn't sound like words she would use, but Naomi is taking his hand and talking in a long, soothing flow.

'I know it was terrible,' she is saying, 'the way she went, but she was ready. And they say it was so quick she won't have suffered any pain. And you were with her, weren't you, at the end? She didn't die alone, did she? If she'd been in hospital, she would have died alone like my dad, but instead she was with the person she loved most in the world. It's so great that you could give her that at the end, you know? So anyway, that's why I've done something I think you'll like.'

'What?' Despite the pain in his heart, he cannot help but smile. 'Nomes?'

'I've only gone and booked the Guildhall!' She lets go of his hand and gives a little shriek. 'Monday August the thirtieth! I tried for the Saturday, you know, your actual birthday, but they were fully booked. But it'll still be summer technically.'

'What do you mean? What for? For a birthday party?'

She laughs. 'No, silly! To get married!'

He is reeling, can't take it in. He opens his mouth, but nothing comes out.

'I know I said I wasn't sure,' she says. 'But I am sure, I am. All I want now is to make you happy for the rest of your life. We'll say goodbye to Joyce this coming Monday as planned, and she'll go up to heaven knowing that we're getting married, OK? I mean, I know you don't believe in that stuff, but it's comforting to think of her still with us in spirit, and this way we won't be too sad. What do you say, Mr Moore?' To his astonishment, she lowers herself to one knee. 'Sam Moore, will you marry me?'

She is looking up at him. She, his guardian angel, has created gold from ashes. She has turned everything on its head. How he loves her. How did he ever let her go?

'I will,' he says, laughing through his tears now, pulling her up, kissing her again. 'Thank you. Thank you for everything. I love you.'

CHAPTER 45

Sam barely remembers anything about the funeral service. He knows he managed to get through the reading without crying, can recall the faces in the small and socially distanced crowd looking up at him: Tommy, in a tiny shirt and trousers, wriggling in Naomi's arms; Naomi's sister Jo, whom he barely recognised with her shorn hair and cream linen trouser suit; Joyce's pals from the Sea Shanty Chanteurs; and Miranda, of course, who stayed at the back, discreet as always. He knows they listened to 'Wild Horses' by the Rolling Stones while the coffin was sent through the saloon doors of the crematorium, and knows that in different, easier times they could have filled the place twice, three times over with Joyce's many friends. What he remembers, what he will always remember, is following the hearse through the town, his breath catching at the sight of all the people standing on the pavements waving and clapping.

I never told Sam that it was me who called round a few of Joyce's friends, told them the approximate time the hearse would be heading up Broad Street, to spread the word. It was quite a sight, I have to say. Even the shopkeepers stood outside their shops, hands raised, some dabbing their eyes with tissues. To know he was comforted in turn comforted me. You feel so powerless in these situations. Especially in the aftermath of such a gruesome thing. I did not, of course, realise the extent of my powerlessness, believing as I did that the tragedy was over. I had no idea at that point that he planned to get married soon after. If I'd known, would I have told him to wait? He was in the eye of the storm of grief – would I have reminded him of that, told him that no one is really in their right mind immediately after losing a loved one, especially in such traumatic circumstances?

I don't know. At the time, I think I would have said his romantic affairs were none of my business. It's possible there would have been a little possessiveness in the mix I would have been keen to hide. A little jealousy. Even petulance perhaps. It was too late by then to let him know how I felt. He had made his choice. I loved him but had no claim on him.

'See?' Naomi said, apparently, as they peered out from the windows of the funeral car. 'She was a celebrity, your gran.'

He was unable to speak.

Now the funeral is over, Sam stands in the magnificent garden of his gran's house, glad of the sunshine, glad they can at least take off their protective masks.

'I'd like to propose a toast,' he says; the meagre crowd falls into silence. 'To my gran, Joyce, who raised me, and to all of you for being her great friends and for coming today to remember her. Thank you. Thank you all so much. Cheers.'

'To Joyce.'

Joyce's friends sip their drinks. Into the silence that follows, a lone, clear voice rises in song. It is Mike, from the Chanteurs, who has stepped into the centre of the lawn, glass still raised:

> *My Bonnie lies over the ocean. My Bonnie*
> *   lies over the sea.*
> *My Bonnie lies over the ocean, so bring back*
> *   my Bonnie to me.*

On cue, the others step forward, their a cappella floating up, up into the air:

> *Bring back, bring back, oh bring back my*
> *   Bonnie to me, to me*
> *Bring back, bring back, oh bring back my*
> *   Bonnie to me.*

Unable to sing or even mouth the familiar words, Sam listens in silence. Even if they cannot embrace one another, let alone continue into the evening, end up round the piano getting slowly drunk and going through all Joyce's favourite songs as he knows she would want, they can do this: sing one last song for her here in the garden she loved so much.

And for those few minutes he is consoled.

Once the song has finished, Naomi flits about, clearing away glasses and empty plates. She has worked tirelessly this morning, he thinks, arriving with Tommy and helping to make sandwiches, arrange sausage rolls on plates, put beer and wine in the fridge. Jo has taken Tommy home. Sam would have liked him here, but Toms is too little to stay, Naomi said. A wake is a grown-up affair, and his routine would have been ruined. Sam did not argue. When it comes to Toms, Naomi knows best.

The guests don't stay long – perhaps because Naomi has begun to wash up, the clank of crockery reaching them in the garden.

Miranda is the only one to give him a hug, arguing that they are, strictly speaking, in a work bubble. He catches Naomi glaring at him, but when he asks her later, she says no, she wasn't, she must have just been tired after working all day. The remaining four guests make their way slowly out. They are exhausted, they tell him as they step onto the driveway, more so since the pandemic; still nervous about socialising but afraid of loneliness, not to mention devastated by the violent loss of their darling Joycie.

'She was the brightest star in the firmament,' Daryll says as he leaves.

'A true diamond,' Susy says.

'We all loved her very much,' Helen adds.

How strange it is not to shake their hands, not to hug them after such a quiet and intimate gathering. He has known them since he was a teenager. Instead, they wave from two metres away and head off to their cars.

He finds Naomi washing the remaining glasses at the kitchen sink, wraps his arms around her waist, kisses the soft skin of her neck.

'Thank you,' he says. 'You've been amazing.'

She turns to him and they kiss. When they pull apart, she says, 'And this time next month, we'll be married.'

'Did you mention it to anyone?'

She shakes her head. 'I thought we were doing just us. I thought that's what you said?'

He can't remember saying it; he thought she'd suggested it on the phone the other evening, but like so much, what is her wish and what is his have melded together. He takes her hand, kisses her again; she responds with more urgency than she has shown since they got back together, and he senses that all her misgivings about him have gone, that she is, finally, ready to be fully his again.

He pulls at her hand. 'We could go upstairs.'

She smiles. 'I thought you wanted to wait? Weren't we going to be born-again virgins?'

'I do. We are. I mean, I do but I also... I also don't.' He kisses her cheek, her ear, her neck. Groans with frustration.

Naomi's eyes glint with a mischief of old. Images of her, of the two of them together, flash into his mind's eye – once in this garden, up by the fir trees, while Joyce was in the front room.

'It's up to you.' Her fingertips trace down to his waist, lower, until she is holding him through the fabric of his suit trousers. 'Although it certainly feels like you're keen.'

He gasps. 'If you do that, I'm not sure I can wait.'

'I won't tell if you won't.' She giggles, bites his earlobe softly. Picks up her phone from the countertop. 'Let me text Jo, tell her I'll be a bit late.'

Afterwards, lying in bed, he tells her he's seeing stars, that he thinks he might have lost the use of his legs. She laughs and rolls towards him.

'I have news,' she says, stroking his chest.

'Yes?' He runs his fingertips up and down her arm. He was feeling silly, giddy even, but now, lying here skin to skin with Naomi, a feeling of melancholy settles inside him.

'I didn't want to tell you until after the funeral, but... we sold the house!'

'What?' He props himself up on his elbows. His heart

quickens. 'How is that even possible? There's no For Sale sign. We haven't had any viewings.' He can't actually remember agreeing to sell it. But he must have done. A pit forms in his stomach. He wonders about asking if it's too late to pull out, but Naomi is talking nineteen to the dozen.

'I told you it would sell. The agents have their mailing lists and there are specialist finder sites, and the world and his dog would kill for a house like this. It sold last week but I didn't want to stress you out so I didn't tell you. Some businessman from London. Had his eye on it for years apparently.'

'Right,' he says, trying to gather his thoughts. But Naomi is still talking.

'I think he wants to do it up for his kids and his grandkids to come to for big family holidays. Joyce would have loved that, wouldn't she? We should have exchanged by now, as he's a cash buyer. The solicitor said he'd give me a call today, then once I get a date, I'll book the house clearance firm, which we'll need if you're moving in with me, yeah?' She reaches for her watch. 'Shit. I need to go. Jo's going out – I said I'd be back before six. It looks like it'll be tomorrow now, the house. These things never go through as quickly as they promise.' She runs her fingers up and down his chest. 'Hey. Are you pleased?'

'Yes,' he says, though he is not pleased, not exactly. There is so much fog and it is so thick inside him; it obscures how he feels, what he thinks, things he might want or not want. He can't remember saying he wanted to have the contents cleared out. There is the tallboy he customised, the piano, Joyce's dressing table he thought Naomi might like, or a daughter, if they have one. Panic simmers in his gut but he is not sure why. It is, all of it, only stuff. It will not suit a modern house, he knows that. And a modern house is what Naomi wants.

She kisses his cheek, strokes his face. 'I'm sorry. I shouldn't have told you today. It's too much. I should've waited till tomorrow.' She kisses the hollow just below his ear. 'We gave her a good send-off though, didn't we? Considering. And all those people out on the street – I've never seen anything like it. How did they even know? And she'll be at peace now, I promise. She was happy.' She shifts, throws her legs over the side of the bed. Her back is a pale guitar. Her dark hair falls thick over her tiny white neck. *Stay*, he wants to say but knows he can't. *Stay and I will fret that thin white neck with my fingers.* She pulls her camisole over her head, turns to kiss him briefly on the mouth. 'I'll see you Wednesday, OK? I'm back at work tomorrow.'

'OK.'

She leaves him in bed. He closes his eyes and lies back. His head has begun to ache, and he feels suddenly unable to get up, gripped by an overwhelming tiredness. He feels like he has the flu.

CHAPTER 46

Dear Sam,

It's all coming together. Bit like us earlier this evening. Sorry, couldn't resist.

Funny, at the start of this horrible pandemic, I thought my life was so over. My horoscope told me to hunker down: Use this downtime to gather strength. I came off Facebook. Sometimes even your fake reality isn't good enough to share, and I didn't want people from Brid gloating, calling me a loser, Oh, did you hear about Naomi Harper? Apparently...

Didn't imagine how handy it would be, seeing no one, hardly anyone at the funeral, no one at our wedding in a few weeks' time. You know how quickly gossip spreads in this place; you can't keep anything quiet, not a thing. And I need things to stay under the radar for a bit longer, so it's just as well you're not up to going out.

You said I was an angel today. I won't lie, I'm tempted to agree – I practically did that whole buffet on my own. It was good, all things considered, that your gran's old mates didn't seem to recognise me. I mean, why would they? I've only met them once, when we went to see Joyce sing in the courtyard outside the Mill Brewery that time. Still, I was glad when they left. And then, what happened between us afterwards... I liked your idea of waiting till we were married, mostly because I don't want to let myself fall in too deep again, but I thought if I didn't give you something, you'd start getting suspicious, or worse, lose interest.

Joyce's death has been a double advantage for me actually. The money, obviously, but also the state it's left you in. Not great, is it, when people you love leave you without warning? It can destroy a person, really affect them, in ways you'll understand now. And part of me thinks that with Joyce on the scene, I was only ever going to come in second. I know you'd say no way, but it's true. I wonder if you'd ever have been able to commit properly while she was alive. Tell you something, of all the women I imagined myself competing with when I was younger, I never imagined someone in their eighties.

So yeah, the mood was right. You were emotional, a flower ready to pick. I always did fancy you, Sam. You were always so tanned, all year round. Weathered. I mean, it's a T-shirt tan, not an all-over tan like the other men I've dated, but no one sees that except me. And I'm sure I've mentioned your arms more than once. So, so fit. I guess I thought I'd give you a taste of what was to come, just to seal the deal. Like a first-one-free type thing, something to get you hooked, something to leave you with withdrawal symptoms only marriage to me will cure.

It was nice, really nice. I want you to know that. You're a good lover, Sam. A bit shy, maybe, but once you get going, you're all right – more than all right actually. A lot of the guys I've been with might be better at getting served in the pub or finding a deal on the car insurance, but when it came to sex, they were selfish, selfish and a bit quick, if I'm honest, and half a minute later you're lying there staring at the light shade listening to the snoring thinking, Oh good, I'm glad you're all right, Jack. You never did that. You always made sure I was OK before you thought of yourself.

I'm going to miss that.

CHAPTER 47

Sam has COVID and has to isolate. I say this as if it's fact, but actually Naomi told me down the phone.

'Did you do a test?' I asked, but she didn't answer, not directly.

She said: 'I'm looking after him, don't worry. He needs rest and plenty of hot drinks.'

I knew she wasn't there in the evenings, because Sam had told me.

'I could do the shopping if you like,' I tried. 'Or I can call and see him in the evenings?' I was thinking I could talk to him from the driveway or something. I knew Naomi should've been isolating too, but I didn't know her well enough to point that out, even gently, and so when she replied no, that the doctor had said no visitors, I said, OK, sure, no worries.

I don't believe Sam ever had COVID. I think that was another of Naomi's lies. If I'd had to diagnose him back then, I would have said he was suffering from debilitating grief and – possibly – the inklings of something not right. The house had been sold from under his nose, but of course

I didn't know that then. It was only my feeling based on the way he told me Naomi was sorting out the money, the banking, Joyce's estate. I got as far as asking, 'And you're OK with her doing all that?'

'Yeah! Nomes is amazing with money stuff.'

Inkling-wise, I can only tell you from four years wasted on Betsy's father, a man who on the surface seemed like a great guy but who I always knew, somewhere deep down, was not great at all... yes, I can tell you from bitter experience that human beings are buggers for ignoring their inklings. So when he said that, like everything else and despite my unease, I left it.

The sale of the house takes longer than anticipated.

'These things always drag on,' Naomi tells him as she checks his temperature and says it's still a bit high. 'Even when they're straightforward. But it's all super chill, don't worry. We'll have completed by the time we get married, a day or two after tops.' These are the words she uses, though Sam thinks she seems agitated.

Sam returns to work. Miranda hugs him tight, the two of them shedding a Joyce-dedicated tear or three on her driveway before they get in the van. Sam thanks her for the bouquet she sent with a note: *Dearest Joyce, keep singing those shanties on the other side, darling woman. With love, Miranda.*

At the site, he is greeted with more hugs and handshakes by the guys, despite regulations to the contrary.

'I'm the safest person in the UK right now,' he jokes.

They tell him they're sorry about Joyce, that she was a great woman, that it's rare to find the likes of her these days.

When his eyes brim, they sigh and pick up their tools, point out what needs to be done next.

That night, Sam packs up the vintage tea set Joyce kept in the sideboard, a leather case of sterling-silver cutlery she never used, and a twenty-four-piece Habitat dinner service, white with silver edging, that Naomi said she liked because it was retro cool. These things he will move into the van before the house clearance people arrive. Despite the burglars turning Joyce's dressing table upside down, her wedding ring and a fine gold chain with a pearl pendant remain, and these he keeps in his pocket for now, his hands finding them whenever he remembers her, which is every minute of every day. The ring he will get resized for Naomi; the necklace he can give her after they are married. The rest is junk, according to Naomi, and he puts it all carefully in a cardboard box, just in case any of it takes the fancy of the clearance company people.

The piano he contemplates for a long while before, in a flash of inspiration, he texts Miranda.

Hey. Do you think you could look after Joyce's piano for a bit? Betsy might like it.

Sure. Betsy would love that! How come?

I'll tell you when I see you. Is Friday OK to have it delivered?

He smiles, feeling something like warmth inside him for the first time since Joyce died. The piano is the only larger thing that really means anything to him, and it is good to know that Miranda and Bets will enjoy it and appreciate it.

He books a company to deliver it on Friday morning and a tuner to go to Miranda's that afternoon. It is the most he's done in weeks, and it gives him a small buzz of satisfaction. When he calls in late on the Friday on his way to Naomi's, Miranda goes through to the kitchen to fetch him a beer, and he finds Betsy sitting on a cushion on the music stool in front of a three-note piece called 'The Typewriter', which she bashes out as if she's trying to push the keys through the piano with her thumb. The sight kindles his heart. He sits next to her and plays a right-hand accompaniment, which makes her throw back her head and laugh.

'Do you have a trumpet?' she asks him, apropos of nothing.

'Ah, no. No, sorry.'

'Do you have a guitar?'

'Yes, but I've given that to my fiancée. It's in her house.'

'Are you going to live in your foncey's house?'

Miranda has come back from the kitchen and hands him a beer. 'Fiancée? Wow! That escalated quickly. I didn't realise you guys were getting married.'

'I thought I told you on the phone?'

'No.' Her cheeks flame. 'You didn't mention it.'

'That's why I needed you to have the piano.'

'Why? Won't she let you have a piano?'

In the background, the keys plink-plonk their three notes: *Tap tap tap tap tap tap tap goes the old typewriter. Tap tap tap tap tap tap tap on the same old note.*

'Of course she will,' he replies over the din. 'But we don't have room in her place. We've sold the house, you see, and—'

'The house?' Her eyes are round. 'You mean Joyce's house? You've sold Joyce's house?'

He nods, feeling strangely like someone is trying to shake him awake.

'Sorry,' Miranda is saying, her eyes glossy. She has sat down opposite him, one hand flat to the top of her head. 'I just had no idea you were engaged until now, let alone selling the house.'

'After what happened, we felt... Naomi said... It should have gone through by now, but as it is, it might not go through till after the wedding.'

'The *wedding*?' Miranda blinks and shakes her head. 'Sorry. It's a lot to take in.'

'Sorry, I... I'm not supposed to be telling anyone, so don't mention it, OK? We'll have a party when things get a bit easier. Next year probably. It doesn't feel right to have a party right now.'

'Sure. Sure. And when is the wedding?'

'Monday.'

'So that's... that's in four days. Wow.' Miranda is nodding, but her voice is high, her face all frown. He should have told her. He really should have told her. And now it is too late.

'I'm sorry. I've been a bit spaced out. I won't be in work until Friday next week. Sorry. I'm all over the place. Naomi said... Hey, are you upset? I haven't upset you, have I? I'd hate to upset you.' Shit. Shit, shit, shit.

'Don't be silly.' She waves her free hand then drinks deeply from her bottle, pauses, drinks deeply again. 'Not at all,' she says, wiping her lips with the back of her hand. 'It's just... I'm just *surprised*, that's all. I mean, I knew you were getting serious and everything, it's just there's getting engaged and there's getting *married*. And it's... in *four days*. Where?'

'The Guildhall.'

'Right.' She drains her bottle, puts it on the table. 'You only got back together, what, a few months ago?'

'We were together a long time though. And with Tommy on the scene now...' His son blooms in his mind's eye; the helpless giggling in his high chair when Sam plays *ah boo!* At the thought, an involuntary smile breaks his mouth wide.

'You love that little boy, don't you?' Miranda's expression is suddenly tender; her voice has returned to its usual low key. She is not cross, not at all. He tries to think if she's ever been cross with him. No. No, she hasn't. Even the idea is ridiculous.

'Do you know, he's almost walking? He only holds my finger ever so lightly now. I reckon he might even walk before the wedding.'

'And *you'd* walk over hot coals for him, gladly, am I right?'

He returns her smile. 'I would. In a heartbeat.'

Gah. This only gets more painful. I want to shake myself back then and say: *Hey! Hey, girlfriend! Miranda! Talk some sense into him. He is being rushed. He is not himself. He doesn't know his own mind. You know this. Do something! Intervene!*

But I don't do any of that. I just drink my beer almost in one go and pretend to be pleased and try not to cry. Why do we do this, in the name of loyalty, in the name of love? Because we feel it is none of our business. Because we do not want to offend. Because we believe we are all grown-ups and that we must all take responsibility for ourselves, our choices, the outcomes of those choices.

Or is it because, deep down, we fear the loss of those we love most?

CHAPTER 48

Tommy is in his playpen on the living-room floor. He squeals when Sam comes into the room.

'Sam-Sam!'

'Hey there, wee fella!' Sam picks him up and swings him around, tickles his tummy, rubs his face into his neck, making him giggle with delight. He goes to join Naomi, who is making coffee in the kitchen, talking to his son all the while. 'How are you, Mr Tom-Tom? Eh? Tom-Tom, the baker's son, stole a... what was it?'

'Piper's son,' Naomi says. 'Tom was the piper's son. Do you want a biscuit? There's some Kit Kats somewhere. Although we'll be having dinner in an hour or so.'

'Piper's son, Tom-Tom,' Sam says, nose pushed against the miniature version of his own nose. 'Stole a pig and away he run.' He looks up at Naomi. 'Away he run? Ran surely? Doesn't rhyme with son though, does it, if it's ran? But it's not grammatically correct.'

'Oh my God.' Naomi is laughing. 'Nerd alert.'

He laughs. Hesitates. 'Nomes? What d'you think about Toms calling me Dad now? I mean, it's only a few days till I move in, and you know I'm not going to run off in the middle of the night. What do you think?'

'Sure,' she says, smiling, brushing a hand down his cheek. 'I think I feel secure enough now.'

'Good,' he says, pulling her close so that she and Tommy are in his arms. 'And that reminds me. I need to pick up the wedding bands from Axminster in the morning. I've had Joyce's resized.' He kisses first one then the other on the cheek. 'This is it. This is all I want. My family. My little family.'

He lowers Tommy to the floor, steadies him on his chubby little legs and steps back.

'Come on then,' he coaxes, crouching down, hands out. 'Can you walk to Daddy?'

'Da-da.'

Sam looks up at Naomi and grins. 'Did you hear that? He said da-da!'

She smiles. 'He did!'

'Come to Da-da!' Sam throws out his arms again.

Tommy mirrors him, his little arms coming up. His expression earnest, he wobbles and promptly falls onto his nappy-padded bottom. After a beat, and seeing he is not hurt, both Sam and Naomi laugh. Sam lifts him, stands him in as stable a position as he can and again steps back.

'Come to Da-da, Tom-Tom. Come on, come to Da-da, that's it.'

Again the boy raises his arms, fingers and thumbs pinched, a fraught and terrible concentration on his little face. He wobbles, then puts one foot forward in its red leather slipper.

'That's it.' Sam's heart quickens. His boy, his son has taken a step.

He takes another, and another, arms up towards Sam, eyes locked on his. Sam inches back.

'Nomes! Did you see that?' Arms outstretched, he has to stop himself from shouting and frightening Toms. 'That's it, little fella, that's it!'

Tommy pitches forward. Sam catches him and swings him up above his head before lowering him into his arms and kissing him on his soft head. Laughing with pure joy, he swirls his son around to face his mum.

'Did you see that?'

Naomi is blushing with delight. 'Tommy! You took your first steps for Daddy!'

Sam leans in and kisses her, still half laughing, shaking his head at the miracle. 'My heart feels like I've sprinted a mile,' he says, taking her hand. 'To think, I might not have seen him grow up if we hadn't... and today I've seen him walk for the first time. And just in time for the wedding. Oh God, I think I'm going to burst!'

But the swell of joy is short-lived, replaced with a blow of grief so strong and so sudden it almost takes his breath away. He closes his eyes, opens them again. Finds himself in his future home with his future wife and his son.

'I just wish she could see him,' he whispers. 'Us. She would have loved... She's missing so much.'

After Sam has bathed Tommy and watched him walk another three times, read him *The Gruffalo* twice and put him to bed, he rejoins Naomi downstairs and together they watch a crime drama on Netflix, the pasta carbonara Naomi has prepared on trays on their knees. Since they slept together after Joyce's funeral, he has been careful not to presume it will happen again, but after dinner, when they start to kiss, he pulls back and asks if they should go upstairs.

She smiles, squeezing his hand. 'I *so* want to. And I know we haven't exactly waited... but we were emotional after the funeral, weren't we? Now I'm thinking we only have to wait till Monday... and I haven't told you my other news.' Her eyes widen, the irises dancing.

'What other news?'

'Well, two things actually. One is that we've exchanged on the house!'

'What? Why didn't you tell me?'

She laughs. 'I'm telling you now! I wanted it to be a surprise! I was going to tell you on honeymoon actually... Oops!' She claps her hand to her mouth, her eyes creasing with laughter.

'Hang on, hang on.' Their fingers intertwine in a kind of wrestlers' grip, sending their hands off in all directions. 'Honeymoon?' he says. 'What have you been up to?'

Naomi throws her head back and laughs again. When she returns her gaze to his, he lets go of her hand and she pushes her fingertips to her eyes, clearly moved. 'I hope you like what I've done.'

'I'm all ears.'

'So. OK. So. The buyer has to come down from London, right?' She smirks. 'Anyway, he's due to pick up the keys next Thursday, which is when we complete, but don't worry, I'll have it all nailed down by Monday. So I thought it best to have the cash go into the joint account for now. We'll need to transfer it into an instant-access ISA or some-thing as soon as we get back, because it's a waste just having it sitting there.' She chuckles, shakes her head. 'This is the other surprise. So there's going to be over three quarters of a million sitting in our account. That's just from the house, without counting Joyce's other savings. Now, I know I shouldn't have done this without asking, because it's your money...'

'Our money. It's ours.' He lifts her hand and kisses it.

She closes her eyes, momentarily flustered, opens them again. 'Sorry, can't get my head round it. Anyway, yes, so I just thought, sod it, you know? Let's have ourselves a proper honeymoon, yeah? I've booked us this *amazing* place in Devon. It's not far; it's just for a few nights – we'll get back on the Thursday in time for a long weekend with Tommy. It's really luxurious and it's overlooking the sea and it's so, so beautiful and I got a really good deal on the honeymoon suite and I *might* have booked us some water-skiing and *maybe* a couples' spa day, and we can go hiking too if you like, and honestly, Sam, it's not like the wedding's costing us anything and you deserve it after everything you've been through—'

He pushes his finger to her lips. 'Nomes. Shh. Relax! Of course it's OK! It's a great idea. I just feel bad because I should've done it. I didn't think you wanted a honeymoon, I thought keeping it super low-key was what you wanted, otherwise I'd have—'

Her finger presses against his lips in return. 'I want us to have the honeymoon of our dreams, babe. It's the one thing we can do, isn't it?'

They sit staring into each other's eyes, tacitly daring the other to lift their finger first, like a lovers' game of chicken. It is Sam who moves, leaning in to kiss her.

'You. Are amazing,' he says. 'You are the queen of organise.'

She shrugs. 'Well, you've been grieving. It was the least I could do. And anyway, you can... you can spot grammatical mistakes in nursery rhymes.'

'No, but you're clever. You're such a whizz with financial stuff and such an amazing mum. I'd say we're a great team... except that you're better. I'm really only good with my hands.'

'I've just had to stand on my own two feet for longer, that's all. You would've taken care of the house sale and Joyce's estate and all that, but you've never done it before, have you? I've sold my place and sorted all the stuff after both parents, so I know the ropes. You would've booked something for us if you'd been in charge of the money. And after your payments for little Toms, plus all the stuff you've bought for him, I can't imagine you've got much saved.'

He shakes his head. 'I am skint, it's true. Well, not now obviously.'

'Not any more, no. We is *well rich!*' She laughs, loudly and for longer than the joke strictly deserves.

Trying not to let her hysterics irritate him, he lets go of her hands. Immediately he feels his shoulders slump, his eyes fill. 'I just wish Joyce hadn't...'

She stops laughing, to his immense relief, and pulls him to her. Her hand cradles the back of his head, a gesture so tender he feels himself slacken, his forehead fall onto her shoulder. 'I know you'd rather have Joyce than all the money in the world, I know that, I do. And I know we're having a super-quiet wedding because that's what's right under the circumstances, even without bloody COVID, so that's why I wanted to do something special. Special but private, just for us, away from it all. And it didn't cost too much. It's just a few days, without Tommy, just for us.'

'*Without* Tommy?'

'Of course without Tommy! It's our *honeymoon*. Jo's gonna take him home after the wedding while we drive off into the sunset. We can go in Joyce's MG. Honestly,

Toms'll be as happy as Larry with his auntie, don't you worry. It'll be just us two – not very romantic if we're changing nappies and trying to find baby-friendly cafés the whole time, is it? So that's why I thought it might be nice to, you know, *wait*, even though we want to tear each other's clothes off.' She giggles. 'That way, when we spend our first proper night together, it'll be in a beautiful suite in a beautiful hotel and it'll be really special and romantic. And really exciting too hopefully. We'll be desperate for each other!'

'It'll be perfect. Like you.' He takes her hands, kisses her knuckles one by one. He kisses her on the mouth again, then, tapping his watch, stands up. 'Now, it's almost ten o'clock, and I for one honour your bedtime, just as I'll be honouring our vows come Monday, milady.' He lifts her hand and presses his lips against it. 'Goodnight, fair princess.'

'Idiot.'

'Will I see you this weekend?'

'Actually, I'm having a hen, just me and Jo and Cheryl. Only a girls' night in. Silly, but... Anyway, I thought I'd see you at the Guildhall on Monday? Three p.m.? In your best suit? I've bought a dress.'

He grins. 'How am I supposed to wait that long? I'll go mad.'

'You'll manage. And you've got the clearance people arriving tomorrow, haven't you? Have you got a witness? I need to tell them if not – they can provide one.'

He presses the flat of his palm against his forehead. 'Bugger. Completely forgot. It's OK, I'll ask Miranda.'

Miranda. For reasons he can't quite put his finger on, it occurs to him that this might not be a good idea.

'Actually, no. I'll pay... sorry, let's just pay for a second witness. Keep it super quiet, like you said. I'll tell Darren and the boys and Miranda when we get back.'

It's a white lie, about Miranda; he's already told her. But not the bit about the boys – they don't know. No one knows how deep he's gone; it's all happened so fast, and he wonders now if part of him, despite everything, has been embarrassed to have returned to a woman he knows deep down his friends don't like. But they don't know her like he does!

'I'll organise a witness.' She walks him to the door, where they kiss a final time. 'See you at three on Monday then,' she whispers, one hand glancing across the front of his jeans. 'Just like that, eh?' She steps back and grins, arms straight down by her sides, fists clenched, like a child who's won a teddy bear at the fair.

'Just like that.'

CHAPTER 49

Dear Sam,

Sorry to break it to you, but they weren't Tommy's first steps. But you were so convinced they were, I didn't have the heart to tell you that he'd been walking for a week.

By now, though, you'll have bigger things to worry about. Whether you were the first to see little Toms take his first steps will be the least of it, trust me.

We're nearly there, Sam. I know the beginning was bumpy, but I think that's added to it all being more realistic somehow. And now we're here, I can scarcely believe it's gone as smoothly as it has. When we first moved in together, I thought you were a keeper, that you'd never leave me. Then you did. But now Tommy has cemented us back together, and in two days' time we'll be married and off on our honeymoon! I've always wanted to stay in that hotel. Any five-star luxury spa hotel, to be honest. I know I said we'll go hiking, but what I meant was you'll go hiking while I hang out at the indoor pool in my fluffy robe, or maybe I'll be in one of my new outfits having a cheeky cocktail in the panoramic bar restaurant or maybe enjoying a mani-pedi in the beauty suite, lol. But I know you won't mind what I do because I'm your angel, your saviour, and you're so, so, so nervous about upsetting me, about getting it wrong, that I can do almost anything. You'll just suck it up like an abused dog. And then when we get back, everything will fall into place.

Funny, I was just thinking about the time you almost fell for that phishing text, do you remember? Just before you left? You thought it was from Hermes. If I hadn't been there to stop you, you would've entered all your credit-card details, your bank account would've been drained in minutes.

Do you remember when we were first together and we went to Paris, you gave that woman two hundred francs? Oh my God, I'm laughing just thinking about your face when I explained you'd been done up like a kipper. You literally couldn't believe it. You actually thought because you'd signed a petition against, oh, I can't remember, cruelty to bunnies or something, and written your dona-tion on a stupid photocopied form, that that made it all legit. What was it, some wild animal sanctuary or some-thing? I forget. But that's what I loved about you when we first met, the fact that you took everyone at face value, that for you, the best day ever would be a long walk, find some-where with a view to sit and eat your sandwiches and drink your coffee from your little flask, and maybe a cool beer as the sun set over Charmouth Bay. You, the Londoner-turned-West-Country-boy; me, Bridport born and bred, desperate to get to the big city.

You needed me, I think, looking back. For your devel-opment, I mean. You never had a girlfriend at school, did you? Too much of a neek. I don't think you'd ever have been able to get a girlfriend on your own, let alone one like me. You needed a woman to make the moves. That's the way with a lot of men, I've found. You're a clueless bunch, you really are, the lot of you. A lot of women don't realise that. And when I say women, I mean single women.

But here we are. Today the clearance company will come and get rid of all Joyce's old junk, thank God: sofas that have seen better days, mattresses that should have been taken away by environmental health years ago, that weird olde-worlde dining table and chairs she loved so much. Thank God you didn't put up too much of a fight there, Sam. I couldn't have kept any of it; it was gross. I want new, new, new all the way, or at least tasteful vintage. Then Monday, that'll be us at the Guildhall: Mr and Mrs Moore, our Jo and little Tommy. I'm going to dress him up as a page boy! I've got this super-cute little outfit – another one of my surprises! The plan is to get Jo and Tommy to walk me in. I'm hoping he'll manage it if he holds our hands.

When all this comes out, Sam, I want you to know one thing. I'm not an evil person, OK? I don't want you to think badly of me. It's just that I've had to fight for every penny I've ever had. Me and Jo. It's not like that for you, is it? It never has been. You can't even imagine it. An eight-bedroomed Georgian villa just begging for a refurb, not to mention the shares, the ISAs, even the current account. That house though. Literally a developer's wet dream. I've always known it'd sell in days, and it did, even quicker than I thought. The market has never been hotter. I made sure I broke that particular bit of news immediately after we made love, because I wanted to make sure you were feeling... receptive. God knows what he's going to do with the place. I just made up some shit about grandkids because I thought that would help me push it through.

I always knew Joyce was sitting on top of an actual gold mine, all alone on the hill. I always thought if I played my cards right, we'd inherit it all. Until you cut me out without a care. I bet she loved you coming back, having you all to herself, away from that pikey Naomi. Don't tell me it wasn't like that, Sam! She was a snob, just like everyone. I saw the way she looked at me, like I was a prostitute or something. But seriously, how can she judge me when she was hogging a place like that to herself in her eighties? What about families with kids who need a home? All those years when you were a kid, just the two of you rattling around like marbles in a box while my family were cramped up like sardines.

Still, she wasn't daft. Property is always a wise investment. I found her bank-account details in the kitchen drawer. I'll bring them with me and we can sort that stuff out while we're away. Faked signature here, sleeping husband's thumbprint there, all into the joint account with the rest.

As I said, now we're getting married, the joint account is what makes the most sense.

CHAPTER 50

At four o'clock on Monday morning, Sam finds himself wandering around the rooms of his gran's house, all empty now save for his own, which has in it his blow-up camp bed, his sleeping bag and camping lantern. One new suitcase, which Naomi bought, contains his honeymoon clothes, also bought by Naomi and including a pair of brightly coloured swimming shorts for the pool and some of the whitest socks he's ever seen. His old clothes are in two holdalls, his shoes in a cardboard box, all in the van, parked on Miranda's drive. His guitar is already at Naomi's place.

Naomi surprised him with a visit on Saturday morning. She brought Tommy, a cake and candles. When he asked her what they were for, she laughed.

'It's your birthday, silly.'

'Oh,' he said. 'I completely forgot.'

She gave him a dark grey shirt to wear at the wedding. No tie, she said. No one wears ties anymore. Tommy gave him a pair of socks to match the shirt and a dark grey hand-kerchief with small white polka dots, which Naomi folded in a special way and put in the breast pocket of his suit jacket.

'There,' she said. 'Don't touch it now I've done it for you, OK? And make sure you wear the socks.'

Then she lit the candles and sang 'Happy Birthday'. The three of them blew out the candles, and Tommy sat on Sam's knee to eat a slice of cake and covered himself and Sam in jam and buttercream. Sam knows he was there, that he blew out the candles and ate the cake, but he has almost no memory of himself, of how the cake tasted, nor of what he and Naomi said to one another.

Now he pushes open the door to Tommy's old nursery, the pale grey-blue walls the freshest in the whole place, a taste of what the house could be – will be, once the new owner takes it over. Sam suspects the whole place will be completely refurbished: rewired, new bathrooms, new kitchen, wireless broadband that works in all the rooms not just the kitchen and the living room. He hopes the new owner will treat it with respect.

Inside the nursery, he turns a slow circle. All that remains is the Roman blind Joyce made. Naomi sold the cot two weeks ago on eBay, along with the customised tallboy – both went for peanuts.

There was no room for those things in her house.

'Joyce,' he whispers into the silence. 'Gran. It's me.'

He wonders what he would say to her now, here in the dark, the night before his wedding. What she would say to him. She'd be awake too, he thinks. The two of them would be out in the back garden, watching the stars, Joyce sipping a sickly-sweet Amaretto, him a meditative whisky. She is in the walls of this place. She is in the air. The fact that she is not physically here is impossible. That he cannot talk to her ever again, only imagine himself talking to her, is a place beyond pain somewhere within him. He will carry her there, in that place, for ever. What would he say to her now?

What happened? Yes, maybe. *Who hit you? Who murdered you?*

At the thought, the waves of guilt that have accompanied his anger and confusion wash over him from head to toe. He should have been here. He should have come home earlier. He should not have called her name. If he had not...

The police have scaled back their investigation. There have been no new leads, only the vague hope that one day soon, the thug who did it will be arrested for something else and a match found for the fingerprints, the E-FIT image. When Sam gave his statement, Robbie Brigstock, who he knew from school and who was a DS now, went in quite hard, going on about the fact that there was so much money in Joyce's estate, that Sam must have realised he was a very wealthy man now. He tried to push him and push him, though both of them knew he had nothing to do with it.

'Sorry, mate,' he said afterwards. 'I have to ask these questions.'

'Don't worry about it. But who would have done that to her? And not even *take* anything?'

'Kids, I imagine. Don't think it will have been anyone local. On your own doorstep and all that. Bungled robbery, everything went tits-up, I reckon. They didn't realise she was in the house or awake or whatever. But with prints that don't match anything on file and no murder weapon, we're stuffed.'

'Do you think...' Sam started.

'Do I think what? Go on, say it.'

Sam studied Robbie's face, but found only concern. A few years younger than him at Lyme Secondary, it was weird to face him across a cheap table in an interview room in such grave circumstances.

'Do you think when I came home... you know, when I called her name... do you think he heard me and panicked?'

'It's possible. It's possible that while you were checking out the back, he made it out the front. We found a partial print to match the back door on the doorknob at the front.'

'Yes. No. I mean... do you think it's possible he panicked and... and hit her? Do you think me coming in and shouting—'

Robbie clapped his arm. 'Mate. You can't think like that. Don't do that to yourself, all right? You can't do that to yourself.'

By which Sam knew he meant *yes*. Yes, it was possible that without meaning to, he had caused his own gran's death at the hands of a mindless thug who didn't even get as far as the safe.

'The safe,' he whispers now, padding downstairs in his pyjamas and slippers. 'Idiot.'

On the way to empty the money from the safe, he stops in the kitchen, where his old camping kettle sits on the range ready for the morning. In the fridge, half a pint of milk, the last scrapings of butter and a jar of the jam Joyce made from the damsons at the end of the first lawn. In the breadbin, her home-made wholemeal bread from the freezer. How can he bear to eat these things, the last of her? How can he bear to leave this house, where she is every-where? How could he have sold it? What was he thinking? He could have persuaded Naomi to sell *her* house. That would have given them enough money to modernise this place surely? They could have done it bit by bit, enjoyed the journey. Why didn't he think of that? He has always, always wanted to open a gardening activity centre for primary school kids here, somewhere they could come on school trips and learn how to plant, prune, make grow. He even voiced this to Naomi a week or two earlier, but she told him it would never earn any money, and immediately he saw, or thought he saw, that she was right. Now, in the silence, feeling Joyce so close, he is not sure.

'The safe, Sam,' he whispers to himself. *The safe, the safe, before you forget it.*

He flicks the light to the basement and heads down the cold stone steps. The coal is still there, damn. He has forgotten to clear out the tins of paint, the white spirit, Joyce's paintbrushes and collection of old rags, her round-ended trowel, her tools. The coal will serve the guy who is moving in, if he decides to keep the fireplace, if indeed he is even moving in. Possibly he will want this place as a grand holiday home overlooking the sea. Whatever, it is too late to shift any of it now, at 4.30 a.m. on the day of his wedding.

He inputs the combination and opens the safe. Immediately he sees that the money is no longer there, no large manila envelopes with hard cardboard backs. He never counted it, but he knows there were three envelopes, and at least two hundred thousand pounds.

'If the banks go down the pan,' Joyce said to him once, 'we go down the pan with them.'

The cash was her insurance policy. And now it is gone. The burglar didn't know where the safe was, let alone the combination.

So how?

When the police were here, he told the cop – Stuart, was it? – he told Stuart the combination, or did he tell Naomi? Did Naomi offer to check the safe? Whatever, Naomi was there, she would have heard him tell Stuart. Surely the cop wouldn't have taken it? Surely neither of them would have? Unless it was Sam himself and he's forgotten. God knows he's been spaced out these last weeks.

He climbs the cellar stairs, preoccupied. He can't call his bride on the morning of their wedding and ask her if she took Joyce's cash, can he? It would ruin everything, stain the perfection Naomi has worked so hard to create from disaster. But he has to know. If it wasn't her, then he will have to contact the police.

He returns upstairs, finds his phone by his camping mattress. At the sight of what remains of his things, the misery of his last night in his childhood home hits him harder even than before, so hard he gasps. He should not have stayed here tonight. He should have asked Miranda if he could stay at hers. She would have said yes; they could have stayed up drinking beer and having a few laughs, maybe even talked about his dream of an activity centre. He knows, or feels he knows, that she would get it, or at least encourage him, brainstorm ideas with him, maybe even help him set it up one day. Or set up as a landscape and design company. As business partners.

He brings up the text thread with Naomi. Her last message, sent at 9.55 p.m., reads: *Off to bed. See you tomorrow, Mr Moore. Love, soon to be Mrs Moore xxx*

He types: *Hey, Nomes. I know it's nearly 5 in the morn, but hopefully you won't get this until you switch your phone on, but I've just checked the safe and the cash has gone. I've been so spaced out, just wondered if you can remember me taking it out? Starting to panic. Sure I must've put it somewhere but can't remember. Let me know if you remember anything. Can't wait to see you later, love, Mr Moore xxx*

He reads it carefully. A bit wordy, but it doesn't sound in any way accusatory. He sends it. It's not the perfect message for her to wake up to on her wedding day, but he can't go through the ceremony not knowing where the cash has gone, and he can't greet her at the Guildhall with an ugly question about money.

He closes his eyes, but sleep is nowhere now, and after another half hour of tossing and turning, he gives up, puts on his T-shirt and tracksuit bottoms and heads out. Run. It is all he can think to do.

It is still dark, grey cloud thick and low on the land. Slowly the sky lifts: a pallid white-blue. He runs. Cannington Viaduct looms, its arches legs of giants. Almost beneath, he tips back his head and looks up. Remembers himself there at the top, looking down. A year and a half ago and yesterday all at once, the twist in his gut somehow still fresh, a memory of a feeling brought to life. He looked down, stared at his own boot raised and hovering in nothingness, felt the pull to lean into that nothingness and let himself plunge.

His phone buzzes. He pulls it from his pocket. Naomi.

Two laughing emojis.

His heart speeds up.

What are you like? is the next message. He stops in his tracks and waits in the lane, directly underneath the arches now.

Don't you remember I said I'd get it?

A sigh that seems to come from his feet leaves him. 'Oh thank God,' he whispers. He is about to reply, but Naomi is still messaging.

I've got it here at the house dw. Really sorry haven't banked it yet, have just been so busy but will do it as soon as we get back OK? I've hidden it somewhere safe.

He doesn't remember, not at all. He replies, almost panting now with relief. *I knew it must be somewhere safe! Thanks for letting me know. See you at three!* He hesitates, chooses what look like celebratory party-type icons, although one of them looks distinctly like a jellyfish. He sends, adds a second message: *I love you, Naomi Harper xxx*

Waits, feels the skin sticky on his face. For reasons he cannot name, he is relieved when she replies.

Love you too, babe xxx

CHAPTER 51

It is a warm, bright, dry day, the sea glittering yellow, the sky cloudless. As he walks past the amusement arcade, the bars and restaurants, the ice-cream parlour, Sam is full of anticipation. It is only when he is standing outside the iconic turret of the Guildhall and staring up the steep rise of Broad Street in his best – his only – suit, his new shirt and socks, that he begins to wish he'd told the guys about today. They could at least have had a pint together up at the Nag's Head and wished him well. He wishes too that he'd asked Miranda to be his witness, can't think now why he didn't, or why he has the impression Naomi doesn't like her when she's never said a word against her.

Or Darren, yes, Darren. Surely Naomi would have no objection to Darren?

How quickly, he thinks, really, how quickly the last few months have gone.

In normal times, the guys would have found out. There would have been several after-work beers he would have missed on account of the rekindling of his old romance, questions he would have tried to dodge but on which he would have had to come clean eventually. Teasing he would have had to endure.

But the world is only just coming up for air, and there are rumours of another lockdown as soon as next month. The situation is being closely monitored. The tourist season has been busy, but the pubs and eateries have been plagued by staff absences, having to close when business could have been booming. It has been a strange time, a time where to stay in and see no one has become normal. And now, to invite everyone and be in a large celebratory group has become abnormal. A little frightening even. Until this moment, perhaps, he has felt fine about so little social life, lost as they have all been in the surreal and sustained monotone madness, himself lost in the whirlwind of Naomi coming back into his life, then, of course, lost in a grief that has at times felt utterly overwhelming, days when he has struggled to put one foot in front of the other.

Now, waiting for his beloved son and the woman who in one hour will be his wife, it feels so strange – strange and wrong not to have told the guys about something so monumental, to not even have mentioned it that night at the pub, the night he left Joyce alone, the night he lost her for ever. Maybe if someone had asked him that night, he would have said yes, actually... In fact, he did tell Darren there was someone, though not who. They have all been so used to having little in the way of news, have sustained conversations over days and weeks really only about the latest television drama, the latest podcast, the government figures, who's got COVID. Perhaps at a certain point, sure that no one was doing anything interesting, they all stopped asking questions that had to do with real life.

A Causley Cabs taxi pulls up at the kerb. A second later, the back door swings open. Naomi steps out and his breath catches in wonder. She is wearing a pale pink dress with puffy elbow-length sleeves, the skirt falling generous and loose to her slim calves, burgundy high heels with a T shape at the front. Her black hair, possibly to match this theme, has been curled at her forehead, a pale silk scarf tied in a wrap around her head. Like something from the history books, a woman from World War II. She is wearing burgundy lipstick, and the smoky make-up around her eyes makes them appear larger than ever. She looks, he thinks, as if she has stepped out of a postcard.

Their eyes meet, and in hers he reads the enormity of what they are about to do, and that she too is thinking the same thing. The moment is fleeting; she bends and helps little Tommy out onto the pavement. Behind, an SUV stops and beeps. Sam raises his hand: wait. Sorry. Won't be a moment. From the other side of the cab, someone he thinks at first is a boy gets out. But it is Jo, dressed in the same cream linen trouser suit she wore to the funeral, her hair even shorter than he remembers. She gesticulates at the impatient driver of the SUV, tells him to calm down, to keep his wig on, before grinning and joining her sister and Tommy on the pavement.

Naomi walks slowly so that Tommy can keep pace with her. His face set in determination, he clings on to her finger. He is wearing a pale-yellow suit, a white shirt and a tiny floral bow tie. In his chubby little free hand he has a basket filled with what look like rose petals. His clothes are a small wonder; this miniature guy, still a baby, inside the formal attire of a man.

Sam blinks to clear his eyes of emotions he is struggling to keep under wraps. Naomi pulls him to her and kisses his cheek, then rubs at it with her thumb, laughing that she's put lipstick on him. She smells of perfume, of soap, of shampoo – exactly how she smelt the night Joyce died, and for some reason this makes him feel strange while at the same time making him want to sink his face into her soft, long neck. Gathering himself, he pulls away and greets Jo with a peck on the cheek before lifting Tommy onto his hip.

'Long time no see,' he says to Jo, who nods, her expression a little cagey. She does not hold his gaze. She asks if they can wait while she smokes, rolls a thin cigarette, which she sucks at deeply, causing it to burn away in no more than a couple of minutes.

Inside the Guildhall, the registrar, a woman of around forty, serious glasses and long brown hair threaded with white, greets them and explains how things will go. Sam confirms that yes, they will need one witness please, if that's all right, pays the fee in cash. After some form-filling and signing, they are shown through to a formal room with red carpet and blue chairs, where after a few seconds he hears the first notes of the Bon Iver album he and Naomi used to listen to all the time. When he turns to her, she is smiling up at him.

'You thought of everything,' he says.

'I did.'

'I love you,' he mouths as they are positioned to exchange their vows. Eyes fixed on his, Naomi presses her fist to her heart, points at him and holds up two fingers.

The ceremony is simple and brief. He is aware of the witness, a stranger; of his friends who are not here, who do not know this is happening. The words are eerily unemotional, almost perfunctory. They slide the wedding bands onto each other's ring fingers and then it is time to take Naomi in his arms.

'Mrs Moore,' he says and kisses her on the mouth. But he is not as lost in her as he imagined he would be, is too aware of the quietness, the absence of any kind of celebration, the lack of warmth from people who do not know either of them. There is no confetti, no cheering, no excited hubbub. It is as if they are watching themselves on television with the sound off. But then they're taking turns to sign their names in the register, and Naomi is holding his hand and saying, 'Hey, let's get out of here, shall we?'

He scoops Tommy up in one arm and lets himself be led out of the building. At the walled promenade overlooking the sea, Tommy lifts rose petals and watches them fly out of his hands.

Coaxed by Jo, who is holding her iPhone to take a photo, he and Naomi embrace again, but still he is self-conscious, half afraid that someone he knows will shout his name and ask him what the hell he is doing. I don't really know, he thinks. But the idea flies away, chases the rose petals out to sea.

No one they know passes by. There are tourists, who turn to look, then pretend they are not looking. Beyond the wall, a group of women are wading into the waves, shrieking and laughing, their belongings heaped like a bonfire on the pebbles. Jo takes photographs, calling instructions for how they should pose. They swap places to take different shots, make sure everyone has a photo they are happy with, but again it doesn't take long, and he finds it hard to relax or to feel the elation he expected to feel. Rushed. That's how he feels. Like it has all gone in a flash, like he wants to throw up his hands and say, *Please, please just wait, can we just slow down?*

It will take time, he supposes. It has all been a bit of a blur.

'Did you want to grab some cake and tea or something?'

he asks his wife, the word in his mind so familiar and yet so new. 'We could take Toms and your sister?'

'Nah. Let's just get going. I've parked my car at Joyce's. We can walk up.' She crouches down to Tommy and wiggles his little bow tie. 'OK, Tom-Toms, you're going to go with Auntie Jo, OK? Mummy and Daddy will see you when we get back.'

'Mummy,' he says. 'Da-da.'

She hugs and kisses him, and Sam picks him up to do the same.

'See you soon, little fella. Be good.' He hands him over to Jo, his heart clenching. Jo's skin is greasy, he thinks. Her fore and middle fingers are yellow at the knuckles. She is not who he wants Tommy to stay with. Tommy doesn't look particularly happy to be palmed off on his aunt. Instead, he is leaning away from Jo as if repulsed, staring after Naomi with an expression of longing and what looks like worry.

'No,' he says. 'No, no.'

Surely they should take him with them? He wouldn't be too much trouble. The hotel would find them a cot. These places accommodate anything, if you have the money.

'See you,' Jo says and offers that same unnerving grin. She lowers Tommy to the ground, crouches beside him and lifts his arm as if he is a puppet. 'Wave to Mummy and Daddy! Wave bye-bye! Say ta-ta!'

Tommy says, 'Ta-ta, ta-ta,' his voice a sad little sing-song.

This is wrong, all wrong, but Naomi is already taking his hand and leading him away, telling him to come on, come on, that she can't wait to jump in the hotel jacuzzi.

They round the little car park by the fudge shop and take the seafront back to the Cobb. On the beach, the swimmers hobble towards their clothes, chatting, pulling off their goggles. Under the creamy sun, the wide ocean sparkles.

Overhead, seagulls screech and wheel. One dives, snatches an entire sandwich from an unsuspecting tourist. She shouts in protest, outraged, but it is too late. The people close by laugh and shake their heads in sympathy. You can't trust the seagulls; they steal everything.

Sam turns back to wave to Tommy one last time, but his son is already out of sight, and for reasons utterly mysterious to him but which he attributes to the anxiety of grief, he feels a cold, creeping fear he cannot name. Until it crystallises enough for him to recognise.

He is afraid he will never see his son again.

CHAPTER 52

I went on the hotel website and had a good look, just to torture myself. I know, that was sad. Pathetic really. A super-posh five-star place right on the coast, which I will not name here for fear of damaging their reputation. Not that they could have had any idea they were harbouring a violent criminal. But I looked and I looked and I couldn't help thinking, *Oh Sam, we wouldn't have needed any of that, you and me.*

As for the honeymoon itself, I only know that Sam said he'd felt happy during those few days, but then qualified it and said if he was one hundred per cent honest, he felt like he was convincing himself he was happy. They had spent so much money. They had made this huge commitment to a new life together. There was no choice but to be happy.

Naomi spent a lot of time in the spa. She didn't come walking, so he went on his own but didn't go far in case it made her angry. She had little appetite for the delicious food, saying she didn't want to put on a load of weight she would then have to lose. She spent a fortune on beauty treatments, which made no discernible difference as far as

Sam could see. She ordered a lot of champagne. A lot of room service. It made him think of the documentaries she used to watch on television: lifestyles of the rich and famous.

He missed his son. Naomi wouldn't let him call, said it would upset him, and this stressed Sam out a great deal. Naomi often seemed agitated, but when he asked if she was all right, she said of course, why wouldn't she be?

As for the rest, to be honest, I'd rather not know the details. We all know what happens on a honeymoon. I didn't ask about that.

Sam and Naomi return from Devon on the Thursday. They have travelled in Joyce's old MG. On the way back, Sam drives. Naomi is glued to her phone.

'Hey.' He reaches over and lays his hand on her knee. 'You OK? You're a bit quiet.'

'I'm just sorting out house stuff. The buyer is coming over late afternoon, so we'll go to Joyce's first, yeah? I'll pick up my car and you can hang on for him. Does that work?'

'OK.'

'I thought you might want to show him the place, you know? His name's Peter Barnard. Do you want me to text you the name?'

'No. It's OK, I'll remember.'

This is it then. He is going to give his home to a stranger. And then it will no longer be part of his life, only his past. It will belong to someone else.

'Hey,' Naomi says, breaking into his thoughts. 'Don't be sad. Jo's dropping Tommy off, but she won't stay on or anything, so when you finish up, you can come straight over and I'll cook us a nice dinner, OK? I put a bottle of fizz in the fridge before I left and told Jo to keep her dirty hands off it.' She laughs lightly. 'It'll be our first proper night in the house! And I won't be kicking you out at ten this time.' She lays her hand over his and squeezes it. 'You can sleep over.'

Naomi's red Golf is on Joyce's drive where she left it. She tells him she'll see him in a bit, reminds him again that this is their first night together in their home, and to be sure and come straight over once he's met with Peter Barnard.

He waits while she loads their luggage into the car, then waves her off before stepping into the house that is no longer his. He is, he supposes, trespassing. But this was the arrangement.

Inside is a shock. He supervised the clearance company himself, but still, after the sumptuousness of the hotel, the unfurnished rooms of his childhood home, the scuffed walls and near-threadbare carpets strike a note of doom in his heart. Again he has the feeling that everything has gone too fast, even his marriage. In the last few days there have been flashes of the old Naomi – the pursing of lips, the silences, and the cruel asides followed by loud laughter, a hard slap on the arm, the phrase she used to say all the time: 'Only joking!'

He wanders up the hallway. Late summer, but the house is cold, unaired, a little musty. He digs in his jeans pocket, rubs his thumb and finger over the pearl at the end of the gold chain. The wedding band he slid onto Naomi's finger in the Guildhall as he promised his life to her. He wonders now why he didn't give her this necklace. It is all he has of Joyce now perhaps. And he needs to keep something for himself.

There is nothing to eat or drink. No kettle, no coffee, no

tea. There is nothing to sit on either, so he walks around the vast garden, back towards the veggie patch, where the courgettes have ballooned as if inflated. The carrot tops have pushed through. He pulls one out, washes it at the outside tap, eats it sitting on the back step. After a moment, he walks over to the shed. All the tools are in the back of his van with the boxes. His van is parked on Miranda's drive. The spade is still missing. For the thousandth time, he wonders where it is. In the sea, he guesses. Where Joyce promised herself she'd swim one day soon.

A feeling of fathomless sadness settles inside him.

He returns to the sitting room. Sits on the floor near the window. Waits.

At the sound of a car, he stirs, stands, goes to the window. But it is a Land Rover for next door.

He checks his watch. Five thirty. There has been no familiar warble of song thrush from his gran's clock. Late afternoon, Naomi said. How late is late? When does afternoon become evening?

Give it another half hour.

He sits, leans his head against the wall. Remembers Joyce bringing him into this room in his pyjamas and his Spider-Man dressing gown after he'd had a nightmare. She read to him, as she often did to calm him down. He remembers the two of them when he was about fifteen, painting the walls this pale pink colour. In the coving, a white patch where Joyce repaired it a few months ago. He should paint the whole lot, he thinks, before reminding himself he doesn't live here anymore. In a few minutes, he will leave this house for the last time. In about an hour, he will see his little boy. He will bath him, blow bubbles from the cup of his palm, make him laugh. He closes his eyes, sees Tommy's head thrown back, his little baby teeth.

He stirs, shakes himself awake. Checks his watch. It is a little after six; he must have dozed off. He is exhausted, he thinks. He has been tense these last few days on honeymoon, though he doesn't know exactly why. And tired – from grief, from stress and from something that feels a lot like guilt. That he has sold this house perhaps. That he has moved on before he was ready. Before Joyce was ready.

He texts Naomi. *Still no sign. How long do I give it?* X

His phone rings: Naomi.

'Hey,' she says. 'Someone wants to say hello. Say hello to Daddy.'

A moment later, Tommy's voice comes down the phone. Relief hits him – so hard he feels his eyes prickle. Why is he so relieved to hear his son? 'Da-da.'

'Hey there, Toms. How you doing, little man? I'll see you soon, OK? Daddy will see you soon.'

A shuffling; Naomi is back on the line. 'So he's not come yet?'

'No. I mean, I fell asleep, but I'm in the front room so I would have woken up if he'd rung the doorbell.'

'OK. If he's not there by seven, just come. Leave the keys under the mat or something, OK? I'll text him.'

'OK.'

Minutes pass. Naomi texts to say she's tried to get hold of Barnard but he's not picking up.

He replies: *OK. Love you. Xxx*

His stomach growls. More than anything, he is bored, his own thoughts weighted with heavy sadness despite the promise of the evening to come. He wonders if he will ever stop missing Joyce, if this is what his life is now: walking into a room and not finding her there. Except he won't be walking into these rooms now, not anymore.

Just before seven, he texts Naomi again: *Any news?*

A minute later, she replies: *I've sent him a message to say the keys will be under the mat in the porch, so just put them there. And leave the outer door on the latch, OK? I've told him it'll be open.*

OK, he writes. *On way xxx*

He leaves the keys under the mat and clicks the latch on the heavy red front door. As he steps slowly out of his former home, it occurs to him that they could have made this arrangement in the first instance, that there was never any real need for him to wait here. It's not as if there are any valuables left inside.

Still looking up at the house, he retreats until his back hits the MG. The small white rectangles within the larger white frames stare down at him. How many times did they paint those windows? Windows that will now undoubtedly be replaced. On the red front door, the brass lion's head is impassive, the bull-nose stone step a little green now with moss.

'Goodbye, house,' he says. 'Goodbye, Gran.'

He gets into the car. The finality of it all rolls through him in one great rushing wave. Gripping tight onto the steering wheel, he makes himself breathe in and out, in and out, until the need to cry abates.

Once he is sure he is able to drive, he pulls out of the driveway and heads up Lyme Road. As he takes the A35 bound for Bridport, he switches on the radio and, finding one of his favourite Pixies tracks, turns it up loud and sings words he knows off by heart but whose meaning he has never understood.

A little after 7.30 p.m., he pulls up outside Naomi's house. Their house now. Tommy goes to bed at seven. Hopefully

Naomi has kept him up.

As he gets out of the car, he spots Naomi's Golf opposite on the road. She must have parked it there because Jo's car was on the drive. He realises he could actually have parked on the drive, which is empty. This is his home now after all. Funny, he hasn't even seen all of it. He never asked for the tour; she never offered.

He strides down the path and rings the bell. As he waits, his chest swells with anticipation and something darker, something that contains a seed of dread. But when Naomi opens the door, she looks glad to see him, and at the sight of her, he relaxes a little. She puts one finger to her lips. Tommy is in bed then. Perhaps reading the disappointment on his face, she steps outside and kisses him.

'Sorry, babe,' she says. 'He was so tired, his eyes were literally closing on their own.'

'Oh,' he says, still fighting it. 'No, that's OK. I'll go up and see him.'

'Let him settle a bit first.' She reaches for his hand and pulls him inside. In the living room, she kisses him again and holds him tight. He tries to focus on her, but anxiety is climbing the walls of him. He wants to see his little boy. Why can't he?

Naomi pulls back, her eyes full of apology.

'Barnard called while you were on your way over,' she says. 'He got stuck on the M3, so he's going to pick the keys up later tonight. Sorry. Things haven't really gone to plan, have they?'

'It's OK,' he says. 'I'm shattered too actually. I think the last few weeks are catching up with me. Are you sure I can't just pop up and see Toms? If I keep super quiet?'

'In five minutes. Give him a chance to get to sleep. OK?'

He nods, reluctantly sits on the sofa. His legs ache, his

shoulders, his neck. It is a little painful to swallow; perhaps the glands in his throat are swollen.

Naomi sits beside him and again takes his hand.

'Listen,' she says. 'I feel bad saying this, but something's come up. You know Cheryl? My childminder?'

'Yes.'

'Well, she just called me in floods of tears. Her boyfriend, Harry's dumped her and she's in absolute bits. Don't be cross, but I said I'd go and meet her. I mean, I won't if you don't want me to, but if you're really tired, maybe it'll be good for you to just chill in front of the TV for a bit. I won't be long. An hour, couple of hours tops.'

'Sure,' he says. 'Of course. The evening's gone a bit pear-shaped anyway.'

'I'll be back before, like, ten? And then... well, we've got the rest of our lives, haven't we?' She smiles, her eyes flashing with promise. After her bouts of coldness on honey-moon, this kind concern for his feelings is a return to who she was before they married. But he can't tell whether he feels reassured.

'Sure,' he says. 'I'll watch a movie or something.'

'There's a pizza in the fridge. Pepperoni, your fave. And there's some watermelon cut up into slices for dessert. Can I bring you a beer or anything?'

'Please. Yeah, cheers.'

She heads into the kitchen, returns a moment later with a can of Peroni, which she snaps open and pours into a glass, then sets down on the table in front of him.

'Can I bring you some crisps? Snacks? Do you want me to put your pizza in?'

He shakes his head, no, though her solicitousness too is a change from how she was on honeymoon, where twice she let him eat breakfast alone, saying she needed a lie-in. It should set him at ease, this return to kindness. But it doesn't. More than anything, he wants to see his son. He wants, he thinks, the anxious feeling clarifying, to check he's there.

'Don't worry,' he says, almost rushing her now, knowing he will run upstairs the moment she leaves. 'I'll sort myself out. Go to your friend and I'll see you in a couple of hours.'

'Sure?'

'Sure. Go.'

She bends to kiss him. 'Stay right there. You'll barely notice.'

'Idiot.'

She giggles. 'Love you.'

'Love you too. So much.'

She strokes his cheek. A moment later, she is gone. He leans towards the front door, listens to her footsteps recede. Another moment passes. The click and slam of a car door. The rev of the engine. Silence.

CHAPTER 53

Sam takes off his shoes and creeps upstairs. It's quarter to eight; Tommy will be fast asleep by now, and if he isn't, who cares? He can sing him a song, read him an illicit story. He pushes open the door to the nursery, his heart fat in his throat.

Tommy is there, in his cot. Once again, relief hits Sam in the chest, so hard he has to grip the cot railings while he gets himself together. Tommy's arms are up, his tiny fists closed. The unease Sam has felt in some deep, dark part of him has come from this, he thinks: he expected to find the cot empty.

He has no idea why.

'Hey there, little guy,' he whispers.

He reaches over the side of the cot and strokes his son's head. The room smells of baby soap, of nappy cream and freshly laundered clothes. It smells of Tommy.

'Sleep well, little one. See you in the morning.'

It is a wrench to leave him, but Sam forces himself to creep out of the room, lingering a moment at the door before shutting it. On the landing, he hesitates. Instead of going downstairs, he decides to have a peep at the other bedrooms. This is his house now; surely it's OK to have a look around? But as he walks along the landing, a sense of foreboding grows in his belly: this time the feeling that he is intruding, that he should wait to be shown the more private rooms of the house.

But no, that's ridiculous. They are married now. He *lives* here. If Naomi hadn't been called away, she would have shown him the remaining two rooms, told him to make himself at home, since that is where he is.

A pang of homesickness then, for the wide hallway and staircase of his childhood home, the high ceilings and ornate cornices, the rounded corners, the deep skirtings, the cool air, the sense of space. By comparison, this house feels small, overheated, stuffy. The wall-to-wall carpets absorb all the noise, so that he has the impression of being in a kind of padded cell.

He opens the door to what he immediately realises is the guest bedroom. It is functional and neat, painted off-white, with pale grey curtains, a small white double bed, white wardrobe and chest of drawers. On the far side is his guitar, propped against the wall. On the top of the chest of drawers, a framed photograph of Naomi and Tommy, and a white leather jewellery box.

He sits on the bed a moment. The bedding he recognises from their old flat – white with blue swirls and flowers; IKEA, he thinks. On the bedside table is a red book called *The Book of Spells*, which makes him laugh; the copy of *Persuasion* he gave Naomi, which he tries not to notice is untouched; a tube of hand cream; a cluster of bangles; and a vial of some sort made from dark blue glass that on closer inspection turns out to be lavender pillow spray. On the back of the door is a white towelling bathrobe. He stands up, crosses over to the door and pushes it to his face. It smells of Naomi, and he holds it a moment longer to his nose, breathing her in before leaving the room and crossing the landing on tiptoes.

The last room is obviously the master bedroom. In contrast to the off-white, the walls are decorated in a similar peachy colour to the bathroom. The furniture is oak, he thinks. Solid, like the dining table downstairs. The duvet set is sumptuous and floral – camellias, roses and hibiscus in soft oranges and creams. There is one painting above the bed. It is similar to the art downstairs: a neutral abstract of the type you can buy in a department store – pleasant enough but not really what he would've picked out as Naomi's choice, not until this new, even-tempered, grown-up incarnation of her.

An epiphany then: she is trying to be something she's not. Maybe, a little bit. Maybe she's trying to put some distance between herself and her family, the notorious Harpers. He remembers her father's ramshackle and frankly grimy chalet down in West Bay – the smell of stale tobacco, the ancient Hotpoint cooker stained with years-old grease, scabbed with rust. Yes, maybe this is at the heart of all this brand-new stuff, the fact that she now wants to live in a clean house with straight walls and fitted carpets, doors that close properly, a kitchen with built-in appliances. Having had to make do with second-hand all her life, she turned it into a style choice in itself – that pride was always there in her, and he admired it. Now that she is earning good money, she wants to show the world that this is the case, of course she does. She wants to show *him* – he can remember how proud she was of her home the first time he came here.

It all makes such perfect sense, he is amazed this idea

hasn't dawned on him before. With a little wealth and a child to raise, she has made a new kind of life. And why shouldn't she?

He wanders over to the double bed and presses his fingertips against the bedding. Yes, he thinks: crisp and thick, like a hotel. It would be typical of Naomi to buy new bedding for their first night in their family home. At the thought of what might happen later, he decides a shower might be in order. He heads towards the door on the right of the bed, to what he suspects is the en suite. Yes, it is. A shower room. Similar colours, fluffy cream towels.

He strips off, steps into the shower, smiles to himself at the men's shower gel next to the women's on the shelf. Good old Nomes, thinking of everything.

He lets the water run over him, washing away the stress of the day, waking up a little after the lethargy of his after-noon snooze. When he grabs the shower gel, it is only half full, which strikes him as a bit weird. Unless maybe Jo sometimes stays over and this is hers. It smells good though: mint, but also, he thinks, lavender in the mix, maybe eucalyptus.

He washes his hair, rinses and steps out. On the towel rail are two towels – so thoughtful. But they are both damp. Nomes must have used one to dry her hair. He helps himself to a fresh one from the stack folded neatly on a wicker chair and wraps it around his waist. It is thick and soft, so unlike the scratchy towels he was used to at home. His former home. Joyce's home.

On the shelf above the sink, there are his-and-hers toiletries. He helps himself to the spray deodorant. It is not the brand he uses, but then Naomi often used to buy new things for him to try: clothes, shoes, an aftershave she liked, wanted him to smell of.

In the bedroom, he looks around for his boxes. There is no sign of them. Of course, they are still in the van, at Miranda's. He wonders now whether Naomi organised the timings on purpose. She will not have wanted a load of cardboard boxes in this tidy house, did not even suggest storing them in the garage. His honeymoon bag, he imagines, will still be in the boot of her Golf.

He smiles. Going forward, he will have to try and be neat or there'll be trouble.

He grabs his clothes from the bathroom floor, gives them a quick sniff. They are not too bad – all he's done is drive and sit about today – so he puts them back on, all except the socks, which he throws in the wicker laundry basket.

Downstairs in the kitchen, he puts the oven on high and unwraps the pizza. While the oven warms up, he cracks open another beer and wanders through to the living room, switches on the telly and flicks back and forth through the channels. Finding nothing of interest, he returns to the kitchen and slides the pizza into the oven. He is hungry actually. Starving. It's quarter past eight.

As he waits for his dinner to cook, he feels again the uneasy sense of being an uninvited guest. He wonders how long it will take him to think of this as his home instead of Naomi's place, himself a visitor.

Two hours later, he has eaten the pizza, drunk another beer, put his plate in the dishwasher and is sitting in front of the news with a cup of instant decaf coffee. It is getting on for half past ten. Naomi has been longer than she said she would be. But then if her friend is upset, she won't want to leave her.

At quarter to eleven, bored of the television and finding himself a little antsy, he texts her.

Everything OK?

No reply.

He stands up, wanders around the living room. Notices that the photograph of Naomi and Tommy has gone from the mantelpiece. On the sideboard next to a candle in a jar there is a smaller framed photograph of Naomi with what looks like the woman who answered the door that night. Cheryl, yes, of course. Cheryl is holding Tommy in her arms; the two women are grinning at the camera. Tommy is younger here, much smaller. A larger photograph shows Cheryl and a blonde man with a really tiny Tommy, what looks like a couple of months old. They are smartly dressed and holding him between them. That must be Harry, he thinks. Or was it Henry? It looks like a christening or something. Did Naomi say they were Tommy's godparents? He can't remember, but it would make sense – not like she has anyone else, apart from Jo. Whatever, they look so happy in this picture. What a shame things appear to have gone wrong between them. Poor Cheryl, he thinks then. Hope she's OK.

A key rattles in the lock and he feels a mix of joy and anticipation swell his chest. Naomi is home. Now their life together can start, truly start.

The living-room door opens. But it is not Naomi. It is Cheryl. And... is that the man from the photograph? It is, he's pretty sure.

'Hi,' Sam says, confused, holding up a hand.

But the woman's eyes widen in what looks like fear. She takes a step back, bumping into the man who Sam is convinced now is the man from the photograph. Harry.

'What's going on?' It is the man who has spoken. 'What are you...'

'I'm...' Sam begins, but a shallow simmering of fear has started in his gut. 'I was waiting for Naomi. She said she was meeting her friend, Cheryl?' Perhaps Naomi managed to reconcile them. Perhaps she has invited them back for a nightcap and is just parking the car.

'I'm Cheryl,' the woman says.

'Yes,' he says. 'Sorry. I know that. I recognise you from... the other night. Is Naomi with you?'

'I'm sorry,' the man says, pushing in front of Cheryl, his tone a little aggressive. 'What's going on?'

Cheryl raises her hand. 'Harry, it's OK. This is... you're Sam, aren't you? Naomi's boyfriend? Has she gone out?'

'Husband actually. And yes, she—'

'Husband? She never said.'

'No, well, we've just got married.'

'Right. Wait, why would Naomi be with *us*? We thought she was here.'

'Here? No. She said she was with *you*. She said...' Sam glances at Harry, back at Cheryl. 'Anyway, it doesn't matter. We... we just got back from our honeymoon this afternoon and she said you'd called her and you were upset so she was going to have a drink and a chat. I stayed to look after Tommy. Obviously.'

'Upset? Upset about what?' Cheryl looks across at Harry, frowns, returns her gaze to Sam.

Sam throws out his hands. 'I'm sorry, that's just what she said. She said you and Harry had split up or had a fight or something.'

'*What?*' Harry's face creases with incredulity.

'There must be some sort of misunderstanding,' Sam says, beginning to feel flustered. 'I can try and call her? I'm sure she'll be able to tell us what's going on.'

He pulls his phone from his pocket and dials. As he waits for the connection, he is aware of Harry muttering to

Cheryl, his face turned to her so that Sam cannot hear. The call goes straight to voicemail.

'Voicemail,' he says flatly, pocketing the phone. 'No reception maybe. I'm sure she'll call back in a minute. There's obviously been a mistake. Maybe I wasn't listening properly. I was really quite tired when she left.' He pushes his hands into his pockets, unsure what comes next. Really he wants them to leave, but politeness stops him from asking them outright. He still has no idea why they're here.

'So,' he says after a moment, 'you said she was supposed to be here. Were you meeting her here?' But even as he asks the question, it sounds ridiculous. It is after eleven at night.

'*Meeting* her here?' Harry is taking off his coat. 'She was supposed to be in this evening. She lives here, for God's sake.'

'I know that!' So intense is Sam's relief, he actually laughs. 'But... no offence, but what are you guys doing here? Do you have a key, or...?'

The couple exchange a glance so purposeful it is almost comical. But instead, a ball of something close to terror lands in his gut. When they look at him, they do so as if he has lost his mind.

'What do you mean, what are we *doing* here?' It is the woman, Cheryl, who has spoken. The man, Harry, is frowning hard. His face is dark pink. He looks livid, frankly. Furious.

'I mean...' Sam falters. 'I mean, why are you here so *late*?'

Cheryl gives a rather unpleasant half-laugh, her eyebrows drawing close together. 'Er, we live here.' Her tone is sardonic, as if she is explaining to an idiot.

Sam feels the rims of his eyes strain, air cold on his eyeballs. 'You *live* here?'

Harry laughs – like Cheryl's, the laugh is not kind. It is not a laugh of amusement but something meaner, a kind of scoffing disbelief.

'Of course we live here,' he says. 'This is our house. And I'm sorry, but I think I'm going to have to ask you to leave.'

CHAPTER 54

'Leave?' Sam looks from one to the other, bewildered. 'I can't leave. I only moved in this evening!'

'What the hell are you talking about?' Harry has raised his voice. His hands are fists, the knuckles white.

'I live here.' Sam too has raised his voice. 'I should be asking *you* to leave!'

Cheryl throws up her hands. 'Guys! Let's just... let's just take a step back, shall we? Nothing to be gained by falling out. I think we should all sit down. Let's sit down and sort this out like grown-ups, eh? Come on.'

For a moment the two men stand looking at one another, before Harry throws his coat on the sofa and sits down next to it. He sighs, pinching the bridge of his nose. Cheryl sits next to him. Sam takes the armchair, perching on the edge like a kid in a waiting room.

'Maybe one of us should go first,' Cheryl says. 'Whoever speaks speaks to the end; the others don't interrupt, OK? Does that work for everyone?'

Sam nods, chastened by this woman's natural authority. 'OK.'

'OK,' Harry says.

When neither Harry nor Cheryl says anything more, Sam clears his throat.

'Shall I go first then? OK? OK. Naomi's my ex. Well, she was my ex...'

He does his best to explain, throwing up his hands but persevering when Cheryl fails to suppress her gasps of incredulity or a frantic *She said what? She did what?* He tells them how he and Naomi met by chance after a year apart, how they got back together slowly after he learnt he had a son. He ploughs on doggedly. As he speaks, he keeps his eyes on theirs, which grow wider and wider with shock, willing them not to interrupt; the words are becoming more and more painful, the weight of dread in his belly getting heavier and heavier and heavier. If they stop him, he doubts he could carry on. But he does. He tells them about looking after Tommy on Wednesdays, about how he and Naomi fell in love again and how, because they knew each other so well, things went really quickly from that point on. He has the impression he is telling a story, the details of which are hazy. He tells them about Joyce's violent death, how in the aftermath Naomi took care of everything, literally every-thing, and how they returned this afternoon from their honeymoon in Devon in order to hand over the keys to his gran's place.

'Naomi told me to wait at the house,' he says, pausing a moment, only then noticing light leaking between the bare boards of all he has said. It is the truth, everything he has told them is the truth, and yet... 'Naomi told me...' he says again. 'Naomi told me...' He can get no further. Naomi told him. She told him to wait for a man who did not come. And when he got here, she told him she had to go and see Cheryl, her friend, her childminder, who had split up with her boyfriend. And yet here are Cheryl and her boyfriend, holding hands. Naomi said boyfriend earlier, he's pretty sure. But they are both wearing wedding rings. They have told him they live here. With Naomi.

'You guys are married,' he says. 'To each other.' It is almost a question.

'We are.' Cheryl glances at her husband, back at Sam. 'So, to clarify, Naomi told you this was *her* house and that Tommy was *your* baby?'

The noise that leaves him is no kind of word but a strange choking sob. When he makes himself look up, he sees two faces locked in incredulity and something else – a terrible, terrifying sympathy.

'Sam.' Cheryl says his name so softly, so gently.

Please, he thinks, don't say anything else. Please don't tell me. But she does.

'Tommy is Harry's child,' she says. 'He's Harry's.'

And although he has known this for seconds now, still her words send the breath from him, a thick pain like a kick to the chest. He glances from Cheryl to Harry, his head throbbing, blood pulsing in his ears. And sees the likeness. The blonde hair, the blue eyes, but also the same mouth, a mouth not his, nothing like his, and actually now he sees that the set of Harry's brow is the same as his son's, as Tommy's, his baby's... not his baby, though, not his son.

Not his.

'No,' he says, hands flat to his face. 'That can't... It can't... She said he wasn't mine. At first. It was me who had to ask, but she said no. It was me who...' He suspected it. He put the idea into her head. He *gave* it to her. She left him sitting there stewing and returned with a different story, a story he took for a reluctant admission of the truth. But it wasn't the truth. It was his own notion, his own dream reflected back at him, used against him.

He looks at Cheryl, who shakes her head, her eyebrows creasing in sorrow. 'I'm so sorry.'

'But... I mean, are you sure?'

They nod.

'But... don't you *mind*?'

She narrows her eyes, shakes her head a fraction as if she hasn't heard. 'Mind what? Mind her using Tommy to lure you into marriage? Yes, I do mind. I'm beginning to suspect we won't see Naomi again, to be honest. I suspect we're all victims here – I'm just not sure what of.'

'No.' Sam raises his palms: stop. 'Not that. I mean, don't you mind Naomi having a son with your husband?' And then it dawns. Of course. 'Oh my God,' he whispers. 'She's the surrogate. She's your surrogate. That's why she lives here. Did you keep her on for the breastfeeding?' Though he never saw her breastfeed Tommy. Only bottles. Only ever bottles.

'No,' he hears Cheryl say, so softly. 'She's not our surrogate. She's our live-in nanny, that's all. Tommy's mine and Harry's. He's mine and Harry's little boy.'

'*What?*' But as he looks from one to the other, he sees that they are telling the truth, and that this too is a truth he has known, for how long he is not sure. From the moment they walked in? Or before that, when he used another man's shower gel? The spare room is Naomi's. Of course. That's why her books are there, the bathrobe that smells of her. When he explained, he didn't even mention that Naomi had claimed to be Tommy's mother, because it had never occurred to him that she was not.

Harry and Cheryl's hands are clasped tight. The look of shock on their faces is, he suspects, a mirror of his own.

'I'm going to check on Toms.' Harry lets go of his wife's hand and runs upstairs. A moment later, he returns and nods to her. 'He's fine. Asleep.'

Sam wants to say, *Of course he's fine. I'm his father, for God's sake.* But finds he cannot speak. Upstairs, his beautiful baby boy sleeps, a child so much part of him he no longer feels whole without him. A child he will never see again after this night. A child not his, never his.

'Are you OK?' It is Cheryl. 'Do you want a glass of water?' She rummages in her bag, hands him a tissue. 'Do you need anything? You look like you're going to be sick.'

Sam shakes his head. 'I'm fine,' he manages. 'I'm...'

'Naomi came to us in January,' Harry says after a moment – calm now, almost conversational. 'We'd advertised for a live-in nanny because we both work long, sometimes unpredictable hours and need flexibility. Plus, we didn't want Thomas going to a nursery because of the whole pandemic thing. Naomi had a great CV, a lovely way about her, not to mention a driving licence. We were looking for someone independent, who could basically see to Tommy's needs, look after the house and generally be a third pair of hands. Someone who could hold the fort, you know? Who wouldn't be waiting for us to get in so she could dash off. Naomi said she was looking for a private arrangement because the nurseries were closed.'

'She never worked in a nursery,' Sam says. 'She was a doctor's receptionist.'

'Right.' Harry's eyebrows rise and fall. 'Right.' He exhales heavily, scratches his head. After a moment, and with apparent effort, he presses on. 'She said she was keen to live in because her partner had recently walked out on her and she was finding it lonely by herself. She...' He throws a questioning glance to his wife. 'Did she rent out her place?'

Cheryl nods.

'So she *didn't* sell her flat?' Sam asks.

Cheryl shakes her head. 'I think her sister rents a room off her. I could be wrong. Anyway, when she told me she'd hooked up with her ex, she said she was saving hard for a house. She encouraged us to go out, said she'd babysit whenever, we could just pop an extra tenner in her wages. She even took Tommy out on a Saturday morning sometimes to give us a lie-in.'

She came to him. She came to wish him happy birthday.

'When I came here,' he says, 'you were here. You were here that night. I thought *you* were the babysitter, but...'

'I get why you would think that. Why would you think anything else? She didn't go out much, did she?' She looks at Harry, who shakes his head. 'When we went out, I paid her a bit more obviously, but if you're saying you came here in the evening a few times, well, it probably wasn't about extra money, was it? She was getting us out of the way to make you think this was her house.'

'But I always had to leave by ten. She said it was because she had to be up early with the baby. I was so impressed with her dedication. It was unlike her. I thought she'd turned over a new leaf. I was so taken with Tommy, I was so wrapped up in...'

He makes himself breathe. When he thinks he can continue, he adds, 'I didn't want to lose him. I just did what I was told. I didn't want to scare her away. I wanted her to trust me.'

'You poor lamb.' Cheryl sighs.

He shakes his head. 'We only met again in April and then Joyce... my gran... it's all been so up and down. Whenever she came to mine, she said she'd taken time off, but she always left around five, five thirty.'

'To get back here before us,' Harry fills in. 'We tend to get home around seven.'

'I thought she was taking time off, but... she was doing her job, there, at my place. Joyce and me, we were helping her do her job. On Wednesdays we were... we were giving her a day off.'

A shocked silence falls.

'And when did you say you got married?' Harry asks.

'Monday.' Sam has the impression he is floating, looking down at himself having this conversation here in this room with its grown-up fixtures and fittings, with its furniture that is not Naomi's taste. It is not Naomi's furniture. It is not Naomi's house. It is not his house. Upstairs, a baby sleeps, arms thrown up, fists tight, an angel child who is not his, was never his. This angel child is not Naomi's. There is no blood link. No link at all. He has no right to see him ever again. He never had. He has no son, no family, no home.

No Joyce.

Does he have a wife? Was the woman at the Guildhall a plant, an impostor?

'Monday,' Cheryl is saying, though to Harry, not Sam. 'That was when her sister had Tommy for the afternoon, wasn't it? Naomi said she had a dental appointment and then she was off on holiday.' She looks at Sam. 'She took this last week off. Well, Tuesday to Thursday. She said she was going on a minibreak. A cheap deal, she said. We had no idea. She said Jo could cover, but... well, we decided to take a few days off, didn't we? To be honest, we weren't over-keen on the sister. Then this evening we were out with friends and she said she'd be back and that she could cover it.'

'But she just isn't the type to...' Harry says. 'Her sister perhaps, but not Naomi.'

'She is the type,' Sam whispers. 'I thought she'd changed. But she hasn't. She's exactly the same. Worse. Oh God.' He plunges his face into his hands. 'Tommy's my son,' he says, unable to stop himself from weeping in front of these strangers. 'I mean, I understand. He's not. I know that. I know I have to... accept... but he's my little boy, you know? He was. I loved him.' He looks up, searches their faces. 'I *love* him.'

CHAPTER 55

'I should go,' Sam says, wiping at his eyes with the backs of his hands.

'We can't let you go like this,' Cheryl says. 'You're traumatised. You're probably in shock. I mean, we're all in shock, but at the end of the day, we've lost our nanny, whereas you... you've lost everything, haven't you? We need to try and get hold of Naomi. There might yet be an explanation.'

Harry stands up. 'I think we should call the police.'

Sam shakes his head. 'I'll call her.'

But it goes straight to voicemail again. He suspects her phone is off.

'What about her sister?' Cheryl asks.

'I don't have her number.'

'I'm going to check on Toms,' Cheryl says and leaves the room. Sam watches her go, understands her need to see her son with her own eyes. Didn't he feel that need too? Doesn't he still?

'Sam?' Harry is sitting down again, inclined forward, keen for information. 'What's your financial arrangement with Naomi? They say follow the money, don't they? You said she'd pretty much sold your grandmother's house from under you, by the sounds of it. I'm beginning to think...'

'I was barely paying attention. My gran had just been murdered.' Something in the fog. A smell. The smell of soap. Naomi smelt of soap when she came to him that night, in the small hours. He had roused her from her bed and she had come straight over. So why did she smell of soap, like she did at their wedding, as if she had just taken a shower? Did she care so little that she stopped to take a shower when he needed her so urgently? Yes. Yes, she did.

'Sam? Sam? Do you know where the funds were transferred to?'

Sam looks up to find Harry staring at him.

'The funds for your grandmother's house. Do you know where they are?'

'She set up a joint account. For both of us. For Tommy. She said it was for Tommy.'

'Oh Christ.'

'She said the house funds went in there. She was going to transfer them to an instant-access ISA when we got back. She said that would put us in a stronger position for buying our own place...'

'Oh Christ,' he says again.

Cheryl reappears in the doorway and shakes her head. 'She's taken her stuff. Cleaned out. She's left the photo of her and Toms.'

Harry stands up again, stares down at Sam. 'Do you have a banking app? Can you check it?'

With shaking hands, Sam manages to access the Barclays app. Once in the joint account, he stares at the number for a long time. Seventy-five pounds and forty-five pence. He continues to stare at this number after he has relayed the figure to Harry, after Harry has said oh Christ for the third time.

'Maybe the funds haven't cleared,' he says. 'Let's just... let's just wait for her to call, shall we?'

Cheryl shakes her head. 'I don't think she's going to call. This is fraud – I think we need to look it in the eye now. Let's just call the police, shall we?'

Harry pulls out his phone, strides over to the sideboard. He picks up the photograph of Naomi, Cheryl and Tommy, puts it back.

'Yes, hello, yes, police please.' He leans forward, presses his fingertips against the top of the unit before putting the flat of his hand to his forehead. 'Yes, hello. I need to report a... I think it's a fraud... a serious financial fraud.'

As he talks, Harry wanders into the kitchen. When he returns, he shakes his head. 'They're saying they'll send someone over when they can. It could be tomorrow. We're all safe and well, so it's not urgent apparently.' He looks at Sam, his eyes troubled. 'Do you... do you want a hot drink? A tea?'

Cheryl stands up. 'Yes. Let's make some tea. We could be here a while.' She must make some sign to her husband, because a moment later, Sam finds himself alone in the living room. As the door to the kitchen closes, he hears Cheryl say in low, soft tones, 'He won't have anywhere to stay, will he, poor thing?'

His heart quickens. Blood rushes through his veins. Before he is aware of what he's doing, he is on the stairs, then on the landing; he is scooping Tommy from his cot, shushing him, pressing his soft head into his neck, wrapping his thick fleece blanket around his precious little shoulders. *Shh, little guy, it's OK, it's OK.*

Creeping down the stairs now, one painstaking step at a

time, lifting the latch, quietly, quietly – *shh-shh-shh* – opening the front door, silently, silently. From the kitchen, low voices reach him without the sense. Sam steals outside.

Cool air hits him. He runs to his grandmother's car, pulse hammering in his temples. Another minute, Tommy is in the passenger seat, himself behind the wheel. He leans over and unwraps the blanket. Tommy is in his quilted sleep suit. He will be warm enough. Talking to him all the while, Sam rolls the blanket into a kind of pillow and tries to prop him up a little, then pulls the seat belt around him, under the crook of his arm. *That's OK. It'll be OK.*

Another second and he is starting the engine. Another and he is turning out of the cul-de-sac of yellow street lamps, dark sleeping houses, neat strips of lawn.

He drives, socks slipping a little on the pedals. To where, he has no idea.

In a lay-by somewhere along the A35, he stops the car. He is crying too much to see, sweating, unsure which is which as it runs over his chin, down his neck, into his shirt. He breathes in and out, in and out, sobs breaking, a high keening of panic and terror.

What now? What the hell happens now?

In the front seat, Tommy's eyes are round.

'Da-da,' he says, and again Sam hears this high and terrible noise coming from his own mouth.

'Yes,' he whispers. 'I'm your da-da. I'm your da-da, little man.'

CHAPTER 56

I was of course ignorant of all of this until later that night.

As for Cheryl and Harry, they are bewildered and confused, shocked and deeply dismayed. In the kitchen, they confer in low voices about what to do next, how to help this poor man, how to track down this morally bankrupt woman they believed to be their lovely nanny. Whether they will have to take her to court. What exactly is the nature of her crimes with regard to them. She has stolen everything from this man, this Sam, that much is obvious. Conned him into parting with everything he owns, into thinking he was a father, that she was a mother. My God. Doesn't bear thinking about. They just can't believe it. There is no way, no way they'd ever have—

The click of the front door. They stop talking. For a moment, their eyes meet.

'Naomi?' Harry calls out, his voice shaky with doubt.

Cheryl stares at him, her heart beating fast.

Is it Naomi, returned to explain the unexplainable?

Hearing nothing more, they open the kitchen door.

Seeing no one in the living room, again their eyes meet in question. A pit of nausea has formed in Cheryl's belly.

'Sam?' Harry strides across the room, throws open the door to the little square of hall. There is no one there. 'Sam? Sam?'

In the house, silence. Total silence. Nerve endings tingling, Harry runs up the stairs. The nursery door is open.

He is already calling for his wife when he sees the cot is empty.

'Cheryl! Cheryl!' He leans over the banister and shouts down the stairs. 'He's taken Tommy! He's taken him, oh my God, call the police, call 999, I'm going after him.'

This time, there is no delay. Ten minutes later, sirens wail. Harry has come back to the house, is holding his wife to him when the blue lights flash through the sitting-room window. A police officer is at the door with a woman, also in uniform, who tells them she is the family liaison officer and who offers tea, which they decline. They sit down on the sofa where moments ago they found out that their highly experienced childminder was conducting a long and very personal fraud, the motive for which appears to be money.

But when questioned, they have no description of Sam's car. The cop, whose name is DC Jacobs, writes down the name Sam, but that is all Harry and Cheryl have. They don't know if he's from Bridport, no, sorry. He might be from Lyme Regis. He might be from anywhere. They're so sorry. Cheryl thinks he did tell her his last name the one time she met him on the driveway, but no, she can't... oh God, she can't remember, think, Cheryl, think. No, it's gone. So sorry.

Harry can describe him – he is blonde, like Harry

himself, with blue eyes. He is tall, slim, fit-looking, with broad shoulders, muscly arms, perhaps from a gym. Thirty-ish. Softly spoken. Gentle in his way. Sensitive. But trauma-tised. They saw it in his face. His eyes looked crazy. Recently bereaved too, under violent circumstances. His grandmother was his primary carer growing up. Murdered, he said, yes, he definitely told them that. Only weeks ago. A close bond, that much was obvious. And he was very much in love with Naomi Harper. Was with her for years before. But Harry and Cheryl only moved here recently so they wouldn't really know.

'Wait a second,' DC Jacobs says. 'His grandmother was murdered, you said?'

DC Jacobs makes a call. The grandmother's case rings a bell. It's still live, he thinks. It was in Lyme. A nasty affair, burglary gone wrong. Terrible. He tells his colleague to search the violent death of an elderly lady last month over in Lyme. Failing that, search for deaths recorded last month in West Dorset, women aged seventy and over, next of kin listed as Sam. Surname unknown. Find the surname.

'He was completely destroyed.' Cheryl is crying now; the tears come in waves. 'He would do anything, anything at all. He thought Tommy was his. He... he loves him. He loves him like a father. Like blood, you know? Oh God, he'll be desperate.'

What else? Anything, even if it doesn't seem relevant, anything else at all?

No, sorry. Nothing.

They move on to Naomi's car registration, but the Golf is immediately found to be parked on the road outside the house.

'She might have gone with her sister,' Cheryl says.

'Joanne Harper. She has a black Ford Focus. Or dark blue. Dark grey maybe. Dark anyway.'

'Registration?' On the cop's forehead, a vein twitches.

But as he predicted, Cheryl and Harry shake their heads.

'No, sorry,' Cheryl sobs. 'I mean, you just don't think people are criminals, do you? You don't go round thinking that about people.'

While the copper phones it in and they wait for a registration trace, the family liaison officer brings tea that no one except her drinks. The trace comes in. Joanne Harper's car and registration are then relayed for an ANPR. And that's when DC Jacobs calls the dog unit and Cheryl becomes hysterical.

By now there are three police cars outside Harry and Cheryl's house. At the windows of the other houses, curtains open; on doorsteps, neighbours stand in their dressing gowns, arms crossed over their chests. Officers go door to door. They search the area. In the gutter, they find an iPhone, which will turn out to be Sam's and which, I presume, must have fallen out while in blind panic he was bundling the baby into Joyce's low-slung MG.

'We'll need to unlock it,' the cop says, standing in Cheryl and Harry's living room. 'Unless you know the passcode?' He takes a photograph of the screen saver with his own phone: Sam and Tommy, grinning. Father and son. No longer. 'At least we have a photograph now,' he says.

'Can I try it?' Cheryl says. 'The phone? It might be Tommy's birthday.'

Her hunch is correct. It feels like the most monumental breakthrough.

'That's saved a lot of time,' DC Jacobs says then calls Naomi Harper – the most frequently used number. There's a long text thread to read, but for now he needs to find someone, anyone who knows this guy.

'Miranda Clarke?' he says. The second most frequently texted number. 'That name ring any bells?'

'No,' Harry says. 'As we keep telling you, we don't know this guy. For God's sake, we don't know anything about him except he was our nanny's boyfriend. Husband, sorry.'

'Try and stay calm, sir. We're doing everything we can.'

And that's when Jacobs calls me.

CHAPTER 57

Sam is about to start the engine again when the glove compartment catches his attention. Hours ago, on the way home from Devon, he saw Naomi putting what looked like a document of some kind in there.

'What's that?' he asked her.

She smiled. It was that same slightly unnerving smile she had used on honeymoon. Smug, knowing, a little mean.

'You'll find out soon enough.' A different smile then: flirtatious, inviting, full of promise.

He focused on the road, on the evening ahead. Naomi put on Radio 6 Music and they listened to New Music Fix until she complained she didn't know any of the tunes and put on her own Spotify playlist, full of their old favourites: Outkast, Franz Ferdinand, Ezra Furman. They sang along loudly and, he thought then, joyfully. They sang like they were two people in love driving home to their baby boy. The document dropped out of his mind.

But now he opens the glove compartment and pulls out a thick A4 envelope. Inside is a typed letter, which begins:

April 2021

Dear Sam,

When I saw you today, I so wanted to tell you the truth, but I couldn't, I just couldn't.

CHAPTER 58

Dear Sam,

This is probably the last thing I'll write. The last chapter, if you like, in the story only I knew I was telling. By now our time zones will be very different. At first, I didn't know when you'd read this letter, but now I know that it'll be after Cheryl and Harry have told you the truth and I'm long gone where no one will ever find me. I'm writing this last bit on our honeymoon, in case you're wondering. By the time you get to HERE, your heart will have broken a thousand times. You'll know that I killed your precious granny, and that baby Tommy wasn't even mine, let alone yours!

You're such an idiot, Sam. Apart from the blue eyes and blonde hair, he looks nothing like you or me. Still, you wouldn't be the first bloke to fall for a claim that he looks more like his grandfather on his mother's side, his great-granny on his father's side – that'd be Joyce; even she was fooled. So you see, I did her a favour, when you think about it. She would have been heartbroken, finding out the truth about her so-called great-grandson, the love of her life after you. It was better this way. As for you, I wanted you to hear the whole story from me so you'd understand it better.

Funny, when I started this letter, right at the beginning, that very first day I saw you, I really did intend to tell you the actual truth, but I just couldn't. How could I? There you were looking like your life hadn't changed one tiny bit, all fit and healthy with the wind in your hair and not a care in the world. You looked like you were doing brilliantly, Sam. Doing brilliantly without me. And there's me with someone else's snotty kid I'm forced to look after unless I want to actually starve, roaming around in the cold like an absolute loser. If I'd told you the truth, I'd have had to admit I'd lost my job because of some ridiculous and completely untrue claim that I was bullying other employees and taking fake sickies. I knew when I got my first warning they were jumping through hoops, trying to make it look like they'd gone through the correct procedure. They had it in for me from the start, so I left after the second written warning, because if they fired me without a reference, I'd never find a job again.

But of course there were no jobs, were there? The pandemic was an absolute nightmare. And I couldn't even get furlough because I didn't have a job anymore, and I was a key worker, for fuck's sake. I was fucked, completely fucked, and that's on you, Sam Moore, so don't even try and say it isn't.

If you hadn't left, if you hadn't been such a coward, none of this would have happened, none of it.

All I could find was some poxy babysitting job, which Jo found actually, online. At first, I was like, no way. I hate kids, as you know. But she convinced me it would be *an absolute earner because it was live-in, which meant I could rent out my flat. You'll be loaded, she said. And you only have to do it till things ease up again. So I agreed. Jo wrote it all down for me, what I had to say in the interview. She rehearsed me, helped me with the paperwork. It was her who had all the childminder qualifications, not me. Easy enough to stick a mugshot on there and pass it off as my own, especially with a couple new to the area. Not like they're going to think, Hang on, isn't she one of the Harpers? Best avoid. It was easy to stand out from the other mouth-breathing applicants – after all, it's not like women in their early thirties and looking for a live-in position grow on trees, do they? Plus, I had my own car.*

So yeah, Cheryl and Harry couldn't believe their luck. As for me, it suited me down to the ground as long as I didn't have to see anybody. Which I didn't. Cheryl and Harry were the sweetest people, like, ever. I told them my partner had recently left and that things had been tough. I pretended I was fighting back the tears. I just want to be part of a nice family, I said, and live in a nice house with nice people. Not that I'd ever invade their space, mind, oh no. I told them I was doing an MA in child psychology – where the hell that came from, I do not know. Evenings I'd be in my room studying. They wouldn't even know I was there. And they didn't. Except I was watching Netflix on my laptop with my voddie and Diet Coke.

As for the flat, it was easy enough to rent out: two bedrooms, perfect for a couple of young professionals. I had it looking well funky by then. After you left, I'd painted it and ordered some cool throws online. Well, I had plenty of time, didn't I? Stuck in day after day staring out of the window. Then when one of the tenants found another place, Jo took her room; I didn't charge her full whack, obvs, but by then we had a whole other money-making plan going, which you now know all about. Plus, I needed her help.

So yeah, that's the truth I couldn't tell you that day on the beach. It was just one humiliation too many, to be honest, and I wasn't about to let you and Joyce gloat over me and my reduced circumstances: Naomi Harper lost her job? Always knew she'd come to nothing. Skank. Loser.

And maybe that would have been it. Maybe it would have. But you had to add insult to injury, didn't you? Typical Sam. You had to come out and ask me if the baby was yours, except you were too much of a coward to put it in actual words. You thought I'd try and pull a stunt like that? I mean, seriously? What the hell do you take me for? Actually, don't answer that. I knew in that moment what you took me for, what you always had. I knew it before that moment really. I knew what you'd think when you saw me with baby Tommy, knew you'd put two and two together and get five, and that's why I heard it loud and clear in the words you didn't have the balls to say. When we were first together, I thought you saw me differently, but deep down you're just like all the rest: the Harper girls are lowlifes, criminals, trash. That was the lowest blow ever and you didn't even know you were striking it, did you? I couldn't believe you had the nerve to basically ask me: Naomi, are you a monster? Are you a monster that would keep a child secret from a man who always wanted kids?

And then you were all, like, I didn't mean to upset you, Nomes. Sorry, Nomes. Forget I said it. Too right I was upset! And no, I didn't forget you'd said it – how could I? I knew then that your opinion of me was less than nothing, that you'd asked to meet me for your own selfish reasons that had nothing to do with loving me or missing me or thinking I looked hot when we bumped into each other. And there was me, making myself all nice because I thought, I actually thought, you wanted me back. Can you imagine what a slap in the face that was? After everything you'd already done to me? To find out that all you wanted was the fucking baby?

Oh my God, Sam. Literally though.

So I went into the toilet and I sat in that cubicle and had a little cry, and then I thought it all through. He wants a baby, I thought. Why not give him a baby? Why not have some fun for a change? Why not see how far I can take it before I bring his world crashing down like he did mine? If he thinks I'm so low, then fuck him, I'll go even lower.

Yeah, I thought. Why not? I'll admit, it all went a bit further than I meant it to, but we are where we are and I can't go back. It's not my fault. I'm not the psychopath who left his girlfriend in solitary confinement.

Anyway, I made my decision. I dried my eyes and washed my hands and came back into the pub, and I was like, yes, Sam, you were right, Sam, I've been an idiot, Sam, Tommy's yours, Sam.

The look on your face! I nearly lost it, but I managed to pass it off as being upset. Laughter and tears are close, babe, you should know that by now. This is going to be too easy, I thought, and I called Jo and told her the plan and she was like, Get in. Let's teach that bastard not to mess with the Harper girls.

Jo is literally the only person I trust in this world. I'm not even exaggerating.

After that, I just made it up as I went along. The

biggest thing I remembered about you was that if I ever wanted you to do something, I had to pretend like I didn't care if you did it or not or even that I didn't want you to do it. I pretended I was protective of little Tommy. I couldn't let just anyone into his life. Bingo, you wanted to be in his life even more. I didn't trust you after what you did. We had to take it slow. Bingo, you wanted me back. I didn't have to pretend you'd hurt me; that bit was always true. You tore out my heart when you left and didn't give me a backward glance. But the more I held you back, the more you pushed forward. It was you who asked me to dinner, you who asked me to marry you, you who gave me Joyce's diamond ring, which by the way I'm going to sell first chance I get, along with the shitty second-hand wedding ring. I don't want your family's junk, Sam. I've got enough junk of my own.

Knowing what you know now, you might be wondering where I got all that guff about the sleepless nights and the breastfeeding and all that stuff. You're probably thinking, what the hell? She hasn't even had a baby! All that came from Cheryl. She and I got quite close actually. She gave me the whole deal, warts and all, over coffee and glasses of Pinot Grigio, dontcha know. Why? Because she liked me and because I asked her. I asked her like I was interested. She thought I was so nice, such a great listener, and the funny thing is? I was nice with them, the Baxters. Part of me is gutted I had to leave them. I'll miss them and I'll miss the me I was with them. Funny how when you catch a break from your reputation for five sodding minutes, when people judge you only on what they can see, it's like you're allowed out of the sewer for a bit; you get to swim in the luxury pool where the water is all warm and clean. They were so respectful!

They trusted me, and I think I just enjoyed that trust, the praise, not to mention the fluffy towels and the central heating on whenever I wanted. I felt safe, even safer than I'd felt with you.

And Tommy. I got used to his sweet little face, so I suppose I'll miss him a bit. I'll even miss us, Sam. Our little family. It was nice, wasn't it? I'm thinking I might like a little family one day. Not with you, obvs. That would be mental.

I'm not sure when my idea became more like an actual path, like I was going to see it through. But Pisceans, once we decide we're in, we're in, you know? I think it might have been when I saw Joyce limping, after the first attempt at removing her. Maybe then, yeah, I knew that if it was going to work, I had to really make it count. No more failed attempts, no more half-arsed efforts. Killing someone is probably the most decisive thing anyone will ever do. You can't mess about. I think I realised that the day Joyce measured her length on the stairs. So once I'd finally figured out how to remove her and get away with it, well, the rest was mine for the taking. They say revenge is a dish best served cold. Mine was on ice, mate, the kind of ice that's so cold it literally burns right through you. Plus, there was all that money to be made, enough to set me and Jo up for life.

I wonder if you've checked the bank account yet? I bet you haven't. You never think about that stuff because you've never had to. But you might want to do that round about now. I'm wondering where you'll be when you read this, over there in your time zone. My guess is, you've left Cheryl and Harry's in a proper state. You've driven back to Joyce's, but it's not your house anymore and you're like, shit, boohoo, what am I going to do? Maybe you've gone straight to that cow Miranda to blub all over her. She'd love that – you know she's into you, don't you? So obvious. Tell her from me she needs a haircut, will you? And some decent clothes. No wonder she's single. No, I don't think you'll go there. It'll be late at night and you've always had that overprivileged thing of not putting anyone to any trouble, haven't you? Again, because you've never had to.

You've got nowhere to go, have you, Sam? No safety net to catch you now you've fallen. And if you have checked the Barclays account, you'll have found it like Mother Teresa's initials. M. T. Empty, get it? I left you a little bit, enough to tide you over, which is all I've ever had. Hand to mouth, mate. Stressful, isn't it? Not having the cushion of wealth, knowing that if you mess up, no one can help you out, no one will catch you. I'm not cruel, by the way. I'm just a survivor. The Harpers are all survivors. You? You're a spoilt little rich boy. You've been spoon-fed, that's your trouble. Joyce has made a soft touch of you, her precious little grandson. You wouldn't know you were being conned if a bloke tried to sell you a watch from the inside of his jacket. I transferred the cash while we were on our honeymoon and you didn't even notice.

Once I've dropped you off at Joyce's, the plan is to go back to Cheryl and Harry's, bundle them out of the door and throw my bag in Jo's boot. Not like I'm going to use my own car as a getaway vehicle, is it? I'm not stupid. Then you'll come over, thinking you're going to spend your first night with your new bride and your baby son... Well, you know the rest. I just wish I could be a fly on the wall when they walk in and see you there. Actual lol! They'll be like, What the hell? And you'll be like, What the hell? And then, if they don't throw you out or call the police, they'll tell you they're Tommy's parents! Actual. Massive. Lol.

I wonder who's going to be most shocked, you or them. What am I even saying – you! You'll have a heart attack, I guarantee it. Like Nonna Joyce.

By then, Jo and me will be halfway to London, if everything has gone to plan, which, if you're reading this and weeping, I'm hoping it has. No one will find us there. We're going to ditch the car and get a train. The biggest pain in the arse was not realising we couldn't get the money for the house until bloody probate was granted, which in the case of a suspicious death could take over a year. A year! By then, my cover would be well blown. Still, you won't know that when the Baxters tell you what a fool you've been, will you, and that's what counts. All I really wanted was for you to feel worse than I did when you left. Much worse. And we've got the savings Joyce had already put in your name, plus nearly two hundred grand in cash, so that should give us time to figure out what's next. I'm just fantasising about you walking out of the Baxters' place completely empty-handed: no Tommy, no Naomi, no money. No gran. And until you read up to HERE, thinking you've got no home.

Humiliated. Abandoned. Just like I was.

Doesn't feel great, does it, Sam?

Your 'wife',

Naomi xxx

PS. One last thing. I love you, Sam. I do. But you don't deserve me.

CHAPTER 59

The call comes a little after midnight. I'm awake, which is unusual. Some might say that somewhere inside me I must know Sam is in trouble. I don't believe in that stuff, but I am awake in that moment, Sam actually is on my mind, and I have a weird and quite unpleasant feeling of doom. At first, I think the feeling is caused by a nightmare from which I've woken only to forget it. But then my phone rings, and when I see it's Sam calling, my guts flip with dread. He never calls so late. Never has.

'Sam,' I say. 'Hey. Are you OK?'

'Is this Miranda Clarke?'

'Speaking.' My hair follicles lift; my entire scalp tingles. 'Where's Sam? Is he OK?'

'This is DC Jacobs from Dorset Police. We're trying to locate a man called Sam. I take it you're a friend of his?'

'Yes.'

'Can you tell us his surname please?'

'It's Moore. Why? What's this about? Is he OK?'

There is a moment; I hear him relay Sam's surname to someone else before he comes back on the line.

'I'm calling you from Mr Moore's phone because yours is a frequently called number. He left his iPhone at the scene.'

'Scene? What scene? What's going on?' I make myself shut up.

'We're looking for Mr Moore in connection with an abduction, and I need to ask you if you can help us identify his whereabouts.'

'*What?*' Obviously, I am reeling. It's the middle of the night and a cop is telling me Sam has—

'Hang on,' I almost shout. 'An abduction? Sam? That's absolutely impossible. Sam would never... Who of, for God's sake?'

'Thomas Baxter. One year old. Known as Tommy.'

'Tommy?' I laugh. Incredible, but I do. 'This is a mix-up. You mean his son? Tommy Harper? Actually, Tommy's mother and Sam got married this week. It'll be Moore now, I guess.'

'The infant's name is Tommy Baxter. He belongs to Cheryl and Harry Baxter. We understand that your friend found this out less than an hour ago and is now on the run with the child. We have a trace on his vehicle.'

'What?' I am reeling. DC Jacobs has to repeat himself twice before I can begin to grasp what he is saying.

'So,' I manage. 'Tommy isn't Sam's son? He's not even Naomi's?'

'That's correct. We're trying to locate his vehicle and—'

'I can save you the trouble,' I interrupt. 'His van's on my driveway. It's empty. Hold on, I'll check.'

I climb out of bed and run down the stairs, grab Sam's keys from the hook in the hall. The van is in darkness. I can tell it's empty before I open it. 'Yep,' I say. 'There's only boxes and a load of gardening tools.'

'Right. Do you happen to know if he has any other vehicle besides the VW Transporter, registration—'

'His gran's sports car,' I say. 'It's an MG RV8. It's vintage but nineties, not like sixties or anything. It's bottle green, but I don't know the reg, sorry.'

There is a pause. I hear voices, the cop telling someone the details of the car, reiterating Sam's last name, then Joyce's name. My heart is pounding, my head throbbing. *Sam*, I'm thinking. It is all I can think. *Sam, my darling, what have you done?* The facts are not with me yet, not completely. I just know the man I love is in trouble, that he is alone and in a dreadful, dreadful state.

'Look, where are you?' I ask. 'Can I come to you? I might be able to shed light on things.'

He gives me the address. I wake Betsy, wrap her up in her dressing gown and blanket, though the night is warm. She is dozy, her eyelids heavy and swollen. But when I tell her we need to look for Sam, she is instantly alert, excited. Excited because she knows none of it, is thinking only of her pal, of funny Sam who lets her start the van, who makes jokes about broccoli and plays duets with her on the piano.

'We need to find our friend,' I tell her. Before it's too late, I don't add.

It takes us a little under twenty-five minutes to reach Cheryl and Harry Baxter's address. Talking to Betsy as if everything is fine is enough to make me feel like I'm losing my mind, but needs must and she doesn't seem to notice the strain in my voice.

The Baxters' front door is opened by a woman in police uniform.

'I'm Miranda Clarke,' I say. 'Sam Moore's friend? Sorry, I had to bring my daughter.'

I am ushered inside, Betsy on my hip, legs swinging. In

the living room, a woman with sandy hair and a man with blonde hair sit shrunken and pale like a two-headed person on a tasteful dark grey couch. They are holding hands. The woman is holding a screwed-up tissue and her eyes are rimmed red. Betsy holds up her plush octopus and tells them it's an octopus and that its name is Ollie, but even she is fazed, her voice growing smaller with every word.

'I'm Miranda,' I say, sitting on the armchair, Bets on my knee. 'I'm a close friend of Sam's. This is my daughter, Betsy.'

The woman looks up, a terrible note of hope in her face. 'You know Sam?'

I nod. 'I know him well. And trust me, he will not harm Tommy, I promise. Not a hair on his head. Sam is the gentlest, kindest person I know.'

'Are you sure?' Fresh tears course down her face. I wonder if I've ever seen pain etched into a face like that before.

'One hundred per cent,' I say, though I am not one hundred per cent anything. I know he won't hurt only the child is what I mean, I think. I dare not look at what lies beneath that thought. 'Sam gets upset if a plant dies,' I add. 'He'll be somewhere. He'll be traumatised, I know that, but he won't harm the kid. No way.'

The woman nods vigorously, pressing her lips tight. 'Thank you.'

I try and smile. 'So you're Tommy's actual mum and dad?'

The man squeezes his wife's hand. 'We are. This is Cheryl. I'm Harry.'

'Yes. The... DC Jacobs told me. And you knew nothing?'

'Nothing. Nothing at all.'

'But how... how did she get away with it?'

'We don't know.' Harry sighs and proceeds to fill me in on the details. That Naomi was a live-in nanny, that she was a godsend, a nice woman with a bit of maturity, great with Tommy, the answer to their prayers. Described herself as a hermit. He got the impression she'd always wanted children, that she loved Tommy almost as her own.

'Kept Tommy's picture in her room,' he adds, like an afterthought. 'There were no alarm bells, none whatsoever. She didn't go out much, but then no one did, did they?'

'I'm so sorry.' What else can I say?

'Please,' Cheryl says in a storm of fresh tears. 'Do you know where he might have gone?'

The Cobb flashes into my mind. The dark harbour. The treacherous slant of the wall. The roaring white waves. The drop.

'No,' I say. 'He didn't come to mine. And he doesn't have his phone.'

I look up at DC Jacobs. 'Have you traced the MG?'

'Not yet. We're running Joyce Moore's name to find the plate number.'

He wanders out. I wonder if he's as confident as he sounds. The woman from earlier asks if I want tea. I tell her yes please, milk and one sugar. I don't take sugar, but I am craving sweet tea like I did in the moments after Betsy was born. I have started to tremble from head to toe.

'Mummy,' Betsy says. 'Stop shaking.'

'Mummy's a bit chilly,' I say. 'You need to warm me up.' I pull her close and throw her blanket over both of us, though I am not cold.

The tea arrives, strong, hot and sweet. I sip at it even though it is too hot. I am a little dehydrated, I realise, my blood sugar low.

Sam, I think. *Where are you?*

A moment later, DC Jacobs returns and tells us they've found the MG in Lyme. He repeats a familiar address.

'That's my house,' I say. 'Were they in the car?'

'No. But I think you should probably come with me.'

A minute later, Betsy and I are in the back of a police car, siren wailing, speeding towards Lyme. I comfort Betsy as best I can, but she has picked up that something is wrong.

'You know like that time you hid under the bed,' I whisper into her hair, 'after you cut your fringe with the bathroom scissors and you were worried I'd be cross?' I feel her head nod against my lips. 'Well, Sam is hiding somewhere because he's worried people will be cross with him.'

It strikes me that this is in fact the truth. That it could be. Please God, let this be the truth.

The MG is parked diagonally across the road at the end of my drive, as if by someone drunk. There are cones a few metres either side of it, a fluorescent hazard sign. Jacobs parks on the far side. We get out and walk towards my front door. I open it and get Betsy into the warm.

'Does he have a key?' Jacobs asks me.

'To my house? Yes. For emergencies.'

'What about his gran's house?'

'I don't know. They sold it. I'm not sure if they've exchanged yet. He might do.'

Jacobs radios a colleague to check Joyce's house. 'The fugitive may have reached the Moore property. He may have a spare key.'

'Fugitive?' I say. 'Really? He's terrified, you know that, don't you? He's just found out the kid he thought was his is not his and his wife's run off to God knows where. He's not a fugitive, he's a victim.'

At this point, as far as I'm aware, this is all Sam knows.

It is only later that I find out he has read Naomi's letter, with all it contains, and that it has pushed him over the edge of reason.

Another unit arrives. A man and a woman get out, both in the by now familiar black and silver. They open the back of the van to release two Alsatians. Above, a helicopter passes overhead. Shit, I think. A helicopter. Dogs.

Sam, where are you?

Needless to say, Sam is not in my house. Nor is he at his grandmother's former residence, as the other cop puts it. But he is somewhere in Lyme with the child. *Alive, hopefully*, is how Jacobs puts it, and my body fills with heat. Is that what I really thought when I pictured the end of the Cobb? That he had thrown himself and the child over the edge? Maybe I did, but this feels different, as though earlier it was just fear; now it is a real possibility. *Oh, Sam. Sam, my darling.*

'If he was going to throw himself in the sea,' I say, 'he'd park by the harbour. Otherwise, I can't think where... Wait.'

Of course, I think. I have already feared the most drastic outcome, but I have not thought about how he would...

Sam does not know that I know. Joyce told me in confidence. I am torn. Should I tell these people, who don't even know him, about his most private moment? A moment so shameful he has not felt able to tell me himself?

If it could save his life, yes.

'I think I know where he might be,' I say. 'We need to get back in the car.'

A female officer tells me to leave Betsy with her. I am reluctant, but Betsy is thrilled with the idea of being allowed to eat a honey sandwich and stay up late with the nice lady, whose hat she asks to try on. I kiss her and let her go, turn away before I have to watch her disappear into my house with a police officer.

Five minutes later, we are parked in the lane beneath the sinister arches of Cannington Viaduct. I have not been here since Joyce told me about Sam that dreadful night. Now I know why. The thought of him alone up there contemplating the unthinkable is too much. I begin to cry.

'Oh, Sam,' I whisper. 'Please God, don't have done that. Please don't.'

From the ground, there is no sign. The police torch shows no evidence of footprints, though the ground is grassy and dry. Myself and two cops scramble up the bank, half running, calling his name, that we're here to help, that he's not in trouble. To please make himself known.

'Sam!' I yell at the top of my lungs. 'Sam, love! It's me, Miranda.'

Every few seconds I crane my neck and peer up to the impossible heights, but I can see no one. We reach the ridge and walk through the brambles to the entrance. The barbed wire is intact. Beyond, completely overgrown.

'He's not gone through there,' Jacobs says. 'No way.'

'Thank God.' I press my fingertips to my eyes, to another bout of sobbing.

'Is there anywhere else he might have gone? Anywhere you can think he would go if he was afraid?'

A second epiphany. And just as I sensed in the dead of night that he was in difficulty, so it comes to me now where he is. Where he might be. Where I hope to God he might be.

CHAPTER 60

We reach the Higher Mill gardening project a little after 2 a.m. The lane is silent, the garages a white row of teeth in the dark mouth of the driveway.

DC Jacobs parks up. 'Is this the property? This one on the end?'

'Yes.' I follow them out of the car.

Flashing torches, they run up the steps to the house, bang on the door, ring the doorbell.

'No one in,' Jacobs says after a moment, striding to the side of the house. He reaches over the top of the gate, feeling for the lock. 'It's bolted.'

'There's another way.' I move towards them so that we are standing close enough to murmur. 'But I think we should stay super quiet. If he's there, he'll be frightened out of his wits. Is it possible to let me go alone? If he's in there, and if they're alive, I don't want to frighten him into doing anything stupid. Not that he will.'

They agree to let me go ahead but accompany me silently down to the riverbank, where they switch off the torch. There is enough light from the street lamp on the lane. After a dry week, the river is low. The grass slope is easy enough to clamber down. I see the sandstone archway in the bank and my heart constricts. I hope I am right. I hope I am not too late.

Dipping my head, I enter the tunnel. Inside, it is pitch-black.

Singing. I can hear singing. So faint, it barely reaches me:

... little star, how I wonder what you are...

I stop, breath held in my chest.

... Up above the world so high, like a diamond in the sky...

Sam. Oh, Sam.

I switch on my iPhone torch. The singing stops.

'Sam?' I call gently. 'Sam, love. It's me. It's Miranda, sweetheart. It's OK, darling. I've got you. Everything's going to be all right, I promise – I just need to talk to you, love.'

A sob. As my eyes acclimatise to the shadows, I see the shape of a man hunched over a bundle of blankets. He is rocking, weeping, and my heart almost stops.

'Sam? Is the baby OK? Is Tommy OK, Sam?'

I hear the child.

'Da-da,' he says. His tiny fingers reach up to Sam's face. 'Sam-Sam. Da-da.'

My throat aches with tears.

'Sam,' I say, so gently. 'It's OK. I'm right here. I've got you, darling.'

I move slowly towards him, praying the two officers don't burst in all macho aggression and cries of *you're under arrest*. My friend is frightened, I try to communicate to them by sheer force of will. He needs us to be very careful with him.

'Sam? Sam, darling? It's OK. You're not in any trouble.'

I bite my lip. He is. But I need to get him and the baby out of here safely.

I reach him and sit next to him on the hard stone floor. It's cold in here but dry at least. He does not look at me. He is crying, his head bowed low. In his arms, Tommy coos and babbles softly. I hold the child's hand in mine. It is still warm; they have not been here long. Thank God. Thank God, thank God, thank God.

'You're a hard man to track down, Sam Moore,' I say. 'What do I keep telling you about not having your phone?' I lean my head against his shoulder.

'I'm so sorry,' he whispers. 'I was going to come back. I'm so, so sorry.'

'Don't be. Tommy's safe. This is not your fault, my love.'

'I just wanted a few more minutes. Just a few more minutes with him.'

'I know, love.'

'I wanted to say goodbye. He's not mine. He's not my son.'

'I know, I know.' In the dark, I find his hand and hold it tight.

'He never was mine. He was never even *hers*. It was all... it was all a lie.'

'I know.'

We are both crying now.

'I thought...' he sobs, 'I thought I *knew* it, you know?'

'I know you did. It's not your fault. Why wouldn't you think that? He's your double.' But even in the torchlight, I can see this is not true. His colouring is Sam's, yes, but his features are all Harry's, in miniature.

The tunnel darkens. At the entrance, I can see Jacobs and his colleague. I hold up my hand: wait. Turn back to Sam, who flinches.

'It's OK. They're good guys. Let's get this little one into the warm, eh?'

It takes Sam a long time to get up. Finally he sniffs and nods: I'm ready. Stooped low, we make our way in shuffling steps out to the river.

'It's OK,' I say, over and over. 'You're doing great. That's it, one foot in front of the other. Nice and easy. I'm right here. It's all going to be OK.'

All he says is sorry, over and over again.

The cops help us up the bank. On the silent lane, DC Jacobs is kind as he makes the arrest. Dust and tears carve tracks down Sam's face; his clothes are streaked with mud. He has no shoes on. When he holds out his wrists for the cuffs, Jacobs shakes his head and tells him it's OK, there's no need for that, let's just get this little fella home.

In the back of the car, we sit close. The other officer starts the engine while Jacobs calls ahead, presumably to a colleague at the house.

'Found him,' he says. 'If you can let the Baxters know... Cheers, yeah... ETA half an hour... Yeah, yeah, he's unharmed but call an ambulance anyway.'

Tommy sits on my knee. I try to hold him to me, but his arms reach out for Sam.

'Sam-Sam.' He begins to wriggle and groan and strain. 'Da-da, Sam-Sam.'

'It's all right,' Sam says quietly and lifts Tommy from my lap onto his. 'Hey, little man,' he whispers, adjusting his position, holding him close, arranging his blanket over him. 'Let's get you home, eh? Let's get you home to Mummy and Daddy.'

I think this is the bravest thing I have ever witnessed.

'Car,' Tommy says brightly, and Sam tells him yes, this is a car. Unharmed, unaware of the drama or of the pain his question might inflict, the child asks: 'Where Noo-noo? Where Mummy?'

'Mummy's at home,' Sam whispers. 'Noo-noo is on holiday.' Roughly he pushes aside tears, sniffs deeply. Turns to me in the darkness. 'I'm sorry. I'm so sorry.'

I find his free hand and squeeze it. 'We'll get through this. We'll get through it together.'

CHAPTER 61

Gently DC Jacobs lifts Tommy from Sam's arms and takes him into the house. Sam plunges his face into his hands and sobs. Jacobs tells me he'll have Betsy brought straight out – the female officer has already brought her back round to the Baxters' at Jacobs' request. I stay in the car with Sam and the other cop, silent in the front seat, but I guess in my role as storyteller here I need to let myself drift into the Baxters' home and imagine the emotional reunion taking place in that cosy modern living room with its grey sofas and nice cushions. Harry and Cheryl breaking into shrieking sobs and cradling their child between them. *Tommy, Tommy, Tommy. We thought you'd... we really thought... Oh God, the relief. He's safe he's safe he's safe, honestly, Officer, there are no words to express our thanks. Thank you, all of you, so much.*

If I sound distant from their emotions, it is because I am. I am pleased for them obviously, but any feelings I have for them and their little boy are drowned by my fathomless sorrow for Sam.

'I...' Next to me Sam's voice is as small as a child's. 'I

don't know how I can carry on.'

'You can. You will. I'm here. Me and Bets are right here. We'll look after you, I promise.'

What else can we do for our friends? Perhaps I should have intervened, told him to get away from that woman, that if she reduced him to a suicidal wreck the first time, she would do it again. But he didn't ask for my opinion and it was not my right to give it. It was not my place to criticise the love of his life, no matter what my feelings were for her – or for him. All I could do was hope my misgivings were unfounded, and if not, be there to pick up the pieces. Which is what I'm doing. All we can do is be there, isn't it? Be there, wait, be there again on the other side.

Betsy appears on the driveway of the Baxters' house. Spying me through the window, her face lights up.

'Mummy!' She breaks into a run; I open the car door and let her in.

'Hey, Bets. Looks who's here.'

'Sam!' Her face is puffy and pale from lack of sleep but full of joy to find her big pal there beside me. She is much more excited to see Sam than me, her mother.

'Hey there, Bets,' Sam says with only the slightest tremor. 'What are you doing up so late? It's way past your bedtime.'

'We had to find the baby! You were hiding like me under the bed when I cut my fringe. The baby's called Tommy.'

'Is that right?'

'That's pretty accurate, to be fair,' I say.

'It is.'

We are putting on a brave face for the sake of the child. I am still holding Sam's hand. We are behaving like grown-ups. Like parents.

CHAPTER 62

At the station, Sam gives his statement and is taken to the cells. DC Jacobs drives me back to my place, where Joyce's MG is still parked like the aftermath of the maddest night out. The Baxters don't want him to go to jail, Jacobs tell me, but the CPS will most likely still charge him with abduction of a minor, a serious crime.

The following morning, Jacobs receives a call from DI Jennifer Whitehead in St Peter Port, who tells him that Naomi and her sister were arrested a little after 9 a.m. at Guernsey airport after Jo's car was traced to Exeter airport car park. Seemingly they had a change of heart about their destination, perhaps thinking a plane would be their best bet but, bizarrely, choosing a small island to flee to.

As for the buyer of Joyce's house, Mr Barnard, he offers to pull out of the deal, but Sam says no. There are too many bad memories. If he avoids prison, he will need a fresh start.

In custody, Naomi confesses to conspiracy to defraud, naming her sister as her accomplice. It seems that blood is not in fact thicker than water and that Naomi's trust for her sister did not run to loyalty when the shit hit the proverbial fan. Joanne Harper is duly charged.

When they find Naomi's letter to Sam, the police rearrest both her and her sister on suspicion of Joyce's murder.

Sam is released on bail pending the CPS review. When I pick him up from the station, I tell him about Naomi's arrest, and though his eyes are dead, he seems to take it in. I know he knows what Naomi did, but I worry the arrest will confirm the horrible truth of it somehow.

'The prints found at the house match Jo's,' I tell him when it's clear he isn't up to speaking. 'And the trainer prints by the back door were hers. They're still searching for the murder weapon.'

'She wanted me to find that letter,' he says, his voice hoarse. 'I can't figure that out.'

'It's strange. They'd have found it on her laptop anyway, I guess.'

As part of the ensuing investigation, the police search the Baxters' residence but find nothing. They also search the outbuildings at Joyce's place as well as the house itself, even excavating the vegetable patch. They turn up nothing more. Jacobs stays in regular contact. Sam manages to have a cup of tea with Darren, who makes him laugh with anecdotes about the Colyton job.

'Soon get you back to work, mate,' he says when he leaves, and this moves me.

Finally – I think this is a day later – the police try Naomi and Sam's former flat back in Bridport. Nothing is found in Jo's room, nor in the rest of the flat. But in a small outhouse to the rear of the property, secured with a flimsy padlock, they discover a spade, and two keys on a cast-iron key ring. The keys fit Joyce's shed and the back door of her house. The spade, which is covered in Naomi's fingerprints, matches Joyce's head injury, and there is a small sample of blood and hair, which turn out to be hers. The keys too are covered in Naomi's fingerprints. It appears neither they nor the murder weapon were cleaned, simply hidden behind a load of old junk and wrapped in a threadbare towel.

When I relay this to Sam, he closes his eyes and sighs. I ask him if he's OK and he says, yes, he's OK, he'll be OK, but he looks like a ghost, his eyes blank.

Naomi and her sister are charged with the murder of Joyce Moore. They plead guilty, we assume on the advice of their solicitor. Owing to a huge backlog of cases at Bournemouth Crown Court due to the pandemic, they are still awaiting sentencing. Their crimes are as notorious as they are odious to the people of Lyme Regis and beyond. Momentarily, the Harper sisters become a hotter topic than COVID.

As for rumours concerning Sam, they die along with early headlines such as *Lyme Man Abducts Child*; *Man Hides Stolen Child in Secret Underground Grotto*.

Reading Naomi's epic letter, it is hard to pick out what is true. She was after all a compulsive liar. My own, perhaps deeply biased feeling about why she did what she did is that, more than anything, she was offended. I know from talking to Darren that she had no shortage of male admirers, and Darren reckoned she picked Sam because she thought he'd be easy to push around. Sam never knew how good-looking he was, Darren said. Never knew when a woman fancied him. Naomi was convinced he wouldn't leave her. And of course, he was the only living relative of a seriously loaded old lady, which can't have hurt. So when Sam did leave, as well as her pride being injured, she lost out on the jackpot, and she couldn't handle it. Hell hath no fury and all that. In this case, not infidelity but the sheer blind gall to walk out on her, Naomi Harper, a woman who did the finishing with and was never, ever the finishee – invented word, sorry, but I like it so I'm leaving it.

And yes, if you believe her letter, it is completely possible she suffered from depression after Sam left. When the police followed up her claims to have had counselling, they found that she had in fact attended three of six prescribed sessions with an NHS therapist called Dawn Mellors. When questioned, Ms Mellors said that the sessions came to an abrupt end but that she could not divulge the reasons for this due to patient confidentiality. My take on that, considering her words in the context of Naomi's letter, is that Dawn said something Naomi didn't like, by which I mean something that implied, or that Naomi felt implied, criticism. Naomi writes about taking responsibility for her own part in the failed relationship, but if you read that letter closely, she never did. She just pretended to, for her own benefit. I think to the end she blamed it, all of it, on Sam.

It was as if the longer she pretended to be in love, the more her feelings spiralled into hate. A hate that became self-fuelling, independent, almost, of its source; as if the reasons for it were altogether lost – a little like a terrible argument, or a war, when no one can really remember why it started. Again, my theory, for what it's worth, is that her hatred for the world and the hand it had dealt her centred on Sam. Sam, of all people. Sam, who would lift a ladybird to safety. Sam, whose only crime was falling for her in the first place.

Right now, the situation is best described as dormant, but there are still days when I'm washing up or cooking or taking a break from a technical drawing and I stop dead in my tracks and think about those Harper girls.

I have become used to flying into other people's heads of late, trying to imagine what they are thinking and feeling, and in these moments I see Naomi and Jo, dressed in their prison sweats, miserable and raging in their holding cells, full of the injustice of it all. There is the evil, yes, but mostly I am astounded at how *stupid* they both were. Naomi was the so-called brains but, despite her flair at moving money, she was a perfect idiot as far as I'm concerned. So caught up in this all-consuming emotion, she chose to leave a venomous, self-righteous letter that would only incriminate her. Why? I don't know. Perhaps because she just could not resist really driving home her punishment of her ex-boyfriend, who had done her a great wrong. The letter was the salt in the wounds she took such joy in inflicting.

As for the carelessness in leaving the murder weapon in a place only she and her sister had access to, rather than, say, throwing it off the Cobb into the sea – pretty handy after all, no? – for me that hints at someone almost not in their right mind, someone so bent on the destruction of another that they lose all ability to think logically. And don't even get me started on her thinking she could sell a dead woman's house in a matter of weeks, or leaving her bank account in her own name.

Alternatively, she must have truly believed she and Jo would never be found... in Guernsey. If it hadn't all had such unspeakable consequences for my beloved Sam and Joyce, it would be laughable.

Maybe they watched too many crime dramas on television. Maybe Naomi's horoscope said, *Now is the time to get away with murder.* I don't know. I can only suppose that with great arrogance come delusions of grandeur: in

Naomi's case, thinking she was so much cleverer than she was, cleverer certainly than anyone she knew. Perhaps this is how you feel when you're pulling the wool over someone's eyes; perhaps that's part of the thrill. I get the impression the Harper girls' mother was a fierce if misguided champion of her daughters, but they lost her. Their father, by all accounts, was a poor substitute. In that sense, perhaps, I feel almost sorry for them. Almost.

CHAPTER 63

In late September, after a thorough investigation, and perhaps taking into account Sam's spotless record, his GP's diagnosis of his complete nervous collapse, and the Baxters' desire to forgive and forget, the CPS decide not to press charges against him, concluding that it is not in the public interest. When we hear the news, both Sam and I cry for a long time.

A week or so later, when the dust has settled, I drive to Bridport one evening and call on the Baxters without appointment. When they open the door, I simply say that I was passing and thought I'd swing by and ask after little Tommy. It is a white lie; I have come here quite on purpose. They recognise me immediately and invite me in. Tommy is sitting on the living-room floor playing with large Lego bricks. My first thought is that he has grown, my second that he looks even less like Sam now. They offer me coffee. I say, sure, thanks, and sit in the armchair where Sam had to hear the annihilating truth of his situation. Over coffee, they ask after him.

'He's getting better,' I begin. 'But it's going to take a long time.'

A small silence stalks across the room.

Harry edges forward. 'Was there... was there anything specifically you wanted to discuss?'

'There was actually.' Nerves rise. But I have come here encouraged by their refusal to hate the man who took their child, by the CPS deciding not to prosecute.

'They had such a deep bond,' I say. 'It might not have been founded on the truth, but Sam really did love this little chap, and I think one reason why he's so low now is because he feels like part of him is missing.' I smile down at the kid. His hair is turning strawberry blonde now, more like his mother's. 'Obviously he knows he's not Tommy's father. He's not in any way delusional about that, trust me, and he has no idea I'm here. What you've got to understand is, he is the sweetest, kindest guy. He's so good with my daughter. I trust him with my life. I trust him with my daughter's life. I know he did a desperate thing at a desperate moment, but he would always have brought Tommy back. It was the first thing he said to me when we found him. He just wanted to have a few more minutes, you know? Just to hold him one last time, maybe keep the lie alive for a little longer before he said goodbye.' My voice breaks, but I cough and get myself under control. 'He just wanted to say goodbye.'

Harry nods. 'I think we know that. We've talked about it a lot, haven't we?' He glances at his wife, who nods then meets my gaze.

'So what are you saying?' she asks.

'I'm saying... I suppose I'm asking, really, without any expectation at all, if there's any chance you'd let him see Tommy? I know I'm asking a lot, but it could be supervised?'

Harry exhales heavily, his head tipping back a little. I wonder about apologising and getting out of there, but Cheryl has begun to nod, her head inclined slightly to the left.

'Sorry,' I say. 'I have no right to—'

'I think,' Cheryl interrupts, one hand rising, 'I mean, we saw him, you know? We didn't even know what had happened to his gran that night, but when we heard that Naomi had done *that* as well as everything else, and apparently told him in a letter? I mean, well, how does anyone recover? We just felt so incredibly sorry for him, didn't we?'

'We did,' Harry agrees. 'I mean, we do, but I'm not sure...'

We talk for over an hour, round and round. The Baxters have had their own share of gutter-press commentary. They are scarred too. But eventually Cheryl gives a deep sigh and turns to her husband.

'We could let him see Toms, couldn't we? With us there? Maybe in a park or something? Just let him see him, give him some closure?'

Harry pushes his bottom lip up against the top. 'I suppose. If we're there with him.'

'Thank you,' I whisper. 'Thank you so much.'

CHAPTER 64

That pretty much brings us to December 2021, when I started my attempt at getting this whole thing straight in my head. The threatened lockdown hasn't happened. The virus has not gone away, but there is talk of learning to live alongside it. With it. What choice do any of us have with something so beyond our control but to try and learn to somehow absorb it into the narrative of our lives, make some sort of peace with it and just... live as best we can?

Cheryl and Harry did let Sam see Tommy. They met him at a park and stayed on a bench at a discreet distance, allowing Sam to say goodbye properly. This extraordinary kindness helped him a great deal. We don't yet know if any future relationship will be possible, but we are in touch with them, and they send us updates on WhatsApp, the occasional photo.

From that point on, Sam got stronger and stronger. He still lives with Betsy and me, and we look after one another. Every evening, after Betsy is in bed, we put on our PJs and pour ourselves a glass of something and just chat or pore over a garden design together. On the landing, we hug, and kiss each other's cheeks, and say goodnight. In the morning, we say good morning and how are you and did you sleep OK? I call him love, without thinking. He calls me Mimes. We talk about working together again soon.

Darren has been brilliant at filling in and at taking Sam out for a pint and a chat here and there. When I can, I go walking with him over the cliffs he loves so much. We have talked and talked and talked, and he is also talking to a therapist once a week.

Last week, it was cold and the sun was out, so we decided to head for Cannington Viaduct while Betsy was at nursery. As I packed flasks and sandwiches, I asked him if he was sure, and he told me, yes, he wanted to face it. We took the tree-shaded path towards Uplyme, headed along the field by the cricket club, up the hill and down the lane.

At the looming sight of the viaduct, we stopped.

'Are you OK?' I asked him and reached for his hand.

He nodded. Holding hands, which we do often, we passed beneath it.

'I'm OK,' he said. 'Honestly, I'm fine.'

'You're doing great. Really great.'

The viaduct was on our left then as we walked up the grassy slope. We looked up, shielding our eyes with our hands. He pointed to the top, to where he had been.

'I'm so glad you're here,' I said.

'So am I.'

As we headed up the hill, the arches receded into the distance, becoming steadily smaller. We climbed over the stile, and seconds later the viaduct was out of sight: behind us, where we left it.

Neither of us said a word.

At a certain point, we took the tiny track that heads up and right, past a few beautiful farmhouses, which we fantasised about buying. Along the edge of a wheat field, over another stile, and we were heading down then into the undercliff.

'I just can't understand why I ever thought she'd changed,' Sam said as we clambered down the thin track past Chimney Rock. He'd said this so many times, but I guessed he'd have to say it until he no longer needed to. It wasn't for me to tell him when was enough.

Close behind him and focusing on my feet, I answered with a version of what I usually say: 'Because that's all she showed you. Any gut feelings you had, you passed off as coming from a time before you'd worked things out.'

'I thought we *had* worked things out. I thought things were different this time.'

'There was no reason for you to think otherwise.'

'But when I think about it now, I realise I always felt tense around her,' he said, walking a little ahead where the track narrows.

This was new; I hadn't heard him say this before.

'I didn't want to admit it to myself until... well, until now, but actually I was always worried she was angry with me or about to be, or that I'd messed up.' He stopped and turned to look up the track, where I was walking down towards him. 'I never feel like that with you, Mimes. With you, I never feel like I've done something wrong. I feel... relaxed, I suppose. I feel safe.'

I pretended to find my footing on the erratic, root-knuckled ground. I was glad of course, but secretly I wondered if that meant he would never feel anything beyond friendship for me. Feeling safe was pretty far from having the hots for someone, wasn't it?

But then he stopped again – so suddenly I almost fell into his back.

'Mimes.' He looked up at me and then down at his hiking boots. 'Do you think I'll ever find...' He shook his head. 'Forget it.'

I laughed. 'Ever find love again? Is that what you were going to say? It's only been a few months, mate. Give it a chance!'

He laughed. 'Sorry, ignore me.'

And I had no idea what it was, but there was something about the way... I don't know, the way he was standing, the way he was looking and not looking at me, the way his cheeks had gone red – *something*, and I just thought: *go for it*, you know? Life is short. How will he ever know if I don't tell him? If he doesn't feel the same, I'll just have to brazen it out until it blows over. Because that was the thing, that was the real fear: losing my chance was one thing, but I could not bear to lose his friendship.

'I think you'll find love,' I said before he could move off again. I reached for his hand, caught the ends of his fingers with mine. 'I mean, you have found it. With me, I mean. Me and Bets. We love you.'

He met my gaze then and did not look away. Neither of us did. My legs started to tremble. 'Do you mean love me or *love* love me?'

'Eloquent. I can tell you read a lot. I mean... well, Bets loves you obviously. Whereas I...' I couldn't meet his eye any longer, so I stared at my boots instead. 'I, er, *love* love you. I mean, I have for ages. I wanted to tell you before, but I couldn't because... well, you know.' I glanced up, cringing.

His mouth opened, closed. He looked horrified, and regret ballooned in my chest. I wanted to take the words back and stuff them down my stupid throat.

'It doesn't matter,' I said. 'You don't need to do anything

about it or anything. We can still be friends. It'll wear off, I'm sure.'

'But I didn't think you liked me that way,' he replied, taking a firmer hold of my hand. In sympathy, I supposed. 'I never... You're, like, a professional. You're clever. And you're way too lovely for—'

'Don't say *way too lovely for me* – that would be pathetic.' I laughed, embarrassed to the roots of my hair. Joking, that was how I would extricate myself from this stupid conversation I should never have started.

'But you know what I mean.'

'I don't actually. I have no idea. I have loved you for over a year and it's been really quite painful and a bit sad. But it's fine. Honestly. It's fine.'

'You're joking? Why didn't you... Ah, Naomi. Fuck.' He pushed a hand through his hair. 'But when we... That time ages ago when I came over for dinner and we spoke about... you know, and you said you were through with men. I thought...'

I did. I did say that at one point.

'I was,' I said. 'But I could never be through with you. Oh my God, please tell me I didn't say that out loud? Oh dear God. I'm sorry. Really, I apologise. I think someone must've spiked my coffee flask with cheese pills.'

But he laughed, a real ha-ha-ha laugh, and I laughed too, and then he pulled me by the waist of my cagoule and kissed me on the mouth – so hard I almost tripped on a tree root.

And that was the moment when this went from being the story of my friend Sam Moore and how he came to be found underground to the story of Sam Moore and how he came to be my almost boyfriend pending his recovery from the loss of a family that was never his and, oh, the annulment of his marriage to the murderer of his grandmother – you know, the classic girl-meets-boy scenario. We have had that one kiss. We hold hands. Actually, we hold hands a *lot*, and when we sit together, there is not a wafer between us. But we are not, officially, an item. We need to wait, I have told him. Above all else, he needs time. He needs to get better, and then we'll see what we have. And while I'm not the most confident in affairs of the heart, I know without any doubt that I can give him a life as free from conditions, mind games and manipulation as it's possible to be, and hopefully help him to be happy. So much has been lost. Sam and I are like a lot of people right now – striving to pick up the pieces and each other again, to lick our wounds and crack on. It is all any of us can do, I suppose.

A LETTER FROM S.E. LYNES

Thank you so much for taking the time to read *The Ex*. It's an intense read, with a small cast, but I hope it kept you gripped. If you'd like to be the first to hear about my new releases, you can sign up to my newsletter using the link below. Your email address will never be shared, and you can unsubscribe at any time.

www.bookouture.com/se-lynes

The idea for this novel came from a news story. A man was duped by his ex-girlfriend, whom he hadn't seen for a few years, into believing the little boy she had with her was theirs. He formed a relationship with the child and looked after him on occasion over a long period of time before discovering that his ex was in fact the kid's childminder. He didn't get back together with her and things didn't go as far as they do in my novel, but he was devastated when he found out the boy had no link to him whatsoever. The real parents recognised his traumatic experience and continued to let him see the little boy and be part of his life. Their sensitivity and generosity moved me and stayed in my mind.

I set the story in beautiful Lyme Regis, west Dorset, and hope to have made the town as much a character as the characters themselves. I have used a little artistic licence here and there – Joyce's house is entirely fictional, for example – but if there are any glaring inaccuracies, I apologise. I have also touched on the after-effects of the pandemic: the isolation, the anger, the 'hiddenness' that resulted from lockdown, the sense in which it was easy to become an extreme version of oneself during that time without the dilution and mental-health benefits of social contact.

This novel explores whether it's a good idea to go back to a toxic relationship in the belief that it will be different this time – in this case a romantic relationship. We are optimists in love, I guess. Every new relationship is a leap of faith; we go into it believing or hoping that it will be better, that we are somehow better, and that we have learnt from our mistakes. Sometimes we have; sometimes, boy oh boy, we really haven't. In this case, the new relationship is between old lovers, but the same hopes apply – doubly so perhaps.

As in most of my novels, I am exploiting the fact that most of us experience the world through the prism of our own subjectivity: if we have no agenda, for example, we do not attribute an agenda to others; if we act in good faith, we assume the same of others, and so on. We are all conditioned by our pasts, our childhoods, our subsequent relationships. Sam and Naomi are no different. In *The Ex*, Sam's reaction to Naomi is heavily conditioned by the effect she had on him in their first relationship. Anyone who has been in a relationship with a controlling, narcissistic person will recognise how hard it is not to become fretful, to begin second-guessing oneself almost immediately. Sam has not experienced any other romantic love but Naomi's; he has not had time to heal properly or to learn that love comes in other flavours. As for Naomi, she was already hardened by her life circumstances the first time she met Sam, and when he left her, it provoked a crisis from which she has not recovered when she bumps into him a year later at Monmouth Beach.

And in love, of course, we can convince ourselves of all sorts of things, often things that are not true. As Chaucer put it in 'The Merchant's Tale', 'loue is blynd alday and may nat see' – in more contemporary language, simply: love is blind.

Enough blathering on from me. If you'd like to share your thoughts or ask me any questions, I'm always happy to chat via Twitter, Instagram or Facebook, so do get in touch. If you enjoyed *The Ex*, I would be so grateful if you could spare a couple of minutes to write a review. It only needs to be a line or two, and I would really appreciate it!

My next book is well under way – it is a secret, but I hope you will want to read that one too.

Best wishes,

Susie

facebook.com/Lynesauthor

twitter.com/selynesauthor

instagram.com/selynesauthor

ACKNOWLEDGEMENTS

First thanks go to my publisher, Ruth Tross, who in addition to being sensitive and kind, improves my work beyond measure and writes funny notes in the margins to brighten my editing days. Thank you to my agent, Veronique Baxter, who said of *The Ex*: 'No wonder it gave you a headache; it's so intense!' I'll take that!

Thanks to my mum, Catherine Ball, who is always my first reader and who has an excellent cringe radar.

Thank you to the continually amazing team at Bookouture, particularly Noelle Holten and Kim Nash, Sarah Hardy and Jess Readett, plus all the Bookouture authors, who are the best virtual not to mention hilarious colleagues a girl could wish for.

Thanks to my copy-editor, Jane Selley, and my proofreader, Laura Kincaid.

Thanks to Tracy Fenton and all the team at Facebook's The Book Club: Helen Boyce, Claire Mawdesley, Juliet Butler, Charlie Pearson, Charlie Fenton, Kel Mason and Laurel Stewart. Thanks to Anne Cater at Book Connectors, to Wendy Clarke and the team at Facebook's The Fiction Café, and Mark Fearn at Bookmark! Thank you, in fact, to all the online book clubs and the people who gather there to share their love of reading. If I've missed you out, I'm sorry – if you message me, I'll make sure to give you a wave in the next book, which I'll already be writing by the time you read this.

Huge thanks to flag-waving readers like Sharon Bairden, Teresa Nikolic, Eduarda Abreu, Nicky Dyer, Fi Kelly, Laura Budd, Tara Munday, Philippa McKenna, Karen Royle-Cross, Ellen Devonport, Frances Pearson, Maddy Cordell, Jodi Rilot, CeeCee, Bridget McCann, Karen Aristocleus, Audrey Cowie, Alison Terina, Donna Young, Mary Petit, Donna Moran, Ophelia Sings, Gail Shaw, Lizzie Patience, Fiona McCormick, Alison Lysons, Dee Groocock, Sam Johnson and many more not named here. Thank you. I read every single review, good or bad. If you don't see your name here, please give me a shout.

Huge thanks as ever to all the amazing bloggers, who are unpaid and who work very hard spreading the word about the books and authors they love. I would like to thank the following bloggers, using their blogging names in case you wish to check out their reviews: Chapter in my Life, By The Letter Book Reviews, Ginger Book Geek, Shalini's Books and Reviews, Fictionophile, Book Mark!, Bibliophile Book Club, Anne Cater at Random Things Through my Letterbox, B for Book Review, Nicki's Book Blog, Fireflies and Free Kicks, Bookinggoodread, My Chestnut Reading Tree, Donna's Book Blog, Emma's Biblio Treasures, Suidi's Book Reviews, Books from Dusk till Dawn, Audio Killed the Bookmark, Compulsive Readers, LoopyLouLaura, Once Upon a Time Book Blog, Literature Chick, Jan's Book Buzz, and Giascribes... Again, if I have missed anyone, please let me know.

Thank you to the tremendously supportive writing community; you know who you are and are now too many to count. Special thanks to Lauren North for organising super author lunches.

Thanks to my dad, Stephen Ball, who doesn't usually

read if it isn't about rainbow trout or the news, but who makes an exception for me.

Finally, and as always, thanks to my very own ex, Paul Lynes. I'm glad we got back together in 1994; you see, it could have been so much worse.

9 781803 145112